"M...

Reactivate Yel...
   Sixty days of...
   Nessie sightin...
   Let paleontolo... discover previously unknown hominid.

Steve snickered to himself. Whoever had this thing before, this joke PDA, had loaded it up with *years* of fake events. Steve had never owned a PDA, but his new PDA didn't seem all that difficult to work. Steve had managed to make the calendar appear with very little effort, and in no time at all he'd been able to scroll through those crazy events. And there were *decades* of them.

Still, he now owned a working PDA, well worth fifteen bucks. At least it would be once he cleared off all the crap. Steve wasn't worried; he had all weekend to figure out how to get it up to speed.

In the meantime, though, he scanned the events. It'd be a shame not to look at them; they were a hoot. Whatever joker had put this together, the guy had a sense of humor and knew his history.

   Inspire Bill Gates.
   Let someone actually make it to the moon.
   UFO landing at Roswell.
   STOP HITLER! This one was listed as high priority. Naturally.

—From "God's PDA" by Dan Hoyt

TIME AFTER TIME

Edited by
Denise Little

D A W   B O O K S ,   I N C .
DONALD   A.   WOLLHEIM,   FOUNDER
375 Hudson Street, New York, NY 10014

ELIZABETH R. WOLLHEIM
SHEILA E. GILBERT
PUBLISHERS
http://www.dawbooks.com

First Printing, November 2005
1   2   3   4   5   6   7   8   9

DAW TRADEMARK REGISTERED
U.S. PAT. OFF. AND FOREIGN COUNTRIES
—MARCA REGISTRADA
HECHO EN U.S.A.

PRINTED IN THE U.S.A.

COPYRIGHTS

CONTENTS

INTRODUCTION

Denise Little

Time's a funny thing. It's completely out of reach except for that tiny instant of eternal now, the place where we make all our decisions, never knowing exactly what they might cost us in the future, or how they might cloud our past.

I learned the hard way about the nature of time. One bright winter morning in New York City, I decided that I wanted to walk to work. It was sunny out after weeks of gray drizzle and snow, and I wanted to take advantage of the weather. So I suited up for the cold, and headed out. I was meandering along the Second Avenue sidewalk, enjoying the light and the scenery, when I heard an ominous screech behind me. I turned around and saw an Entenmann's truck bearing down on me, unable to stop. The truck had hit an ice patch, the driver had slammed on the brakes (not the best decision!), and the vehicle had gone out of control. I had maybe a second before the truck would smash me into a people puddle somewhere in the middle of the Second Avenue Deli.

I expected my life to flash in front of my eyes, but that's not what happened. I had maybe three distinct thoughts all at once. First: I'd always suspected that pastries would kill me, but this wasn't exactly what I'd had in mind. Second: my obituary was going to be a riot. Third: I probably should have taken a cab this morning.

Luckily, I was able to leap out of the way, the driver got control of the truck full of pastries in time to avoid killing anybody else, and the curb and sidewalk were sturdy enough to withstand the abuse. They build 'em tough in New York City. After a bit of mayhem, things went back to normal again for all of us. But I'd just had a vivid demonstration that even the most miniscule and inane of the decisions I make every day could have devastating and unexpected consequences in my future. (Also that the last thought of my life is likely to be some crazy variation of "Ooops," but that's another story.)

I'm not the only person who has wondered about how the future or past or present could be changed if someone had the chance to rethink, redo, or otherwise rework a moment in his or her life. Writers have been churning out alternate history almost as long as literature has existed. It didn't even take a truck full of pastries barreling at them to make them consider the subject. It's an active subgenre of speculative fiction.

But I wanted to put my own spin on the subject. So, with the help of a number of very talented writers, here's a look at the way life can change when we tweak time—past, present, or future. The characters in these stories range from the sublime to the ridiculous, as do the plots. Some tales work on a global or even a universal canvas. Others cover the small victories of ordinary lives. Every story is a work of pure fiction, of course, even though some of them feel remarkably real.

I loved every single story in this book. I hope that you do, too.

AFTER CAMLANN

Liz Holliday

A falcon broke the azure dome of the summer sky. Below, an old man stopped working in his lord's cabbage field to watch. His knuckles whitened on the handle of his hoe and tears filled his eyes. A village brat playing mumble-jack in the weedy edge of the field stopped his game long enough to jeer.

The old man cursed him, then rubbed at his eyes with his sleeve, the coarse undyed cloth scratching the white scar that crossed his face from brow to chin.

The falcon plunged to take a smaller bird out of the air.

Once, he knew, a falcon had meant something to him. A face, wild-eyed and silver-haired, came into his mind then.

A boy.

A falcon. The old man had given the boy his name. It was a new memory.

He followed it, as once he had followed a mist-shrouded stream away from a battlefield. There had been a time, he knew, when he had worn fine linen, eaten at the top table, carried a sword. A sword, and a falcon. He tried to deny the images they conjured. The clash of battle. Screams of dying friends. The blow that had stolen his memories. Pain, and the stink of blood. Darkness. Hands on him, taking the sword, all the marks of his gentility. Waking in the blinding light, and stumbling away as the crows came to feast.

After that, a time of floating madness where he spoke what he saw, and what he saw made no sense. Beaten for a fool from one village to the next, for there was no one to care for an idiot: not with the raiders at the coast and the northern borders, and the Romans out of Britain, fighting other, winnable battles. Until he had come here, half dead, and the lord had taken pity on him. He had a soldier's calluses, not a peasant's, but he had worked and learned the rhythm of the fields. He was neither happy nor unhappy. But when the lord flew his hawk on the hill, the old man watched and wept and tried to remember.

That night the old man woke, startled by something he could not name. His head hurt, a dull throb at the temples. He lay on his pile of straw, staring across the barn. Moonlight slipped through the wattle walls, and picked out patterns in the old mosaic floor.

Faint music drifted up from the hall, where the lord's house celebrated May Day night. The servants had given him ale to drink, and he had been foolish and drunk it. They had pushed back the heavy tables in the kitchen and beat out rough music with tabor and fife. Some of the serving girls had asked him to dance, beckoning him on with their brown hands and their smiling eyes. Later, they had merely laughed at him, at his clumsy shuffling caper.

He pulled his blanket close around his head. It had not always been so. Gently, he touched the cold tile of the floor. Once, there had been honor and order in the land. Pax, he thought: Pax Romana. There had been peace. That time had long since passed.

The cows whuffled gently in their stalls, and shifted their weight back and forth. The old man lay wrapped in their warm, musky smell, regretting that he had ever woken. The open half door framed a tree silhouetted by the moon. There was warmth and beauty in the world still, he thought, and that paid for much.

An owl hooted softly in the night. The old man stared straight ahead, blue eyes filled with rheum and tears and moonlight. He knew that it was for this he had awoken.

The owl lit upon the half door, a pale bird silhouette against the dark tree. "Gwynhwyfar," he whispered. It was the first name he had remembered. "Pale one."

The owl lifted itself into the night, where it hung for a moment, silver, like a piece of the moon against the sky. Then it flew away, ghost-silent, towards the ancient wildwood.

He followed it.

He had lost her again. His Gwynhwyfar.

The old man leaned his weight against the twisted hawthorn tree and wept. The owl had left him.

He was not where he should be. He felt the need to move on, as if a voice were calling his name. He had no name. He did not know where he should go, here in the deep woods, where the oak and ash were uncut, and there were no paths to follow.

Gwynhwyfar had left him, his pale lady, white owl. In his imagination, the owl flew again; but then the image rippled, as water disturbed by a pebble does. When it stilled, his mind was full of Gwynhwyfar: his young bride, fairest of women, all he had cherished.

Then that too passed. When he looked up, he saw the black branches of the oak tree knit against the indigo sky. A falcon roosted there. It looked at him with its wild eyes, and the cold moonlight turned its grey feathers to silver.

A falcon. A—

"Merlin?" the old man said.

The falcon only stared. Merlin, his friend and teacher. Merlin, who never aged: the fool child his father had rescued from the Christian priests, who could not stop the mad prophecy that poured from his mouth. Merlin, who had come from the wilderness, and often returned there for the druid rites.

Who had led him here. He knew it, as certainly as he knew his own name.

I am Arthur, he thought.

Dux Bellorum; warleader; king in all but name. And he had come to this: to living like a dog off table scraps, and to fawning gratefully not to be kicked.

The old man touched the scar that cut his face. A sword wound. There had been the battle. Medraut, his bastard son, and his mother Morgause had come down from the north to take back what they would call theirs, at the battle of Camlann field.

The falcon stared impassively. Merlin, the fatherless

child who had believed in the old Way; who had
brought about Arthur's own birth and prophesied
dragons; who had shown Arthur the way to unite his
country. Merlin, who had made Arthur all that he was.

Who had left him.

They said his heart had been stolen by the nymph
Nimue, and with it his power. They said he was under
the earth, or bound in the fôrk of a tree, and that
when Arthur had need of him, he would come again.

He had not come. Not when Arthur knew himself
for the maker of an incestuous bastard, and not when
Morgause had come out of the north to make war on
her husband-brother.

Arthur broke away from the gaze of the falcon. He
stared at the ground, where scrubby grass broke the
surface of the cold earth. Something glinted there,
among the roots of the hawthorn tree. He picked it
up. A knife of stone. It was familiar to him. He felt
the power of the old memories, giving him back to
himself. He rubbed his thumb down the flat of the
blade and felt the druidic serpents incised there. Merlin's knife. It was a gift, but such a gift he did not
know how to use.

He looked up. The falcon caught his gaze and held
it. The druids had made sacrifices. It was a part of
Merlin's life that Arthur had shunned. Yet it was Bel-
tane. Sacrifice the falcon? Would that bring back his
Merlin to him, return what was to what had been?
The legends were full of such tales.

The falcon screamed its hunting cry. It flew up. Arthur crashed through the woods after it. Low boughs
of oak and ash whipped his face. He put up his arms

to save his eyes, and found that the branches cut his hands instead. His breath came in gasps, and the roaring in his ears could have been the blood rushing round his body, or the wind, or the distant sound of singing. He could not tell. He would not allow himself to lose sight of the falcon.

There were noises ahead of him: low chanting, rhythmic and guttural. The falcon settled heavily on the branch of an ash tree amid a flurry of falling leaves and snapping twigs. Arthur held himself still, silent.

Ahead of Arthur, the fires of Beltane sent red gold light flickering through the trees. It was the old Way, the rite of the Goddess. Merlin had persuaded him to join them. He had done so warily, as he had also partaken of the Eucharist of the Christos Gwynhwyfar worshipped: he balanced each against the other, and both against the Mithras of the Romans.

Merlin had brought him here. He saw bodies, jewel-like through the trees. There were priestess' robes and painted skin. He was drawn to it, as he had never been drawn before. It seemed to him that the woods were full of voices singing. They called to him. They needed him, for their completion. All he had to do was walk forward. He took one step. Another. He stood at the edge of the clearing. If anyone looked, they would see him. He wanted to go forward, but his life had been built on a warrior's self-denial, the discipline of leadership. He stayed where he was.

He had expected a Beltane festival, where the women chose men to father their children. At such a Night of Fires he had once married the Goddess of the land, all at Merlin's bidding. At another he had, all unknowing, fathered his son on his own sister.

What he saw now was something quite different.

A young man, dressed for kingship, was led to a place before the fire. Arthur recognised the robes, the scabbard, the sword hilt. His. He had been Dux Bellorum, war leader of the tribes; not a king, but almost so. They had set this manchild up to mock him, then. His hand tightened on the stone knife. He should rout them all for their insolence.

Yet the druids had followed him, however reluctantly. He did not believe they would despise him so.

Not mockery. Sacrifice. He remembered Merlin explaining to him, his earnest young voice in one of his lucid periods. The Goddess demanded tribute, but she would accept a scapegoat offering, where the need was great. It was the old rule, the rule of sympathy. In return, she would give back . . . what?

A priest offered the young man a wooden goblet. Firelight glinted on the brass that banded it. Arthur felt compelled to go to them. He would give them Merlin's knife, be their sacrifice, if that was what was needed.

A druid stepped up behind the young man, looped a leather strangling-cord around his neck. The druid put his knee against the small of the young man's back, pulled on the garrotte. Arthur fought for breath. His hands went to his throat. Then the sweet air came into him again.

They did not want his sacrifice, he realised. They wanted something else. . . .

The young man was not dead. Another druid stepped behind him and raised a wooden club. He brought it down on the back of the young man's head. Arthur felt the pain as his own, brought up his hand and was surprised to find no gout of blood and bone, but only thinning hair.

The druids had called him back to himself, called him to lead the people. He had to go to them. The falcon screamed suddenly. It swooped into his face. He brought his arms up to fend it off. It gouged his hands. Blood fell like benediction on his face. The pain cleared his head. Choose, Arthur. Merlin spoke plainly to him. The druids would compel you. They would force you to lead the people, leave you with no choice at all to make. Arthur lowered his arms. The bird seemed to hover effortlessly in the air before him, and its eyes were those of his old teacher, wise but quite, quite mad. I say—I, *Merlin*, say—that this is profane in the eyes of the Goddess. By your blood and by your name, I tell you Arthur, you must choose!

Still, the druids called to him.

He should go to them. He would unite the tribes again. Together they would hold the borders against the Saxons to the east and the Picts to the north. He would become the king he had never quite been before. A vision of the crown danced in his mind. It could be his. He would take back his sword and lead his people. Find Gwynhwyfar in whatever nunnery she had hidden herself. Perhaps get a right-born heir (for such was the right and duty of a king): a son, in the new fashion, and not a nephew in the old way. His

brother Kai might even be alive still, and Bedwyr
(who he would of course forgive for his cuckoldry),
to sit at his right hand in council, as he had before.

The falcon landed on his shoulder. Its talons bit
straight through the poor homespun, into flesh and
muscle. Arthur grunted. The falcon touched its beak
to his face, the place where the scar crossed the jaw-
line. He turned to look at the falcon. He could not
quite manage it, but he caught a glimpse of the silver-
grey feathers, the dark eye.

He saw himself leading the armies of the British
against the Saxons. Succeeding. Arthur, who had come
again to Britain, to be its king. He died peacefully, at
the end of a long reign. His children ruled a strong
nation. It was good.

Almost, then, he stepped forward. The druids had
placed the sacrifice on a wooden bier. The young man
was still alive. Arthur fancied that he could hear his
muffled groaning. He knew, from the things Merlin
had told him, that they would take the still living body
and plunge it into the cold water of the peat marsh,
to complete the sacrifice to the triple Goddess.

You must choose. It seemed Merlin spoke to him.
He did so, took a pace forward. The falcon dug its
claws deeper into his shoulder. Arthur almost
screamed. Then he was in the vision again. His grandson would be weak. The line would fail and fade. War
would be everywhere, and peace something the people
dreamed of. The kingship would pass from line to line.
Arthur's name would be lost to time. In a hundred
years, it would be spoken no more. The darkness

would come, and there would be no light to prevail against it. This, if he stepped forward, into the circle, let them give him back his sword, his loves, his life.

Or this, the falcon seemed to say, in the sweet mad voice Arthur had once loved: Merlin in his prophetic frenzy. If Arthur did not go to the Druids, the Saxons would come and after them, the Normans. Much of the old Britain, the Britain of the Romans, would be lost, and there would be many battles, more pain. In a thousand years, the land would be torn by civil war. Five hundred more, and innocents would die at the hands of enemies who sent death from the sky. Yet even in the darkest, bloodiest moments, the people would have this to hold to: that one day, when he was needed most, Arthur, King—King!—of Britain would come again to lead his people into the light.

The druids finished stripping the sacrifice of its kingly attributes. They wound it round with white cloth, and began the long walk to the peat marsh.

Choose. The falcon screamed its hunting cry. Your kingdom now, and then dark despair for your people for all time. Or pain for you, now, and the golden light of hope unfading. *Choose!*

But Arthur had no choice. He felt himself compelled to walk forward, into the flickering light: to take up kingship, and send his people down into a thousand years of darkness.

He tried to walk away. He could live a peasant's life, pay duty to his lord and work the fields for crusts. He could do that. Yet the druids and the firelight compelled him. The Goddess wanted him. He remembered the night he had married her. It was such a night as this, when the fires burned hot and the flames burnished her skin as she held him.

He was bound to her, bound to his land, to his duty. He could not turn away, could not walk forward. Would not.

The stone knife was heavy in his hand. He tested its blade against his thumb. It was sharp as any sword. He looked once, longingly, into the firelight. To be king. To have Gwynhwyfar at his side, and Bedwyr his companion, and Britain whole again. He would die, and know nothing of the dark that overtook the land.

Yet the dark could last forever. Or not, as Arthur chose. The falcon rose up. For an instant, it was silhouetted against the sky: wild eyes and silver hair, friend and teacher, guide and prophet. Choose, it screamed, for the third, the last time.

And as the druids went to make the final sacrifice that would bind him to their will, Arthur drove the stone knife deep into his heart.

As his lifeblood wept into the unforgiving earth, he whispered, "I am Arthur. And I have come again to Britain."

THE GHOST OF THE
GARDEN LOUNGE

Dean Wesley Smith

I tucked my hands inside my bar apron in a useless
attempt to cut down the wind chill. The cold December wind cut across the open meadow to my right
and through the dark pine trees above me, driving
small crystals of snow into my face. In the on-again,
off-again moonlight I could see the figure ahead moving through the brush. His name was Pete Hansen.
Tall and thin, with broad shoulders and short-cut
blond hair that almost shone in the dim light. Tonight,
he didn't seem to even notice the cold or the wind.
I suppose it was because he knew he was about to
die again.

He led and I did my best to keep up through the
brush on what seemed to be no more of a trail than
a deer path. Ahead, through the cutting howl of the
wind, I could hear the seasonal song "White Christmas" echoing faintly through the trees and the wind.
I had come back in time six years with Pete to the
exact place he was when the song started for him.

With my old jukebox, time traveling back to memories always worked that way. And the song playing the memory for Pete was "White Christmas" sung by Bing Crosby. "White Christmas" brought us back six years to the night Pete died.

At the moment, with the snow taking small bites out of my face and numbing my hands, a white Christmas was not what I was wishing for.

I glanced quickly around. Nothing but the dark forest of northern Idaho, an open, snow-covered meadow barely visible in the moonlight, and a ghost. Or at least a man who was about to become a ghost again. And I was here following the soon-to-be-ghost because he had asked me to.

He had asked me to see how he was killed.

Begged was more like it.

I could think of about a thousand things I would rather have been doing on Christmas Eve.

"Hurry, Stout," Pete, the soon-to-be-ghost said, glancing back as he moved along the trail. "The song is almost half over."

His voice was raspy and sounded almost hoarse. I knew it wasn't because he'd chain-smoked about three packs while sitting at the bar in the Garden Lounge, before we started this crazy adventure into his past. Right now, the Garden Lounge seemed a long way away in both time and distance.

He turned right and headed through the trees away from the meadow. I hurried and caught up to him.

In the faint light I could see he hadn't really changed much since we left the bar, even though he was now six years younger. He stopped and pointed through the trees. I could see a small cabin about twenty steps ahead looming in the dark like a tomb-stone. The music was clearly coming from the cabin.

"When I go through that door," Pete said, point-ing at the wooden door on the right side of the small building. "Mary's ex-husband shoots me in the face."

"Then don't go through the door," I heard myself saying, just as I had said fifty times before while stand-ing behind the bar in the much warmer Garden Lounge.

He shook his head and I knew my comment would make no difference. If he didn't go through the door, Mary died.

If he did, he died.

In over two hundred tries going back through the jukebox to try to change the outcome of this bloody Christmas Eve, it had always worked out exactly the same.

Either he died.

Or Mary, the woman he was in love with, died.

That's why he had begged me to come along this time. I was to see if I could find a different way out of this deadly event. I was here to find another way to change the past. A third door both he and Mary could walk through into the future.

With a long look at me, Pete indicated the cabin. "Let's go."

He took a deep breath of the bitterly cold air, put his head down, and headed for the front door of the cabin.

I did my best to stay close to him. I knew Mary and the ex-husband inside wouldn't see me when Pete opened the door. I wasn't really here, at least in their reality. I was just hitchhiking on Pete's memory, taking an unwanted ride through the jukebox. But Pete was here, in the flesh, in his six-years younger body.

And he was about to die.

Pete didn't hesitate when he reached the door. He just grabbed the wooden handle and pushed.

I could see that the inside of the small cabin was lit by a fireplace and two lanterns. It looked like a warm, comfortable place to hide out against the cold. Pete told me he and Mary loved to be out here. In this tiny cabin they could be alone. They had planned a peaceful Christmas Eve, but Mary's jealous ex-husband had had other ideas.

"Pete!" Mary shouted.

Beyond Pete I could see Mary tied up on the big, quilt-covered bed. She had dark, almost black hair, and she wore a blue jogging suit. Her hands were tied behind her back, but her feet were loose.

Beside her stood a tall, angry man with red hair and a huge shotgun.

"I thought so," the man said. Then he pointed the gun at Pete and pulled the trigger.

The blast sent Pete sprawling back toward me into the snow. Blood and brains splattered everywhere, giving the white snow a diseased, measles-like look.

My stomach clamped tight and I wanted to throw up.

I stood, first staring at Pete's body, and then watching as the man walked forward and stood in the doorway. I could tell he suddenly realized what he had done.

Behind him Mary just looked at Pete, shaking her head from side to side as if she couldn't believe what had just happened.

The song "White Christmas," sung by Bing Crosby, slowly faded behind Mary, and with it the biting cold and smell of the blood of a Christmas Eve six years in the past.

I blinked as the light in the bar hit my eyes.

I was back in the Garden Lounge, standing beside the old Wurlitzer jukebox, staring into the worried faces of my friends sitting at the bar. Mary stood touching me where just a song ago Pete had stood.

I shivered and tried to think warm thoughts. I couldn't remember ever being that cold before. Even the toasty, smoky air of the Garden didn't make me feel much better.

I glanced at the bar. A few minutes ago Pete had left an ashtray full of cigarette butts and the remains of a gin and tonic. They were now gone, because in this time line they had never existed. Mary didn't smoke and only drank orange juice. Her empty orange juice glass sat in its place where she had left it.

She looked at me, her eyes half glazed over with the memory. She knew what I had just seen. She had been there.

I let my left hand that had been touching her shoulder drop to my side.

I gazed across the empty tables and the hazy, smoke-filled gloom of the lounge. There, standing beside the front door, was the ghost of the Garden Lounge.

Now it was Pete's ghost.

A song before it had been Mary's ghost.

*   *   *

Seven years before, when I had bought the Garden
Lounge, Pete had become one of my regulars almost
from day one. The Garden then looked a lot like it
does now.

It's a cozy, warm place, with six black vinyl booths
and ten tables spaced around a windowless, low-
ceilinged room. Artificial plants fill wooden planters
between the booths, and the entire place constantly
smells of smoke.

A ten-stooled oak bar runs across the back wall
with glasses stacked behind it in front of a large,
wood-framed mirror. To the right of the bar is an old
Wurlitzer jukebox that I only plug in on Christmas
Eve. Every other day of the year the music comes
from my stereo system in the back room.

With the normal forty-watt spots over the booths
and bar, the Garden has a feeling of safety in the
shadows. Someone once asked me why I didn't put in
a few windows and brighten the place. Bring in some
of the world, I think they asked. I told them the Garden Lounge had nothing to do with the real world.
My customers came here to get away from that world,
and by and large I believed that.

I liked the place just the way I bought it: dark
and homey.

I remember the year Pete was killed. All the Garden Lounge regulars went to the funeral and then
came back to the bar to hold our own private memo-
rial service. I remember there wasn't a sober person
in the place that night. Everyone had really liked Pete.

Mary came through the door for the first time six months after Pete died. I remember it was mid-afternoon and I had been doing prep work, cutting fruit. She had ordered an orange juice, introduced herself and said she had stopped by just to remember Pete. She said he had always spoken so highly of the Garden that she felt she almost knew us all.

I had made her feel welcome, convinced her to stay around until evening, and introduced her to the regular gang as they showed up. She became a regular, only drinking orange juice.

Two months later, on November thirtieth, I finally got around to fixing the old broken-down Wurlitzer jukebox that the previous owner had stored in the basement. That night I had discovered what it could really do.

That coming Christmas Eve, one year to the day after Pete died, I tested the jukebox and lost two more of my best friends: Carl and Jess.

It turned out that somehow, in some way, the jukebox takes a person physically back to the memory associated with the song being played. The memory rider, as I call them, actually disappears from the bar for the length of the song, as if they don't even exist.

They reappear inside their own memory, inside their younger body with both older and younger memories intact. A turning point in some fashion in their lives that will send them either back to the Garden Lounge, if nothing changes, or into some new future.

It is the new future part that gets me. That's how I lost two of my closest friends that first jukebox Christmas Eve. I gave them a chance at a personal memory through the jukebox, and they went back and changed their pasts.

They changed their memories. Can't say as I blame them sometimes.

But their new futures didn't bring them to the Garden Lounge.

The only reason I even remember them was because I was touching the jukebox when the song each had played ended. Somehow, touching the jukebox allows me to remember both the time line where they were Garden regulars and the new, altered time line where they weren't.

That jukebox Christmas Eve a third friend also went back and changed a memory. He went back twenty some years and saved his wife's life. Somehow he made it back to the Garden, only as a very different man, and he didn't come back through the jukebox, but through the front door.

Playing on that first year's tradition, I have, for the last five years, closed the bar on Christmas Eve and invited only my closest friends to revisit a personal memory of their choice. But now, after that first year, we always agree to only go to pleasant memories that we don't want to change.

Except this year. This year was different.

Very different.

Last year had been Mary's first jukebox Christmas Eve. Honoring my wishes and like all first-timers, not really believing in the jukebox, even though she had seen four of her friends disappear from the middle of the bar, she chose the song playing during her first kiss. When she came back she sat quietly, reliving the moment, as we all had a habit of doing.

Or so I thought.

She told me a few weeks later she was thinking that night of Pete and how, if she went back to the Christmas Eve he died, she might be able to save him by warning him.

She told her idea to some of the other regulars who knew about the jukebox and its special powers and slowly, over the next few months they wore me down, convinced me to give it a try.

On Sunday night late, March first, I plugged in the jukebox and with five of us watching, Mary played "White Christmas" and went back to the Christmas Eve Pete was killed. We all were touching the jukebox when the song ended, so when Mary didn't come back, we all remembered her.

We also all remembered she was killed on a Christmas Eve. And I even remembered going with Pete to her funeral, just to give him some support.

She'd changed her memory, and saved Pete's life.

Now Pete was standing there next to the jukebox, his drink on the bar, as if he had never been killed. It took us most of the night to convince him that Mary had been here earlier.

Three weeks later he convinced me to let him go back through the jukebox again to try to save Mary.

It didn't work. This time he was killed again.

And Mary was back. Telling her what had happened with her and Pete was damned hard. After that all I wanted to do was unplug the jukebox and be done with it. But Mary and the regulars had worn me down, so she and Pete kept trying, back and forth like that through the summer.

Either Mary was there drinking orange juice, or Pete was there smoking.

It was in early September that things had changed again, but not in the way anyone hoped they would. Mary had been sitting at the bar, drinking her orange juice, when suddenly Pete's ghost showed in the Garden, sort of hovering near the front door.

The ghost was more like a fuzzy outline of Pete. But you could really tell who it was. None of us had even tried to get close to the ghost, and it hung around for an hour or so.

The next night, when Mary's attempt to save Pete had again got her killed, her ghost showed up.

The ghosts never did anything, and never acknowledged any of the living. They just appeared by the front door late at night, after all the normal customers were gone.

One night it was Mary's ghost, with Pete sitting chain-smoking at the bar.

Then, if Pete got killed trying to rescue Mary with his newest idea, his ghost showed up while Mary sipped orange juice.

So now, this Christmas Eve, instead of staying warm and drinking my eggnog, I had agreed to ride Pete's memory with him and see if I could figure out a way to save them both.

Mary staggered away from me while I stared at Pete's ghost near the front door. I couldn't believe I had just watched him be killed six years earlier.

"Stout? You all right?"

I turned to the bar and my worried friends. Mary had taken her place on her stool. David, a United Airlines pilot, sat next to Mary and his wife Elaine sat next to him. Their twenty-four-year-old daughter Donna was next down the bar followed by Ernie and then Hank. All except Mary were staring at me with concern.

David was my closest friend and had been for years. He was thin, almost fifty, with a full head of gray hair. In three years he would retire from flying. Elaine, his wife, was an architect who had designed some of the nicer buildings in town. She had short, blonde hair and a smile that could light up a room. Donna, their daughter, was a junior at the university and planned on going to law school. She had the looks of a model and her mother's smile.

Ernie and Hank both worked construction and looked it. Hank was balding and Ernie had a pot gut. Their voices were rough, their actions sometimes rougher, but both had hearts of gold.

"I'm fine," I said to whoever had asked.

I didn't know if I really was or not. I headed back around the end of the bar and to the sink. I doubted if I would ever be warm again as I ran hot water over my hands until they tingled.

"Did you see anything that might help?" David asked after I turned off the water and grabbed a bar rag.

I glanced up at the worried look on David's face. He knew what Pete and Mary were going through. On that very first jukebox Christmas Eve he had gone back over twenty years and saved Elaine from being killed in an auto accident. Somehow, with Elaine, he had found his way back to the Garden Lounge in the new time line. So Pete and Mary's problem was very, very real to him.

I shook my head and finished drying off my hands. "Not right off. But maybe if we go over the layout of the place again, something will come to me."

David glanced down the bar. "Mary, you up for this?"

Mary turned and glanced at Pete's ghost hovering near the front door. "Very much so," she said

David looked at me. "Okay, there's no other way inside that cabin. Right?"

Mary nodded.

So did I. She was right. I had gotten a good view of the small cabin, and the front door was the *only* door, just as Mary and Pete had said. The only window was beside the front door, and Pete had told us he'd tried going through it ten different times in ten different ways without any luck. Mary's ex-husband was just always too fast and too good a shot.

I moved down to the well and poured myself a large glass of warm eggnog, then returned to a position in front of Mary and David.

"Mary," I said, doing my best to remember the quick glimpse I got of the cabin before Pete was shot. "You're tied on the bed when the song 'White Christmas' starts. Right?"

Mary nodded.

Pete had said that her normal way of saving him was for her to yell a warning that caused him to turn and run. A few times she'd warned him just in time so that he managed to duck the shot and then ran. Each time Pete got away, the ex-husband had turned the gun on Mary before killing himself.

Twice she'd gone back and tried making promises to the ex-husband that she would remarry him if he'd let Pete live, but he'd still killed Pete.

"Is there any way," I asked, "that you could kick your ex while he's shooting at Pete?"

Mary shook her head no. "I think we tried that early in the summer a few times."

She pulled out a small notebook and flipped through it, nodding. She had been making notes about each attempt, recording what she remembered and what we told her Pete was trying on his attempts.

"I'm never close enough to do any good," she said.

I shook my head and glanced down the bar at the faces of my friends. "It all happened just as they have told us a hundred times."

"Nothing different at all?" Elaine asked. She was holding David's hand on top of the bar.

"Nothing that I could see," I said. "If Pete doesn't go in, the ex kills Mary. If he does, no matter how, he gets killed."

David glanced down at Mary. "And you tried going back to other song memories during your marriage with him and destroying his shotgun?"

Mary nodded, flipping through her book again. "Eight different times we tried that. He always buys a new one."

David shook his head and no one else said a word.

I stared past them at Pete's ghost. There just didn't seem to be a way out of this deadly cycle, at least that

I could see. And going along for the ride hadn't been a pleasant thing to experience.

Of course, having the ghost of a good friend haunting your bar wasn't pleasant either.

There just had to be a solution.

David glanced up at me again. "What was it like hitchhiking on a memory like that?"

"It was fun and really weird when I did it," David's daughter, Donna said. She had been the first one a few years back to discover it was even possible to hitchhike on someone else's memories by touching them when they went. She had rode along with David back to the delivery room when she was born. That way she got to witness her own birth.

"Almost like I was really there," I said. "I even had to hike through the trees behind Pete." I held up my hands. "They still feel cold."

"And even though you went back with Pete, you came back with Mary," David said. "Don't you think that's weird?"

I glanced at Pete's ghost and then at Mary and suddenly I knew the answer. They had a chance if they both were aware of what was happening at the same time. They both had to go back at once so they could work together to stop the killing.

I turned to Mary. "You ready to go back again?"

Her face turned pale, but she nodded. "If you think it will help."

I patted her hand where it rested beside her glass of orange juice and smiled. "I have an idea I think might work." I glanced down the bar at the faces listening to me, then turned back to Mary. "What happens if you go back and warn Pete just as the door opens."

"He'll run for help and I'll be killed," Mary said.

"But what happens if Pete knows what's happening, too? Couldn't he duck the first shot, you manage to get up and kick your ex-husband to keep him from getting another shot off. That will give Pete time to get back in to stop it all. Wouldn't it?"

Mary nodded. "It would, but how will Pete know if I know?"

The question sort of hung in the silence of the room.

Then slowly David smiled and turned around on his stool to stare at Pete's ghost. "Are you thinking what I think you're thinking?"

I laughed. "Time traveling with music is weird. Who says a ghost can't do it too?"

Suddenly Mary understood what I had suggested and she spun around and looked at Pete's ghost as it hovered near the front door.

"Think we can get him to move to the jukebox?" Donna asked.

"We don't need to," I said. "We'll take the jukebox to him. Mary, you game?"

"Of course I am," she said. That was the first time in over a half year I had heard hope in her voice.

It took Ernie, Hank, David, and I to move the old jukebox to a place near Pete's ghost. The closer we got to Pete the colder the air got around us. By the time we got the jukebox in position beside Pete and plugged in, I thought my hands were going to have frostbite.

All four of us retreated, blowing on our hands to warm them.

"Hope it still plays in that cold," David said.

So did I. It was the closest any of us had gotten to Pete or Mary when they were ghosts. Usually we just watched them from the bar until they went away.

I tossed Mary a quarter that she caught easily. "You're going to have to be touching him," I said. "At least as much as you can when the song starts, if you are to have any chance of taking him with you."

"Do you think he'll know what's going on?"

I glanced at David and he shrugged. "Your guess is as good as ours," I said. "But if it works, this could all be over."

Mary nodded, smiled at us all, and headed for the jukebox beside Pete's ghost.

I could tell when she hit the cold air, because she hesitated, then moved quickly to the jukebox and dropped in the quarter.

As if the jukebox were hot, she punched the keys to bring up her and Pete's death song.

From where we stood near the bar I could hear the mechanical insides of the jukebox bringing up the record and dropping it into place. There was a click as the record started.

Mary quickly stuck out both arms and did her best to wrap them around Pete's ghost.

As the first notes of the song filled the room, both Mary and Pete's ghost vanished.

"I hope it works," David said.

"Me too," Elaine said.

I couldn't agree with them more.

*   *   *

For the first two minutes of that old song we all stayed near the bar. Those two minutes were the longest two minutes I could remember. And if I ever heard Bing sing "White Christmas" again, I would remember the two minutes that night.

We didn't really talk about anything during the wait. But I could tell we were all thinking about that Christmas Eve six years earlier and the fight that was going on out in those cold, dark woods.

We didn't want to think about which one would return this time. We just hoped they both would.

As the song neared its end, we all moved to the cold air around the jukebox. As the song ended, we all reached out and touched the icy-cold music machine.

Not a one of us wanted to forget.

The metal surface of the jukebox felt almost frosty under my hand, like a car handle after a cold night.

"Wow," Donna said. "That's cold." But she didn't pull her hand away.

Then the song ended.

And neither one of them came back.

For a moment I couldn't make myself believe what had happened. Then the new time-line memory flooded over the old one, and I remembered how Pete and his girlfriend, Mary, had been killed on Christmas Eve six years earlier. I had even gone to both their funerals.

We all had.

"Oh, God, no," David said, softly.

Elaine sobbed and hugged David.

Slowly, one at a time, keeping our thoughts to ourselves, we moved back to the bar, leaving the jukebox plugged in near the front door.

I moved around behind the bar, quietly refreshing everyone's drinks.

Now they were both gone.

Both Mary and Pete. I had done it again, only this time it had gotten a person killed. Instead of just having a friend change a past, I had gotten a friend killed.

I kept repeating that, over and over.

I must have been muttering aloud a little as I worked with my head down.

"Stout?" Elaine said, breaking the silence.

I moved over in front of her and she smiled. She reached out her hand and took mine. "I'm here, alive, because of you."

"So am I," Donna said.

I glanced at the two beautiful women who were alive because David had gone back though the jukebox and saved Elaine's life.

And then I glanced at the empty stool where Mary and Pete had alternated for the last year, both working and fighting to save the other.

Both had been willing to die over and over again to save the other.

Now they were both dead.

At the same time.

How was I ever going to live with that?

"Stout!" David said.

I glanced up and saw immediately what he was pointing at. Near the jukebox and the front door were two ghosts.

"Oh, my," Elaine said.

"Amazing," Donna said to herself.

I didn't say a word. I doubt if I could have.

The two ghosts hovered near the jukebox for a few moments while we all stared in amazement.

Then they were gone.

The ghosts of the Garden Lounge were gone for good.

"They came to say good-bye," David whispered loud enough for all of us to hear.

I didn't want to believe what I had just seen.

I suppose I wouldn't have either if Elaine hadn't turned around to face me.

Her face was wet with tears. But not really sad tears. More like happy, relieved tears.

And she was smiling.

I suppose I was too.

She had seen what I had seen. Everyone had. The two ghosts of the Garden Lounge had been smiling.

And they had been holding hands.

THE LAST VAMPIRE

Kristine Grayson

The last real vampire in the world sat behind the desk in his New York apartment. "Apartment" was an awfully grand word for the 8' by 8' room without even a proper window. The only window, proper or not, was in the bathroom; it had access to the fire escape—which he appreciated, given his penchant for traveling via roof—and a view of the brick wall next door—which he did not appreciate, given his voyeuristic tendencies. But what was a poor—literally poor—vampire to do?

He didn't have a lot of furniture, not that he would have had room for much: a ratty overstuffed chair that he'd stolen from someone's garbage, the essential television set with every cable channel possible, and his circular desk, with its five computers. Three of the computers were hooked up to the internet: one on a DSL line (which cost a bit), one on a cable modem (which he buggered off the neighbor's system—just like his cable TV), and one on an old-fashioned phone line, in case of emergency.

He was bent over the corner of his desk, the only spot without a computer, or a modem, or a mouse. He had fingernail clippers in his left hand and was slowly, methodically, chopping off his lovely yellow nails—so perfectly groomed that one human (just before her untimely yet glorious death) had compared them to talons.

No one appreciated talons any more. Plus it was hard to work with them. He'd been trying for the past fifteen minutes to put four AAA batteries into the time machine he'd bought down in the East Village (and yes, he knew the machine was hot; it wasn't like he cared—who was going to arrest him after all?), but he couldn't fit the batteries into their tiny space and get his nails in there too.

The modern era was proving too frustrating for words.

Which was why he'd bought the infernal machine. The twenty-first century had become too much for him.

Women carried guns and knives and mace in their purses. Plus, these no-longer-fragile-flowers had also learned karate kicks and eye-pokes, and Adam's apple chops, things that hurt even the most experienced vampires.

Men weren't slacking either. They hit first, asked questions later. And more than one guy had figured out the vampire-thing too quickly. They'd looked for any sharp object, aiming for the heart, but willing to chop off the head if necessary.

The last real vampire in the world had actually run away from his last so-called kill, screaming at the top of his undead lungs, while the so-called kill chased him with a pool cue, broken so that the ends formed a mighty impressive stake.

Ever since, the last real vampire in the world had been stuck dining off of rats and stray cats.

It wasn't easy being a traditionalist any more.

One of the AAAs fell off the desk and rolled across the floor, finally stopping against the two-dimensional foot of Sarah Michelle Gellar in her *Buffy the Vampire Slayer* mode. The cut-out, which he'd stolen from the trash of a nearby video store, was only one of several reminders he had stashed around the apartment.

He'd been keeping them for years: an original *Nosferatu* poster, now tattered and worn; a series of stills from 1960s vampire flicks; Bela Lugosi's face, remarkably lifelike (deathlike?), hands raised, his ridiculous cape flaring out behind him. The last real vampire in the world even had a first edition copy of Bram Stoker's *Dracula*, with a stake which he had driven through its heart. (An act he now regretted, of course. He could have dined off—or, to be more accurate, rented off—it for nearly a decade.)

Still, he needed these things, reminders of the problem—the thing that had actually caused the death of his kind.

He felt like Richard Nixon, blaming the media for the way his life had come out, but in this case, it was accurate: if the vampire stories hadn't gained an undeath of their own, vampires would have been able to conquer the world in peace.

He wouldn't be the last real example of his kind, chasing a battery across the floor of a darkened room, hoping against hope he had enough juice in this little awkward machine to change the entire world.

Okay. So here was the thing: he could have gone the way of his contemporaries. He wasn't the last vampire in the world. He knew that. There were dozens of others. But he was the last real one, the last true believer.

The rest of these guys had sold out. They had become heroes—he spit even thinking of the word—basing their lives on the works of P.N. Elrod or Laurell K. Hamilton. Or they'd become antiheroes, basing their lives on the works of Anne Rice. Or, worst of all, they'd become tortured heroes, the Heathcliffs of the vampire world, made mainstream and cliched by those wimpy *Buffy* spin-offs: Angel and the misnamed Spike.

Whatever these sell-outs did, they spent most of their time posing romantically in Village cafes, reading poetry, and taking an occasional bite from a besotted goth groupie.

It was embarrassing, really.

His fingers closed over the battery, then he punched the vampire slayer. Even though she was no longer in first run, she was one of the worst—teaching girls they could be tiny and tough, showing people that a little garlic, a little witty banter, and one pointed stake was all it took to kill a nasty vampire.

He growled and backed away.

He would change things. He would change it all. With one easy (well, not that easy) trip to the past.

*   *   *

He had to cut another fingernail, then another, all the while trying not think about the irony of the fact that he was using human technology, bought with human money, to save his own race. He'd kept up to date on science—figuring that was one way real vampires would survive—and it wasn't until time-travel technology became small and portable that it interested him.

Of course, that was about the time governments banned it, thinking the technology dangerous (well, *duh*, in the immortal words of his fictional little blond nemesis), and then he had to go to the black market, trusting human technology even more.

He wiped the fingernail clippings off his desktop and leaned back in his chair. So many years of hiding, of staying away from people who thought themselves latter-day Van Helsings trying to save the world from traditional vampires. The last real vampire in the world had even used his computers to cover his internet tracks.

He was broke, he was tired, and he was ready to stop being the last traditionalist of his kind.

He stared at the time machine, the size of an old-fashioned Palm Pilot, and watched the display run across the tiny screen. The machine came without instructions, but according to the website he accessed a little while ago, all he had to do was punch in the dates, squeeze the plastic sides of the machine, and voila! he traveled to the past. Right here, in New York, because he couldn't smuggle the infernal machine onto an airplane—not that he could afford a ticket.

So he was going to travel the old-fashioned way. He

would gorge himself in post-revolutionary New York and no one would be the wiser. Then he could sleep for part of his trip across the ocean—and for the rest of it, well, he'd kill the crew and pilot the ghost ship himself, arriving in some obscure European harbor, just like Dracula did in Stoker's novel—in a sea of fog and with corpses hanging off the bow.

The last real vampire in the world smiled at that image. Real food, real slaughter, real good times.

Then he'd work his way up the continent to Switzerland, just in time to kill off Lord Byron, his doctor Polidori, and maybe even the Shelleys, just because he'd always hated their writing.

Near as the last real vampire in the world could tell—and he'd researched this, not just on the net, but also in the New York Public Library—the rise of the fictional vampire started with a story fragment that Lord Byron had told during a rainy summer in Lake Geneva—a fragment his doctor, Polidori, later finished and published. The story became famous—a book, a play—and then countless authors started writing their vampire stories.

Without Byron and Polidori, there would be no Stoker. Without Stoker and his (somewhat) fictional creation Dracula, there would be no movie vampires, and without movie vampires there would be no TV vampires and without TV vampires there would be no romantic vampires, and without romantic vampires, there would be no goth movement, and without the goths, none of his colleagues would have gone over to the light side and revealed all the secrets about how to kill—or at least co-opt—the native vampire population.

He had it all worked out. And all it took was four AAA batteries, an expensive hand-held device, and a willingness to put up with the early nineteenth century for little more than a year.

He grinned, revealing his little-used fangs.

Then he followed the prompts on the screen, typing in the date he wanted to travel to and how long he wanted to stay.

He pressed his newly shorn thumb against the start button, leaned back in his chair, closed his eyes, and waited for the particles of light or the spinning sensation or whatever the hell was going to happen next.

Minutes crept by. He didn't fall a couple of stories like he expected (they didn't have buildings this tall in 1815) nor did he end up on a cold, damp rooftop or in a farmer's field.

He opened his eyes, saw the machine blinking stupidly.

Clutch the machine in your hand, the warning said. *This machine will not send inanimate objects into the past.*

He stared at the warning for nearly as long as he had closed his eyes. Then he tried again.

And again.

And again.

Nothing happened.

He resisted the urge to bang the piece of crap time-travel device on his desk, and instead logged onto the manufacturer's website. Sure enough, the damn machine was designed to work only when clutched by a warm, living hand, one with a recognizable body heat pattern.

"No," he whispered.

He went to other manufacturers' websites. Those that still existed (most of them with the machines marked UNAVAILABLE in big block letters) talked about the "life" failsafe. Apparently, too many people had sent their garbage or their broken-down cars or their rusted-out refrigerators into the past—rather than trying to recycle or reuse.

It was easier, apparently, than hauling all that junk to the dump.

He couldn't even piggy-back on some live human. The machines weren't strong enough to send more than one body (*of no more than 200 pounds*, said one instruction) back into the past.

He growled and threw the machine against an image of George Hamilton's tanned Dracula, and then stomped around the apartment until his downstairs neighbor shouted at him to shuddap.

In the past, the last real vampire in the world would have gone down there, shuddap the neighbor, and gone on a spree.

But the last real vampire in the world was out of money, and was afraid of being staked, and wasn't up for a spree.

Besides, he was hungry.

He closed his eyes, rubbed his cold undead fingers on his cold undead nose, and sighed.

His choices had narrowed. He couldn't afford another machine, even if he found one that worked for him. Therefore, he could starve for his beliefs or he could learn how to write poetry.

Starving sounded like a lot less work.

But the poetry slams had free drinks and nubile goth groupies. He just had to give up his ferocity.

Not that he'd been very good at ferocity in the first place.

He grabbed a pen and scrawled on a piece of paper:

> *There was a vampire who grew violent*
> *Whenever he saw a Palm Pilot . . .*

He tapped his pen on his pointed teeth, and realized he was better off writing in the poetry café, where someone would give him a glass of blood and a little admiration.

He wasn't the first vampire to sell out to the media hype that had changed his race, but he was almost certainly the last.

God's PDA

Daniel M. Hoyt

Steve Beneman stared, his eyes narrowed suspiciously, at the pawn shop that shouldn't exist. At
least, it hadn't existed yesterday, despite the months-
old, crusty film covering the only door's glass pane, or
what little was left of it after a dozen duct tape repairs
obscured any view from the familiar cracked sidewalk
into the little shop's contents.

Exhaust from the constant buzz of nearby traffic
choked him as he sipped his afternoon fast-food coffee
and contemplated the view.

A battered sign emblazoned with the words *Deuce's
Pawn and Fire* hung precariously over the entrance,
suspended with what appeared to be several loops of
fishing line. Steve figured that the last word on the
sign was actually supposed to be *Firearms*, but he saw
no indication that part of the sign had broken off.

Strange, he thought. *Very strange.*

But then, the shop's appearance was strange in itself. Steven had been barreling down this street twice
a day for at least five years, fighting the workday traf-

fic with the liberal use of hand gestures and his car horn, but he'd never noticed the shop before.

And Steve knew *all* the pawn shops in the city.

He'd never pawned anything in his life, but he knew a good bargain when he saw one. When life dealt a certain kind of hand, the kind that made people like Steve live day-to-day in middle America, struggling to make ends meet, bargains were an important part of surviving. And pawn shops had bargains—if you knew where to look.

"Pawns got *quality*," he always said to anyone who would listen. "They *have* to. If they can't sell it, they won't buy it. Regular places'll sell you *crap* and they don't care. Pawns gotta be your friend or they're out of business. It's simple economics."

But this place, Deuce's, seemed to have miraculously cropped up overnight. And the name was compelling to Steve, as Deuce had been his nickname with his high school poker buddies, from his habit of *always* calling deuces wild. It was almost like an inside·joke, just for him. Steve just *had* to stop and check it out. Besides, it was Friday and he was going home to an empty house otherwise, the perfect capper for a forty-hour week of pretending to care while tuning out a constant stream of Department of Motor Vehicles customers, all whining about something or other. Yeah, a pawn shop visit would be fun.

There was no sign on the door announcing the shop's hours, and Steve couldn't see through the duct tape and grime even to tell if the lights were on inside. He stood on the sidewalk, traffic whooshing past an arm's length behind him, undecided whether to go in or head for home. A diesel Mercedes accelerated nearby, enveloping him in a cloud of thick, noxious smoke.

Steve coughed and decided to go for it. Gingerly he poked at the door with his free hand, hoping it would open without crumbling at his touch.

It swung solidly and easily open, beckoning him inside, and a cheap door alarm chimed his imminent entry to whoever was watching over the place.

Two hundred and fifty pounds of Steve waddled in. ("A quarter ton of real man," he liked to say to girls at the bars on Friday nights, just before they'd burn him with withering glances that left no doubt he'd been refused—although there was the one redhead who first said he was clearly a math genius, and *then* laughed at him and turned away.) Steve's five-and-a-half-foot frame scraped the sides of the narrow door, but he managed to squeeze through.

A middle-aged woman stood behind a counter, a lit cigarette dangling from pale lips, her disheveled dishwater blonde hair hanging limply to her waist. A large, colored dragon tattoo adorned her bare arm, its tail curling around her shoulder and disappearing under her off-white tank top, presumably continuing to her sagging breasts. She pointedly ignored Steve, feverishly working on some receipts that he had no doubts were already entered. He knew the drill. She'd eye him like a hawk, her busy hands completing the illusion of attention focused elsewhere while she secretly watched for shoplifters.

Steve didn't let that bother him as he absentmindedly ran his fingers over the filthy displays, scanning the electronics merchandise beneath the counter, safely tucked inside locked cabinets. He stopped at a particularly sticky spot and wiped his soiled hand clean on his pants. Nestled in amidst the CD players and miniature black-and-white televisions was a little electronic planner—a PDA, he thought they called them—with a rich, leather case and an inscribed gold plate. He bent closer to the grime to get a better look. PDAs hardly ever turned up at pawn shops.

"You wanna see it, buddy?" the pawnbroker said in his ear, magically appearing beside him as if she'd been there all along.

Steve tensed at the sound of her voice, but forced himself to relax, trying to appear aloof and casual. "Yeah, I guess so. What is it?" he asked.

"One of those electronic planner thingies," she said, blowing acrid smoke sideways out the corner of her mouth. She slipped her crone-like body through a tiny space between two counters and stepped behind the counter. Unlocking it, she grabbed the PDA, removed it from the case, and tossed it on the counter. "It's sold 'as is.' Don't know anything about the gadgets myself," she said, "but I can't get it do nothing." She blew out more smoke casually, enveloping Steve in a gray haze.

Steve coughed, flapped his hand to stir up a breeze and cut the carcinogens, flipped open the PDA case, and thumbed the power switch. The PDA winked on, displaying a prompt for a password. Steve looked up at the pawnbroker.

"I didn't say it wouldn't power up." She shrugged. "Battery's good, at least. A surprise, since I've had that thing for a year or two." She took another long drag on her cigarette and blew upward.

Steve fiddled with the PDA for a few seconds, turning it off and on again, but the password prompt came up every time. Snapping the leather case closed, he scowled and rubbed at the gold plate. Dust wiped off easily, revealing "Yahweh."

Yeah, right, he thought. *Yahweh. That's another name for God, isn't it? So this would be God's PDA? Look, everybody, I've got God's planner here. Somebody in heaven swiped it from Him and pawned it.*

Right.

Steve chuckled and flipped open the case again. He slipped out the stylus and clicked on the little keyboard indicator, making a drawing of a keyboard appear on the PDA's screen.

So, if God had a PDA, what would He use for a password? Adam? Eden? Noah? Maybe Moses? Steve tried them all—just for grins—but they returned him to the password prompt. Of course.

The pawnbroker waited, unconcerned, sucking down her cigarette to a tiny stump while Steve relentlessly tried password after wrong password. "Fifty bucks," she said at long last.

Steve shook his head. "Kinda high," he said automatically, wondering if he could just reset the thing.

"Won't reset," the pawnbroker said, as if she'd read his mind.

Steve stopped punching the stylus at the screen momentarily, looking up to stare at the pawnbroker.

"It's worth a lot more," she said, "but my partner says it won't reset. And it's got some weird kind of battery, too, he says. Never seems to go out, though, so I guess it's okay. Forty."

Steve busied himself with the password search again. *A couple of tries more, and I'm out of here. This is just a waste of time.*

"Look, it's been here for a while. Thirty."

Ten, like the commandments, Steve thought, trying the word. No dice. Hmmm. How long had it been since he'd been to church? What was it he remembered so long ago? Something about Greek letters . . .

Why did he even care about this stupid little PDA? It was just a planner. He didn't need it, but his bargain hunter's instinct and his curiosity were both piqued. Maybe some goofball had it inscribed as a joke, and after the joke played out it wound up here.

Who cares? Leave it behind.

But he couldn't. Just *couldn't.* There was something compelling about Yahweh's PDA. Steve fought off the urge to buy it and set it on the counter.

The minute he put it down, it nagged at him. Greek letters . . .

Greek . . . letters.

Alpha. That was it. Alpha and . . . something. Steve stared away, his gaze resting on some old watches nearby. A Seiko with hands, a Casio with a tiny number pad, a gold Omega, a cheesy Lorus, a Tim—

Omega! That was it. Steve grabbed the PDA again and tore it open. It turned on, the keyboard graphic blinking its request for a password. He poked the little stylus at the letters.

A–L–P–H–A–O–M–E–G–A.

The PDA screen winked out.

Steve's hopes fell.

Then the screen flicked on again. The password screen was gone, replaced by several icons. He'd done it.

Steve's heart stopped; he was sure he went pale.

"Can't go lower than twenty-five, but I've seen you in here befo—"

"Ten," Steve said without looking up, using his best poker face. He snapped the case closed and let his gaze wander back to the watch case, but didn't let go of the PDA.

The pawnbroker sighed loudly. "Twenty."

"Fifteen."

"Done."

Reactivate Yellowstone volcano.

Sixty days of rain in Columbia, SC.

Nessie sighting.

Make holy statue bleed.

Let paleontologist discover previously unknown hominid.

Steve snickered to himself. Nestled into a lumpy recliner at home, the television blaring a game show for background noise, Steve lit a Marlboro and tucked the little machine between his fingers.

Whoever had this thing before, this joke PDA, had loaded it up with *years* of fake events. Steve had never owned a PDA, and this one didn't come with any instruction manual, but he'd seen other people use them and he'd used computers before. His new PDA didn't seem all that difficult to work. Steve had managed to make the calendar appear with very little effort, and in no time at all he'd been able to scroll through those crazy events. And there were *decades* of them.

He wasn't sure how to delete the file, though he'd made a few unsuccessful stabs at it.

Still, he now owned a working PDA, well worth fifteen bucks. At least it would be once he cleared off all the crap. Steve wasn't worried; he had all weekend to figure out how to get it up to speed.

In the meantime, though, he scanned the events. It'd be a shame not to look at them; they were a hoot. Whatever joker had put this together, the guy had a sense of humor and knew his history.

Inspire Bill Gates.

Let someone actually make it to the moon.

UFO landing at Roswell.

STOP HITLER! This one was listed as high priority. Naturally.

How far back did this prankster's fake events go? The novelty of scrolling around in the calendar was beginning to wear thin. It was great fun, sure, for a while, but you could only take any joke so far. . . .

Give H. G. Wells dreams about submarines and aliens.

Give long-overdue dose of talent to Will Shakespeare.

Okay, make that *centuries* of silliness loaded onto the PDA. Steve navigated back to the beginning.

The icons were all of events in the same vein as the calendar.

Create "EZ-world" from 7-day plan in Gods Digest.

Chess in Garden of Eden.

Somebody had really gone all out on this thing.

Choking on his laughter, Steve accidentally poked the PDA screen with the stylus—

—and fell onto the grass, sprawling amidst an aromatic field of flowers. The air was heavy and sweet with the scent of lilies, with an occasional perfumed breath of rose wafting through it—and the PDA was still clutched in his outstretched hand.

He lay there for a few seconds, staring at the impossibly clear blue sky above him. Steve closed his eyes, then opened them again, but the illusion was still there.

A handsome man's head poked into view above him, squinting.

A woman's head appeared beside it. No, not just any woman . . . the most beautiful woman imaginable. Steve's heart flipped over just looking at her angelic face, framed by the sunlight like a living halo.

With some effort, Steve managed to shut his mouth and push himself up to a sitting position, despite maintaining his death grip on the PDA in one hand and keeping the fingers of his other hand twisted around the stylus.

The gorgeous woman was completely naked, and she didn't seem to care that he was staring at her.

Steve looked away, embarrassed, only to find himself staring at the man's state of undress more closely than he preferred. In the midst of his panic, a stream of memories of locker-room comparisons ran through his brain, but he'd never compared as inadequately as this. He yanked the PDA to his face, inches from his eyes, and poked at the screen with the stylus. The event's edit screen disappeared—

—and Steve found himself sitting once again in his recliner, a confrontational talk show blaring on the television. His lit cigarette rested where he'd left it, on the edge of an ashtray balanced on the recliner's arm, undisturbed, the ash still glowing and clinging to the butt.

Shaking his head, Steve stubbed out the cigarette and stared at nothing in particular, ignoring the shouting from the television.

What exactly had just happened? Was it a hallucination? Had he fallen asleep? His mind swam with possibilities.

Steve poked at the PDA screen absently, viewing events at random. And each time he brought up an event, he was . . . there somehow. As if he'd been transported back in time.

He watched Julius Caesar's glorious refusal of the crown in the middle of a stinking crowd of unwashed peasants in dirty tunics. He mounted a skinny old nag and set off on a crusade with badly outfitted teenagers who hadn't seen a decent meal in weeks. The Industrial Revolution cropped up all around him as he flicked through a series of events in rapid succession. The Wright Brothers flew at Kitty Hawk and Steve was there, standing on the beach as they flew over him, low.

It was all here. *All* of it. History.

The World Wars. So many wars in the Middle East

that Steve lost count. The twentieth century in its entirety.

Steve stopped scrolling. The dates were closer now, during his lifetime. He stared at the date displayed, and tried to remember what is was like when he'd been that young. Carefree, the easy life of a preteen. Before he got fat. Just thinking about those days made him feel better, more grounded.

Smiling with his memories, Steve closed his eyes and tried to remember. He'd been skinny then, before puberty really set in; what had happened between then and now to make him so fat? Was it something he'd done? Something he'd failed to do? If he'd done . . . *something* differently, would it have made any difference?

The PDA beeped, breaking his train of thought.

A blank event edit screen was displayed, waiting patiently for Steve to schedule something new.

A *new* event.

Twenty years ago.

On God's PDA.

His heart raced. The garden had seemed so *real*. The man, the woman—so vital, so *immediate*, that Steve couldn't imagine they weren't real. And all the other places, too. Dozens of places, in such detail that he couldn't possibly have made it up. How could they *not* be real?

Yet, how could they be *real*?

This couldn't be real, right? It was just a prank, surely.

But he couldn't seem to convince himself that it was

all a joke, an elaborate illusion. He'd been *there*, in the Garden of Eden. He'd been *there*, in Rome, Spain, Africa, on the deck of the *Santa Maria*, in Antarctica, on the moon. *Everywhere*.

Steve gasped for air, then started to hyperventilate.

Despite the impossibility of it all, deep down he was convinced that he'd *been* all those places.

So what if it really *was* God's PDA?

If it *was*, then Steve held in his hand the most awesome power imaginable. What could this little PDA do?

What *couldn't* it do?

He shook his head.

It was ridiculous. It was a prank, a joke. Nothing more.

Yet Steve's hands trembled, and he shivered.

Subconsciously, Steve knew what he had to do to find out for sure what was going on here. The idea started as a feeling of dread, down deep in his soul, the feeling of wrongness that comes with bucking authority. The plan in its entirety crept over him quickly as it came to the forefront of his consciousness, bringing with it a sheen of cold sweat covering his entire body.

If he really held history in his hands . . .

Maybe, just *maybe*, he could use it for more . . . *personal* events. He had to find out.

With the stylus clutched in nervous, twitching fingers, Steve slowly typed in: "Tell Steve Benemen chocolate cake is *not* the answer."

*   *   *

From his favorite leather recliner, Steve looked out the massive window in his living room, overlooking his Olympic-sized pool, at a glorious southern California sunset. In the background, a muted television displayed the news. Shocked, Steve levered his hundred and fifty pound frame easily out of the chair—his new PDA still clutched in his hand—and gaped at the sunset.

"Anything wrong?"

Steve spun around. In a matching recliner next to his, a trim woman sat, her blazing green eyes looking quizzically over her glasses at him, the magazine she was reading laid in her lap. Sensuous, full lips parted as she repeated her question to him, and Steve's knees went weak as he imagined himself kissing those luscious lips. He could almost *feel* the woman's long, blonde hair brushing his hard chest teasingly while they made love.

Memories flooded through him of the way that they *had* made love, just this morning.

It was impossible. Steve didn't have a girlfriend.

Yet, there was something familiar about her. . . .

Steve's mind struggled with two sets of conflicting memories. There was this . . . fantasy, and there was another reality. In one set of images, he was an accomplished mathematician and successful dot-com millionaire, whose stock trading acumen had led him to pull out just in time, before the technology crash, saving his assets. But in the other, he'd drowned his adolescent shyness in food, and lived a pathetic, lonely life, married to his fat. . . .

In one version of his life, there was Kitty. His wife.

Did it even *matter* which memories were the "real" ones? Steve decided to *make* this one real.

Steve looked down at the PDA in his hand and snapped the leather case closed. There was a gold plaque on the front with the name *Yahweh*.

Steve felt some of those *other* memories slip away. Fine. Let them go. Who needed them, anyway?

But Steve knew he had changed his past with this PDA. Somehow. And with the finely honed intuition of a successful businessman, he knew that that was not a piece of knowledge to be taken lightly.

Plopping into his recliner, Steve flipped open his PDA. Quickly, with a practiced hand, he captured everything he could remember about the PDA from those *other* memories, before they disappeared into oblivion.

While furiously entering the reminder note to himself, mid-sentence, the PDA chimed and a message displayed.

Reminder: [In 3 Days] Destruction of world. Do over.

Steve's heart stopped and his chest constricted so he couldn't breathe. His eyes unfocused. His mouth tasted of copper.

This was no ordinary PDA, he knew that now. This was *God's* PDA, and the events on it were *real*.

The world *would* end in three days.

So it is written, so it shall be done.

But . . . *now*? Did it have to be *now*? After a lifetime of loneliness, Steve found a way to change his fate, a way to have the life he'd always wanted, and now it was scheduled to be taken away?

And not just for him, either, but for the entire *world*?

Why? Was this some kind of cosmic punishment for whoever stole God's PDA? It *had* to be stolen, right? God wouldn't have just *lost* his PDA, right? And what did it mean that Steve had the PDA? Wasn't God supposed to be omniscient? Why would He need a PDA?

Then again, maybe the PDA was what *made* God all-knowing. Maybe He *needed* the PDA to remember things. Maybe God had a bad memory. Steve certainly had had enough trouble sorting out only two timelines, much less the myriad possibilities of this world and the universe that God must track.

In Steve's *other* memories, he remembered viewing events from the past. He'd even changed things and altered the present. But he'd never looked at *future* events.

Maybe he hadn't changed things at all. Maybe the world was already supposed to end.

Would the end of the world still happen now that Steve had the PDA? Or would God forget about it? *Could* God forget about it?

Bile rose in Steve's throat and he went cold, clammy. It was no fun, trying to second-guess God. He felt the blood drain from his face. Closing his eyes, he swallowed. And he thought.

If Steve could *visit* an event just by viewing it, and he could *create* a new event, what would happen if he *changed* the event? Or deleted it entirely, for that matter?

It was worth the chance. Steve navigated forward

and found the event easily. It was right there, plain as could be.

Destruction of world. Do over.

The stylus vibrated in Steve's shaking hand as he poised the tip over the event, ready to delete it. But curiosity overwhelmed him. How would it happen? Was the world going to just stop? Was there the war to end all wars? What? How did God plan to "do over?"

Steve couldn't help himself. He poked at the event to view it—

—and he was in the middle of a city, with massive buildings and a moving mass of humanity rushing along the streets. They were all around him, moving fast, bumping, jostling him as he stood there on the sidewalk, dazed, and they flowed around him like a river current. Cars zipped close by, occasionally splashing his pants leg with stinking, muddy water. Pigeons flapped noisily overhead.

Then a roar rose up from the belly of the great city itself, and the ground shook with the effort. Steve nearly lost his balance as the sidewalk groaned and lurched upward unsteadily. Nearby, the ground cracked open and swallowed some surprised pedestrians. A cab careened front-end into the chasm, its horn blaring on long after the crash.

Chaos should have reigned, but it didn't. All around Steve people just stopped dead in their tracks and gaped, not downward at the disintegrating earth, but . . . upward.

Perplexed, Steve looked up, too. A thick, black

cloud sped across what little sky he could see between the towering buildings, rapidly blotting out the sun. Night fell in seconds, and they were plunged into a darkness that Steve knew would never end.

Steve prayed.

He prayed that God's PDA had a backlight.

It did—

—and Steve was back in his recliner in California, paralyzed with fear.

The sensation passed quickly, but he was still dazed. Shaking, his heart bursting in his chest, he poked at the delete icon so sharply he was afraid he'd drive the stylus right through the screen.

The entry blinked out.

No more destruction of the world. All gone. Deleted.

He hoped.

The weekend passed for Steve with little sleep. The scare with Armageddon on God's PDA had left him too nervous to rest. For the entire weekend, the PDA sat undisturbed on the recliner near the television. In fact, Steve went out of his way to avoid it.

Steve didn't talk about the abandoned PDA and Kitty didn't ask. The pair of them ate and swam and talked and made love, and that was enough for Steve. If the world was going to end, Steve was determined to enjoy his new life until then.

And if it wasn't, well, Steve was determined to enjoy life anyway.

Monday morning arrived and Steve spent the entire day on edge.

But nothing happened all day.

No Armageddon. No destruction of the world. No "do over."

Steve slept soundly that night and woke the next morning refreshed, ready to tackle the PDA's mysteries.

It had occurred to him during the night that if he had thought to enter a memo to himself about those *other* memories after he'd made the world change, maybe he should check for other memos. Maybe—just maybe—this wasn't the first time he'd used God's PDA.

It took only a few seconds to confirm what he'd suspected—there was another memo, just one, that he'd written to himself, titled, "Steve Benemen vs. Armageddon."

God did it. Earth gone. Can't describe it here. You'll find out later. Stole God's PDA. Can't use it here for some reason, but you can there. Stop Armageddon, Steve. Get the PDA back before He notices.

Steve Beneman stared, eyes narrowed suspiciously, at a pawn shop that shouldn't exist. *Deuce's Pawn and Fire*, the battered sign said. But, when he'd found the PDA last Friday, just lying forgotten on the sidewalk in the space where the shop was now, and wasn't then, there weren't any shops nearby.

Steve had never been in a pawn shop before—at least not that he could remember—but he knew this was the right place. The shop was called *Deuce's*, just like the nickname his teenage poker buddies had called him way back when. It *had* to be a sign. He was *sure* this would be the right place.

He steeled his nerves and went in, carefully pushing on the broken glass door checker-boarded with duct tape.

It felt weird pawning God's PDA, almost like he was committing a sin of some kind. Then again, wouldn't it be the *other* Steve, the *original* Steve, who sinned? After all, that Steve was the one who'd stolen the PDA in the first place. This Steve was merely righting the wrong.

With one teensy, weensy little change: that whole end of the world thing.

He handed it over to the scrawny tattooed proprietor, took the ticket, and got out of there.

Steve turned his back on God's PDA and walked away quickly, secure in the absolute knowledge that, somewhere, somehow, the original Steve would get that PDA back to its rightful owner.

Or *was* it the original Steve? Maybe there were other Steves before that one, who hadn't bothered with notes to their counterparts. Or maybe *that* Steve had erased them so that *this* Steve wouldn't get distracted. Or maybe—

It didn't matter. After all was said and done, no matter how many of them there were, he decided that *he* was now the original Steve, master of his own life.

And his wife was waiting for him.

Smiling, he turned toward home.

THE RIGHTEOUS PATH

Jay Lake

1425 Anno Hegira (2004 Anno Domini)

The Amir of Rome rushed through his sermon. "The Hadith tells us that women are naturally, morally, and religiously defective." The congregation gathered within Boutros al-Islamiyya muttered. Words like that might be consistent with tradition, even true, but were not openly spoken in the modern Caliphate. The former seat of the Christian popes was not a mosque normally friendly to Restorationist imams.

"That's our signal," Jorj told Herbert. Torn between relief and excitement, he moved toward the exit. He pulled Herbert along in his wake. "Heat's coming for sure now."

"Women are among the silent beasts," the Amir shouted. His tone pitched up in fear, or perhaps conviction. "But they have been made in human form so that men may speak with them, and not recoil from inter—"

The golden doors at the back slammed open.

"Mutaween!" boomed a woman's voice, amplified to a painful volume. "You read from forbidden texts. Hold in the name of the Calipha!"

"Abomination," shouted the Amir, his voice cracking. "The Calipha spits upon the Prophet!"

Then the armored mutaween troopers swarmed into the ancient building. Shock sticks buzzed as Jorj bolted through a side door, still dragging Herbert behind him as they scuttled down slick, narrow steps. Behind them the crowd screamed.

"That was close." Herbert's voice was ragged with the pounding of his breath. Jorj's partner was a pale, thick-lipped Frank who never seemed fully aware of his surroundings. Even though Herbert prayed faithfully, Jorj could not quite bring himself to believe in Herbert's dedication to the Restorationist struggle. No one with those pallid blue eyes could be a true soldier of God.

"Silence." Jorj kept a careful watch on the catacomb's side tunnels, turned into the eleventh on the left. The last flickering electric light faded to shadow as the tunnel curved away.

The catacombs confused the mutaween's pheromone trackers, with their random drafts, open connections to Rome's ancient sewers, and copious human tissue. The only thing Jorj and Herbert could do about infrared tracking was move faster than their pursuers.

Jorj counted skulls. The slick ones had been touched in the recent past. The cobwebbed ones he ignored. After nine slick skulls, he stopped. "Trapdoor just to the left," he whispered.

"Sewers," Herbert hissed.

"Cistern, actually."

There was distant shouting, and the distinctive sound of bullets ricocheting on stone.

"And we go," Jorj said. He felt a warm surge of pride and fear, a strange but delicious mix. They were committed to the Restoration now.

They vanished into a stinking dampness where even infrared tracking was pointless.

Later, in a sagging warehouse in an alley near the Via Ostia on Rome's outskirts, Jorj and Herbert finally relaxed. The building's foundations were older than Islam itself. The walls leaned in around them, braced with rusted steel bars, held apart mostly by the roof beams of ancient oak. The place stank of mold, stone, and machine oil. Most of the space was occupied by an enormous bulk beneath a tarp.

The slums along the Via Ostia were the dhimmi quarter, where Christians, Jews, and Zoroastrians dwelt. It seemed appropriate to bring about the Restoration of the true path of Islam in such a place.

"You said it wasn't a sewer," Herbert complained.

Jorj laughed. Fleeing the mutaween had been a pleasure so great it must be sinful. They had even stopped for afternoon prayer somewhere in the depths of the city. God had surely blessed their feet.

"That was drinking water," he said. "The sewers are much worse. This is Rome, not Damascus or Cordova." He stalked to a wall calendar featuring a supercharged motor chariot covered with logos from some infidel Annamese tool maker. One finger stabbed against the paper. "Look. Today is 24 Raby al-awal.

We heard the signal in the Boutros al-Islamiyya. The plan is ready, God willing."

"As God wills it," echoed Herbert.

Turning, Jorj spread his arms wide. "So rejoice. We are set to change the world. Make your machine ready."

"I rejoice." Herbert smiled, though it looked strained to Jorj. Herbert walked over to the tarp and tugged it free.

Beneath the tarp was a Rathah Mark Eleven, an Indian-built military hovercraft captured from the Siberians in the most recent of the Ural Wars. The slab-sided vehicle was over two meters tall, four meters wide and twelve meters long. Its armor was utilitarian, rivets and welding seams exposed—nothing like the sleek, glossy fighting machines that came out of the Caliphate's great motor works at Aleppo and Tell Aviv.

Technology was but a tool in the service of God, Jorj told himself, stilling his admiration.

Herbert thumbed open an armored flap and tapped a key sequence. A hydraulic hatch oozed open to admit him, flickering light shedding a blue-white radiance into the musty warehouse.

There were hundreds of fighters in the Restorationist Jihad. Thousands, perhaps millions of supporters. Those outside the wisdom of the Shari'a would see the light soon enough. Jorj was humbled that he and Herbert were blessed to be the tip of God's spear, puncturing the heart of the Damascene Caliphate and the Calipha herself.

Somewhere over the centuries it had gone wrong.

Women in the councils first of the Cordoban Caliphate, then the Damascene, had been obscenity enough. But the Council of Tours had crushed true Islam to dust, elevating women to the status of men in the eyes of God, against all common sense and any rational reading of the Quran or the Haddith. Pluralism and tolerance were transformed from vice to virtue in the space of a few generations.

Now, thanks to some deep thinkers in the Restorationist ranks, all would be put paid.

Jorj had been reading for a doctorate in history at the University of Baghdad when the Restorationists approached him. His master's thesis on the liberalization of Islam under the influence of the Cordoban Caliphate had caught the attention of important people. His thinking was progressive, straight into the arms of God, they said. Then they asked him the impossible question.

Would he like to change history?

Six years later he sat in a warehouse near Via Ostia while a rumpled Frankish geek set the jumpers on an Indian-built time machine. The spirit-sapping influence of the liberal Cordoban Caliphate would soon be erased from history. Islam would be restored to the rigor demanded of all good worshippers by the Prophet himself.

The equations describing time travel were necessarily incomplete. According to Herbert, by definition they could not be fully described. As Jorj had lost track of math somewhere just past algebra, he had to accept that.

What Jorj did understand was that as the Earth
moved around the sun, and the sun moved around the
galaxy, every point separated in time was also separated in space. Herbert had shown Jorj the ferociously
complex reverse spiral required to illustrate the retro-
grade position of their target. Their course moved
over a light-year through space to reach their desired
location in time. It made him uneasy to use such progressive "science"—the Quran was quite clear about
the Earth being flat, for one—but Jorj considered himself a practical man. All in the service of God.

This meant that time travel necessarily predicated
positional change. Somehow, the original Indian build-
ers of the machine had botched this bit of theory, at
least as Herbert explained it. Which was why the Rathah Mark Eleven with the time machine on board
had been captured in a Siberian military convoy in
the trans-Caucasus, traveling under more security even
than a nuclear weapons transfer, trying to get into
position to threaten the Caliphate's Sevastapolis space
base at some time in the recent past.

All of history could turn on one man, in one place.
It had over and over. Jorj had determined where best
the leverage represented by the Rathah-mounted time
machine could be applied.

The man was Abd ar-Rahman.

The place was the Battle of Tours-Poitiers in 114
A.H.

Jorj was armed with faith and good historical analy-
sis of the rise of the Cordoban Caliphate. The hovercraft was loaded with fuel for fifteen hundred
kilometers of cruising, enough explosives to topple

several Frankish castles if the need arose, along with firearms, night vision equipment, and a hundred kilograms of gold carefully rendered sufficiently impure to pass muster with an Iberian or Frankish goldsmith of the era. So equipped, they planned to leave Ostia for the wilds of second century Gallia.

During the rest of that day Herbert emerged from the hovercraft twice for prayers and once for a restroom break and a nap. Jorj went out for food and a fresh bucket of stones—Herbert's seemingly permanent Frankish indigestion fouled even the cleanest privy soon enough. Waking up well into the evening, Herbert stretched and smiled. "Praise God, but I am ready."

"Just like that?" Surely there was more ceremony to such an undertaking than a nap and plate of cold pheasant.

Herbert nodded and stepped back into the pale-lit hatch. A Frankish sort of a light for a Frankish sort of man, Jorj thought. He touched the Quran nestled in his robes, thought of the glory that awaited them, and followed Herbert into the time machine.

"Local effects might be interesting," said Herbert from the right seat, flipping switches on a panel marked only in some tiny, flowing Asian script.

Jorj settled into the left seat before one of the hovercraft's twin control yokes. Herbert would do the gross navigation, delivering them to Gaul in the right framework of time and space. Jorj would do the fine navigation, keeping them out of trees and lakes. They had to trust the gravimeters and other arcane instru-

ments of South Asian science to keep them precisely
on the Earth's surface—as opposed to a hundred kilometers above or below, for example.

"Tau flow potentiometers online," Herbert said.

The Frank liked to talk while he worked.

"Gravity wave benders online."

Jorj checked the idle of the hovercraft's paired gas
turbine engines. Normal. Fuel pressure was fine. Aux-
iliary tanks were full.

"Reverse q-bit stream normal."

Jorj began to recite Quranic verse. "Is not He Who
created the heavens and the earth, and sends down
for you water from the sky, whereby We cause to
grow wonderful gardens full of beauty and delight?"

"Lighting off in ten . . . nine . . . eight . . ."

"It is not in your ability to cause the growth of
their trees."

"Four . . . three . . . two . . ."

"Is there any other god with God?"

"Hit it, Jorj."

He powered up the fans and hit the throttle just as
their warehouse door vanished in a sheet of flame. The
hardened hovercraft plowed through, shooting into an
alley that seemed to stutter like a bad animation.

"Local effects," said Herbert. "As predicted, that
transition really interferes with the ambient molecu-
lar resonance."

"Silence!" shouted Jorj, who was trying to dodge a
rapidly shrinking tree.

They skimmed over land and water at an apparent
speed of well over a hundred kilometers per hour. Jorj

backed down the throttles and concentrated on his steering, trusting the hovercraft's armor to absorb any truly dreadful punishment. Trees, fences, livestock all crushed beneath the armored foreskirt. More disturbing, they burst into flame.

It was as if he were a fiery djinn, traveling along the Mediterranean coast on some mysterious errand.

As Jorj understood the theory, they couldn't *actually* hit something so hard as to destroy the hovercraft. Damage, yes, but objects were either in "leading phase" or "trailing phase." The vehicle was in neither of those states. Which meant that obstacles were not quite as solid to him as he was to them.

He still flinched and cowered from the flickering trees and strobing cycle of the days and nights, much to his shame. "I am a warrior of God!" Jorj shouted at the windscreen. "I fear nothing in pursuit of jihad!"

"Save your energy," Herbert said.

They moved through a spray of crops. Jorj caught a glimpse of a startled Frankish face, then another night flickered by in reverse.

114 Anno Hegira (732 Anno Domini)

Eleven hours later by their internal frame of reference, the hovercraft ground to a halt on a bluff overlooking a river. They were surrounded by woods, with some farmed clearings near a fitful, muddy track headed for a crude stone city on a hill some distance upriver. Fat snowflakes fell from high clouds, obscuring but not completely blocking the view.

"Tours?" Jorj asked.

"Poitiers." Herbert flipped some switches, studied his gauges and displays.

"What year?"

"Need to take a stellar fix to be certain, but looks like 114 according to our onboard instrumentation." Herbert smiled. "We're in the right place and time."

"You're not getting a stellar fix tonight."

"I'm not worried."

They established the position of Mecca, took out their prayer mats and knelt to give thanks to God. Purified, Jorj took a pair of field glasses and an assault rifle, cycled the hatch, and left the hovercraft for the chill Gallic autumn. He needed to find a place to hide the machine while they waited for the armies of Charles the Merovingian and Abd ar-Rahman to meet.

Part of him hated to hand the victory to an infidel Frankish army, but the Cordoban Caliphate had to be broken before it could blossom in Western Europe. Then the Damascene Caliphate would triumph by strength of faith and force of arms, without the liberalizing infection from Cordoba.

"There is no God but God," said Jorj with a smile as he climbed atop the Rathah to scan the area for hiding places. They needed to be hull down in a depression, away from the high ground which would be sought by both Frankish and Islamic scouts.

At least the locals didn't have artillery.

Gallia resembled Rome in some unexpected ways. Both were a long way from Jorj's native Mosul. Alien

trees, alien terrain, alien weather, which vacillated between rain, sleet, and snow. The cold got into his
bones despite his Siberian military surplus arctic-
duty battledress.

Herbert refused to venture out, preferring to stay
inside and plot their return to 1425 A.H. Jorj promised
himself that he was prepared for either outcome—to
become martyr or return to the Restorationists in a
world of righteous Islam. Herbert didn't seem to think
there was a difference. Though Herbert never missed
prayers, Jorj was coming more and more to suspect
his associate's theological purity.

Instead of fighting with the man who would someday soon save his life by restoring them both to the
future, Jorj stalked the woods. He shot deer. He shot
squirrel. He shot a Frankish peasant one day, then
had second thoughts about a search being raised and
was forced to bury the louse-ridden corpse himself.

They were in the right place, within a few kilometers. At the right time, within a week or so. All they
were missing were the opposing armies.

Jorj settled into a shallow, leaf-filled depression on
a slope overlooking the road. The trackway was knee-
deep in mud. Whoever came that way wouldn't be
moving fast. He figured on the battle taking place
where the road forded a swift, shallow river that was
either the Clain or the Vienne. The historian Ibn 'Abd
al-Hakam had written of the battleground being at a
river crossing near Poitiers. Even if Jorj was misposi-
tioned, one of the two armies had to move past this
point to reach the battle.

Something rustled behind him as water ran down

his neck. Cradling his rifle, Jorj turned to look only to find himself jabbed in the neck with something sharp.

It wasn't water on his neck. It was metal. He was trapped, seeing only a narrow slice of earth without rolling his head into the point of the weapon.

How could he be caught like this?

A pair of leather boots appeared in front of him. Still metal on his neck, though. Behind Jorj, a horse whickered.

The boot owner knelt to look Jorj in the eye. His captor had a nut-brown face, wild beard and a great grin. The man wore robes of dark red and blue much like a desert nomad's traditional dress, with a leather shoulder harness for his weapons.

Berber horsemen. Abd ar-Rahman's light cavalry.

"You don't look to be a Frank," said the Berber in badly accented, archaic but comprehensible Arabic.

Jorj had never been so glad he'd read history at university. He tried to match his captor's dialect. "God is great," he said. "I am from Arabia."

"A Damascene." The Berber sucked breath between cracked brown teeth, biting his lower lip. "We're to kill or run from anyone we meet. You do not appear to need running from."

"I come to do God's work for Abd ar-Rahman." It was even true, in a sense. The man was only a Berber. God would forgive the lie.

"Orders and orders," said an unseen voice in the same muddy Arabic. The man with metal at Jorj's neck. Then the unseen speaker rattled on in some barbarous African tongue.

Jorj's Berber grunted, glancing over Jorj's head. "Up, Damascene. Back to camp with you."

The metal vanished from his neck. Jorj got to his hands and knees only to have his captor kick his wrists and grab the rifle. Both Berbers laughed as Jorj staggered upward again to find a leaf-bladed spear nudging his chest.

The second scout, still mounted, held the other end of the spear, a good three meters away. He grinned, wider and toothier even than his fellow.

"No weapons," said the first Berber. He searched Jorj, taking his radio, pen, and pocket comp. He then tugged a rope from his saddle, tied it to a ring worked into the leather then bound Jorj's wrists at the other end.

"Let us see if God made you to be a fast runner."

The horses set off at a trot through the woods, eerily silent as they picked their way along. Jorj stumbled after, thinking of how quickly he could escape if he just got his rifle back. Then he wondered what would happen if Herbert were discovered by ar-Rahman's Berber scouts.

Or would it be worse if Herbert *weren't* discovered?

Jorj fell several times, and was dragged through the leafy mud of the forest, but managed to get up. He never did hit his head, despite his fears. The Berbers ignored him, though they never set their horses to a full gallop. Jorj's shoulders, elbows, and wrists burned as he was yanked along. His feet blistered even within the Siberian boots.

After perhaps four or five hours of hellish, stumbling progress they passed through a line of Berber horsemen. Whistles, catcalls, and shouts greeted his captors. Then the land dropped into wet fields of stubble and mud dotted with the tents of a vast army. The camp stretched across the dale, over the next ridge and beyond. Smoke rose, hammers rang from smithies, horses whinnied, children cried, sergeants shouted— all the noises of war and then some. It was more of a city on the march than what Jorj understood an army to be. The subtlety of the Berber scouts was lost in the brawling immensity of the camp.

Perversely, his captors increased their pace, forcing Jorj to a wild, windmilling run through the crowded lanes. They whooped, one cracking a whip, as Jorj stumbled on something and fell to slide in the mud. He fought to get to his feet, but they were moving too fast. Someone tossed slops on him with commendable accuracy. He began to twist on the end of rope, seeing gray sky, then canvas tents, then mud, then sky again. The breath was pounded out of him as if with hammers.

Then it was over.

He lay on his back, ribs groaning as he tried for breath which would not come. A huge silk tent towered just at the top of his field of view. His captor leaned down and poked Jorj in the chest.

"Be well, be honest, and God willing you will walk from this place alive."

Then with a wink he was gone. Jorj could only nod.

A pair of armored guards, true Arabs, Jorj dimly noted, dragged him into the tent. There was a sort of mud room where water was dashed over him by giggling Frankish maids with buckets. They set to scrubbing him without a care to be gentle, still giggling. Moments later a fat man in pale silks slipped through an inner wall of the tent and inspected Jorj. He had gentle, sleepy eyes like a deer.

"You look like a Frank left too long in the sun," he pronounced. His Arabic was archaic, too, but not as muddy as the Berbers'. Then the fat man took a little pot and sprinkled some stinking perfume over Jorj. "Come."

Jorj slipped down a narrow carpeted hall with walls of silk after the fat man, followed by the armored Arab guards. He had no idea what had become of his rifle. He would be dead soon, his mission failed. That idiot Herbert could not be trusted to dispatch Abd ar-Rahman.

In some strange way, Jorj felt relieved.

Then they were in a small room. The guards chained Jorj to a deep-set chair with high arms before departing. The fat man had many questions, some of them assisted by razors and sand-filled silk tubes. Jorj screamed and shouted and denied everything, never telling the truth through the hours of torture. The lengthy beatings he had experienced in the Restorationist camps in the Balkans stood him in good stead.

The worst was the laughter of women through the tent wall, the little animals listening to his every moment of humiliation and taking their pleasure from the weakness of a man.

Much, much later Jorj was still chained to a chair, sitting in a pool of his own fluids. His battledress blouse was in ruins, a gob of tarry mud blocking the blood flow where his right nipple had once been. He still had most of his teeth, though many were loose.

The Mutaween could have taken lessons from Abd ar-Rahman's sloe-eyed torturer.

There was a rustle as a young man in a linen robe came into the little room carrying Jorj's rifle.

He had a chance after all.

"Is this Chinese?" the young man asked without preamble, tapping the weapon. He was beautiful, vibrating with an intensity of spirit and purpose.

"It is mine," muttered Jorj.

"My eunuch Aabaar says that God sent you."

"I belong to God."

"The Franks march south. We will meet soon. Are you a messenger?"

This was Abd ar-Rahman, Jorj realized. The man who had conquered Western Europe for Islam, swept all the Franks and their Pope under the Caliphate's prayer mat. Jorj could see why men followed ar-Rahman.

"I am a messenger." *Think, think . . .* "Sent to bring lightning into your battle with Charles the Merovingian."

"So Charles leads them." Ar-Rahman tapped the rifle against his other hand. "I expected no different. Their king Theuderich is less than a woman." He sighed. "We will not take Tours before Charles arrives."

Not if you're camped here like this. Respect. Jorj had to command respect from this man he'd come to kill. "I will show you my lightning but once. The rest is reserved for the Franks."

"This?" Ar-Rahman turned the rifle over in his hand.

"Come, then."

It was that simple. Jorj's hands were freed by more armed men who stepped through the door. His rifle was handed to him by Ar-Rahman. Weapon in hand, limping, Jorj followed the general through the silk walls and out into the camp.

I could shoot him here. I could shoot him now. God's work would be done. The righteous path of Islam would be restored.

But the battle might go on. The armies had not met yet. Ar-Rahman's lieutenants had time to elect another war leader. The Saracen and Berber cavalry would shatter the Frankish peasant levies under Charles—history was starkly clear on the matter. Ar-Rahman *had* to die in the heat of battle in order to force a retreat.

"That man," said Ar-Rahman, pointing at a short fellow in a gold and red turban walking perhaps sixty meters away.

Jorj shouldered the rifle. "Has he offended you?"

"Lightning from God shall send him straight to the virgins of paradise. There is no offence."

Sight in.

Jorj's fingers hurt as he gently tugged the trigger partway home.

Breathe out.

He ignored the shooting pains in his beaten ribs.

Easy shot.

Blood pooled in his left eye.

Squeeze the trigger.

The multicolored turban exploded as the soft-nosed bullet struck the man's head. The shot echoed. People near to Jorj and ar-Rahman dropped to their knees, but the rest of the camp went back to its business almost immediately. A wailing woman threw herself across the distant body before a mule train blocked Jorj's view.

He had killed a fellow Muslim. Christian Franks were one thing, but God's people were another.

"God is great," said ar-Rahman. "He had sent me lightning to strike Charles the Merovingian."

"God is great," echoed Jorj. The pain in his mutilated chest was a mocking echo.

For two days Jorj rested amid a small harem of cow-breasted blonde Frankish maidens. These were not the white raisins and honeyed dates of paradise, but it was not far off either. The Franks were hardly virgins, but he experienced more male release in two days than he had before in his entire life.

This was not such a sinful way of life. Their female bounty almost made him forget the pain of his torture.

On the third day the sloe-eyed eunuch brought Jorj and his rifle before the general again. Today ar-Rahman was armored in lacquered steel, ready to ride to battle. The eunuch was barely clothed at all. Arabesque tattoos ran down his enormous belly and across his thighs. A huddle of bright-silked nobles and armed retainers crowded the audience room.

"Are you ready with God's lightning?"

"Yes, lord," said Jorj. He had studied etiquette within the harem.

"We ride for God and the caliphate." Ar-Rahman glanced at the eunuch. "Show my court that this lightning will not strike the faithful. They fear."

It *had* struck the faithful. "I cannot do that, lord. My lightning is reserved for the Franks."

The eunuch's delicate eyes twinkled. The nobles stirred, muttering.

Ar-Rahman tugged at his leather neckpiece. "Show us that God's lightning will not mark me."

This was his best chance. A called shot, no less. They would cut him down where he stood, but Jorj had long ago pledged himself as martyr to the faith.

Except he was supposed to cut ar-Rahman down in battle, so that there would be no transfer of leadership.

Jorj shouldered the rifle.

Sight in.

Gently tugged the trigger.

Breathe out.

Engaged the safety catch.

His body didn't hurt so much today.

Pulled the trigger.

The weapon clicked. The sound was like the fall of a sword in the silent room.

"Mussawa was a pig and a secret Christian!" bellowed someone in the crowd of nobles.

Cheering erupted. Abd ar-Rahman smiled and tugged his neckpiece back into place. The eunuch made a very slight bow toward Jorj, one meant for only him to see. Ar-Rahman stepped forward and embraced Jorj, the rifle pressed between them. "You are my man now, as well as God's," the general whispered.

The armies met two days later after a daylong march through freezing rain, slowed by the heavy wagons hauling tribute acquired in the course of the campaign. Almost no one in ar-Rahman's army was prepared for the harsh Frankish weather. The march took a frightening number of casualties just through exposure, many of them men who could not get up again after kneeling during the stops for prayer. There were still tens of thousands of troops, many of them Saracen and Berber cavalry, but ar-Rahman was at a clear disadvantage in the freezing, muddy woods.

Charles had drawn his Franks up across the ford, arrayed along on a bluff with pike squares immediately in the trackway. The Islamic advance would be highly constrained, throwing a small wedge of force against tightly-packed defenders. History showed that Islamic morale and training would win the day, but the situation still appeared grim.

He avoided looking toward the hillside where the Rathah Mark Eleven was hidden. The hovercraft, explosives and weapons were all in the control of one unreliable Frank. What would Herbert do? If he still had his radio, Jorj might have been able to drive the Frank to action.

Jorj did not believe his partner could kill ar-Rahman. Though he had come to like the man, Jorj must still do the deed himself. He prayed for strength as he rode with ar-Rahman's party. The sloe-eyed eunuch was never far. Berber skirmishers traded ineffective arrow flights across the river with the Frankish line. Despite the miserable weather, ar-Rahman seemed in no hurry to engage. A mob of slaves and peasants already worked to fell trees and draw up tent lines for a temporary camp out of bowshot from the other army.

The general pulled his horse up next to Jorj. "Can your lightning find Charles the Merovingian from here?"

"No, lord. I need to see him first."

"How will you know him?"

The question was far too astute. What he needed was the hot press of battle, to shoot ar-Rahman when the general's death would turn the tide of battle. Otherwise this man would be preaching the Quran in Rome in two years, gathering power for the ultimate feminization of Islam.

"God will guide my eyes," Jorj finally said.

Ar-Rahman nodded and edged away again, already speaking with two of his commanders.

Days of desultory raiding followed. The weather varied between sleet and snow, relieved by occasional chilly rain. That kept the river high, the road muddy and bowstrings damp. The Berbers took to taunting the Franks, whooping as they galloped along the south bank. The Saracen heavy cavalry sulked in their tents, while peasants and pikemen on both sides simply suffered.

Everything according to history. Jorj saw no sign of

Herbert. He spent his days skulking miserably in the edge of woods watching for an unexpected sally by Charles. He spent his nights alone, the bubbly Frankish maidens left far behind.

On the sixth day of the desultory battle, a weak sun shone through ragged clouds. The river lost some of its roar, and Jorj's breath did not hang over his head in a plume.

"Tomorrow," whispered the soldiers. Even the horses seemed eager.

The seventh day dawned clear and cold. Instead of rain, they had frost. The river was down, the ford more accessible. The Franks drew up their tight square on the opposite bank, pikes wavering.

"They are ours," shouted Abd ar-Rahman with his sword drawn. "We shall send them to God."

Battle was joined in earnest. The Saracen cavalry rode out for the first of their many assaults on the ford. Berbers faded into the woods for less reliable fords upstream, seeking to harry the enemy's rear.

All according to history.

The rifle was chill and heavy in Jorj's hand, a narrow metal millstone. "You are history," he whispered to it, his breath leaving fading clouds on the blue-steeled metal of the barrel.

In the third hour of the day, ar-Rahman rode toward the ford in a body of guardsmen and officers. Jorj sighted in on him, ar-Rahman's narrow nose leaping large in the scope.

His finger touched the trigger.

Breathe in.

He watched ar-Rahman.

Breathe out.

The Calipha could not be permitted to come to power through the ultimate consequences of this man's victory.

Breathe in.

She was an abomination against God and man.

Breathe out.

"And pull . . . " he whispered, still tracking ar-Rahman in the scope.

Then Jorj set the rifle down. He could not betray Islam in its march to victory. The problem of the Calipha could be solved in a different time and place.

The sloe-eyed eunuch smiled at him from the back of a mule.

After that, the battle raged in earnest until blood flooded the river. Jorj climbed high in a tree, braced himself, and scanned for Charles the Merovingian. If he could not do one, he would do the other, ensure against a historical accident caused by his presence. The Frankish general liked to lead from the front—Ibn Abd al-Hakam and the other chroniclers were very clear on that. Jorj would have his shot soon.

He still watched his own battle line, so as not to be isolated by a surprise Frankish advance. A flash of steel along the river bank caught Jorj's eye. Jorj swung the rifle to sight in on the sloe-eyed eunuch, who smiled back at him as he cleaned his bloody dagger on ar-Rahman's cape. The general lay face down in the mud. Already the Franks poured over the ford.

Though it would do no good, Jorj shot the eunuch in the stomach. He then curled on his branch and shivered.

Much later, stunned by cold and shock and fear, Jorj heard the roar of the Rathah Mark Eleven's gas turbines in the gathering dusk. Screaming mules fled the hovercraft's advance as Frankish rear guards hurled spears and fired arrows before following the lead of their animals.

They advanced through time in a swirling sheet of fire, aiming for Rome. Herbert drove. Jorj curled in the left seat, chilled to his soul. "What did I do?" he whispered.

"Huh?" Herbert drove badly.

"The Calipha will still hold all of the faith beneath her woman's heel."

"Uh."

Jorj stared across the flickering sunrises and sunsets of thirteen centuries until the hovercraft finally ground to a halt in a muddy, deserted alley sometime late at night.

"Where's our warehouse?" Jorj asked.

"We destroyed it."

"How long ago—" he began, before realizing the question was meaningless.

Herbert scanned the comm channels. "No traffic on the usual frequencies." He pulled in voice in several half-familiar languages, bastard Roman Latin, perhaps.

Nothing in God's language.

They finally paused on one of the frequencies at the sound of a familiar word badly pronounced—

"Baghdad." They listened carefully, catching other words. "Mosul." "Damascus."

"Where are we?" asked Jorj.

"Where we should be in time and space," answered Herbert. "Wherever this is."

They armed themselves and left the hovercraft. The fifth person they caught and pinned down spoke Arabic. His story was incredible, what they could get out him.

No Calipha. No Caliphate. Jews ruling Palestine. Frankish armies in the streets of Baghdad, on the way to Damascus. Some power called the United States murdering Muslims around the world.

They clubbed their informant into insensibility, then hid in a doorway to confer.

"What do we do?" Jorj asked.

Herbert shrugged. "We could go back. But there is no Cordoban Caliphate here. This is the world of the righteous path. We have succeeded."

"But our people are powerless, living under Frankish guns." The rifle felt hot in Jorj's hand, as if it had absorbed some of the energy of their trip back through time. Jorj had never imagined regretting the elimination of the Calipha. He should have killed the eunuch Aabaar earlier. His chest still ached from the man's tortures. "Can we go back and set things right?"

"We can try."

Keeping to the shadows, they returned to the hovercraft. It was surrounded by motor chariots with flashing blue lights, and armed Franks shouting in debased Latin.

Many, many armed Franks.

"We must return," Jorj whispered. But instead he raised his rifle and took the shots he'd meant to take thirteen centuries earlier.

CHAIN

Ray Vukcevich

1
Eastern Turkey

Nathan had turned off the kerosene lamp before they made love so they would allow a silhouette to show on the side of the tent; now that they were finished, he lighted it again so he could catch up on his reading. Tomorrow they would both be back on the dig, desperately trying to get what they could before the ancient city of Zeugma was drowned by the rising waters of the Euphrates River behind the new dam. There was so much to do and so little time to do it.

Darcie turned away and snuggled into the covers. He leaned over, lightly brushed the hair from her eyes, and kissed her cheek. She sighed and settled into sleep. He watched her for a moment and then found his book on the upended cardboard box that served as their bedside table.

Nathan had not read more than a paragraph or two

when Darcie sat straight up in bed and said, "I've just realized I'm a time traveler with a mission."

He figured she was coming up out of a dream, so he said, "And I'm a deep sea diver with an octopus in my pants."

"What?"

"Never mind."

"This is going to be hard to believe," Darcie said, "but I have come back in time to tell you what you must do at the dig tomorrow."

She got out of bed and found her robe. Sitting on her heels, she lighted the camp stove and put the coffee on. She opened a canvas chair and pointed at it, and her message was clear. Get up and sit down.

He got up and got into his pants and sat down.

She handed him a cup of coffee. She got a chair for herself and put it right in front of him and sat down. "I'll start with the nature of time," she said.

She was acting so strangely. They had been married for nearly 20 years.

Who was this woman?

2
The Nature of Time

"Aliens have finally landed," Darcie said.

"Oh, wonderful, first time travel and now we've got aliens," he said. "What's really going on here, Darcie?"

"Be patient," she said. "There is a lot to fill in, and you need to understand it all before morning. In the year 2210, aliens make themselves known to humanity."

Nathan sipped his coffee and was quiet. He wondered if she were sick. If so, there was nothing much he could do about it tonight. He would sit up with her, all night if necessary, and listen and then tomorrow he could get her back to town or even on to Istanbul for medical attention.

"This was not the first time they had visited Earth, of course," Darcie said. "They have been dropping in for thousands of years. But in 2210, they figured we might be ready to know about them. But there was a test to pass."

"Isn't there always?" Nathan asked.

She flashed a smile on and off to let him know that she had heard him but didn't really think his remark was very funny. "They had planted Items around the planet over the years. Our job was to find them all and put them together. If we assembled them correctly, the terrible plague that was wiping us out would be cured. But all the pieces could not be found. Or more precisely, one piece could not be found."

"That's a lot on our plate," Nathan said. "Items to assemble, a worldwide plague, and then one of the pieces is missing."

"Yes, well, to repeat myself, in order to understand the real problem," she said in her lecture voice, "you must understand the nature of time."

Well, time was something she should know about. If she were delusional, wouldn't it be just this sort of fantasy a geophysicist would come up with?

"Here's how time works," she said. "It starts sometime after you're born and ends when you die. Actually saying when it ends is usually easier than saying when it begins. But both 'ends' and 'begins' imply something beyond time, and there is nothing beyond time. Each of us is an isolated universe. Your time is not my time and my time is not your time even if we might spend some time together."

Was she trying to tell him she wanted to leave him? He leaned forward and took her hand. "Darcie?"

She didn't seem to notice that he held her hand. "The thing is," she said, "time travel is not only possible, it turns out to be relatively easy. The catch is you can only travel *in time* when you time travel. That is, you can only travel in your own time—birth to death. And Zee needed to travel back from 2240 to now."

"I thought you said the aliens come in 2210," he said. "And who is Zee? Who would call themselves 'Zee' anyway?"

"It did not become evident that we did not have all the pieces until 2240," she said. "And Zee is the guy in charge. This is a time when single names are back in fashion. Oh, and it's not entirely clear to me that these people are really what we'd call 'people,' what with augmentation and the increase in computing power and all, but I suppose that doesn't matter."

"It doesn't matter that our descendants are not really people?"

"You knew that would happen sooner or later, didn't you?"

"Yes, I suppose, but 240 years seems kind of a short time for it to happen."

"In order for Zee to send a message to you from

2240, he had to use a chain of people. That is, he had to go back in his own time and find a person who was alive before Zee was born and who would carry the message back in his or her own time, and then find someone who was born before they were and convince them to carry the message back. And so on until someone delivered it to Nathan Moore, the archeologist Zee has chosen to change history so the item at Zeugma could be found."

Her delusion reflected the disappointment they all felt. Soon, the dam would back the water of the Euphrates River up and flood Zeugma. There were decades of work to be done, and even then, they probably wouldn't find everything. They didn't have decades. They had been lucky to get the Turkish government to agree on a few more weeks. So much would be lost under the new lake. It was getting to them all. Was this Darcie's way of handling it?

"Why me?" he asked.

"Oh, I don't know," she said. "Maybe he found your name in an old book or something."

"So, you've come back in time to deliver the message to me. Why didn't Zee just have you deal with the Item yourself?"

"No, it has to be you," she said. "I won't be in any shape to do what is required."

"What do you mean by that?"

"Of course, it still might not work," she said quickly. "You might follow my instructions exactly, and nothing might change. If our great-great-grandchildren were doomed before, they might still be doomed now."

"How would we know?" Nathan asked.

"We can't know," she said, "but that doesn't mean Zee's theory is wrong. There is the problem of introducing error. It's like that game where everyone gets in a circle. You start it off by whispering a sentence to your neighbor who passes it on, and so on all the way around until it gets back to you. You say it out loud, and then you say what it was when you started—and they are nothing alike."

"And everyone laughs," Nathan said.

"If you don't do it or if it doesn't work," Darcie said, "no one will be laughing in the future."

3
The Chain

Nathan was still not clear on all the points, so Darcie got a legal pad and drew him a few diagrams.

"Zee was born in 2160," she said. "He was eighty in 2240 when he started the chain project to change the past. He could travel back in time no further than 2160, so he needed someone who was born before that to carry the message on. There are many things to consider when picking someone to time travel for you. To minimize the number of people you will need to reach your target point in the past, you might pick someone who was already old in your younger days. Zee picked a man named Ralph who was born in 2110 and who died just at the new century in 2200. Zee traveled back to his own past in 2185. Zee was 25 that year and Ralph, his old teacher, was 75. It's true people live longer, and, well, differently in those days, but in 2185 both Ralph and Zee are still using everyday bodies not too different from those we use today."

"Were do you get this stuff, Darcie?" Nathan asked.

"I memorized it," she said. "It's important to understand all the details, although to be honest like I said before, we have no way of knowing if any of these details are true. Every time the story is passed on to another time traveler, it probably changes."

"So, Zee went back into his own past and told his old teacher about the emergency with the aliens and the missing Item and taught him how to travel in time and sent him back?"

"Exactly," Darcie said. "Ralph traveled back to 2120 where he found a woman named Mary Odell who will someday marry our great-great-grandson."

"I suppose this means David will get off the sauce and get his life together?"

"Yes," Darcie said, "It must mean that. Thank goodness."

"Anyway, when I was nearly eighty, Mary came to me and explained how I must go back in time to the Zeugma dig and get you to make a few changes."

"Why didn't she tell me herself?"

"She wasn't born yet, of course," Darcie said and looked away again.

It didn't take Nathan long to figure out that the convoluted math running around in her brain predicted that he would not be alive when she was eighty.

Let's see, he thought, I was born in 1956 and she was born in 1960 and . . .

"Stop it," Darcie said. "I see what you're doing. Just stop it. That's not the important part."

"So what did this distant child of our child of our newly dried-out child or whatever say to you?"

"His wife, actually," Darcie said. "Mary is his wife."

4
What She's Not Telling Him

Darcie said, "Listen carefully, Nathan, I have to hurry now. I must make you understand what you have to do while I still can."

"What do you mean 'while you still can?' "

"They will discover the sewer system in Seleucia tomorrow or maybe it will be the next day. It will be a big eye opener. You'll be able to see the whole of the place from an underground perspective. In fact, you will be able to map all of Zeugma in reverse from underneath the city."

"That sounds wonderful," he said.

"But it will be quickly clear," she said, "that there is no time to use this new knowledge. It would take months to map everything. So they will give up on it."

"Yes, it would happen like that," he said. "The water will cover everything before we could finish."

"You must convince Leriche to let you continue exploring the sewers," she said. "You must find the Item and move it to higher ground, so it may be found when it's needed in the year 2240."

"How will I know it?"

"I don't know. I'm sorry."

Her eyes rolled back in her head, and she slumped

forward. He caught her by putting his hands on her
shoulders, and her coffee slopped into his lap. He
pushed her back up and came around to her side. She
was totally limp. He picked her up and carried her to
the bed.

He must get a doctor! But he couldn't leave her.
He put his face down close to hers. Yes, she was
breathing. He peeled back an eyelid and saw that the
pupil was a pinpoint.

"Help!" he said.

Then he was shouting it. And when no one came
at once, he ran out of the tent yelling and waving his
arms in the air. Soon everyone was awake and a doctor was summoned. It took a long time for him to
get there.

5
Too Late

The sewer system in Seleucia was found the next
day, but Nathan didn't hear about it for over a week.
He had ridden with Darcie to the hospital in Istanbul,
and he'd seldom left her side since then. The medical
staff chased him out, but he always came back, and
soon they stopped telling him he should go get some
rest and maybe something to eat. The doctors said
Darcie had suffered a massive and destructive stroke.

Word was sent from the site that he should take his
time and not worry about his work. Darcie came first,
of course. As she had predicted, the emphasis was
moved away from the sewers.

Later someone told him about the mosaics that had

been found in the Roman villa—the Minotaur and his mother Pasiphae and Daedalus who built the labyrinth to contain the monster forever. Moasics in almost every room. Fabulous finds. Bittersweet since that meant there was probably so much more to be found. It would all be covered by the rising water and lost forever.

He did not really believe Darcie was a time traveler, but he had some trouble understanding how she had known about the sewers. And he felt guilty. If she were a time traveler and if such travel destroyed the brain of the traveler, she had done it for nothing, since he had not gone into the sewers to find the Item the aliens in the future would insist humanity produce. Even if there were a chain of time travelers from some guy named Zee back to him, it was unlikely any of the details were true. There might not even be any aliens. Did that really matter? Almost certainly they had lost something of immense value when Zeugma was flooded.

He imagined himself as this Zee guy. You go back and say to Ralph, "It is vital that the strategy of mapping the sewers in Zeugma not be abandoned." But even as you're saying it, your mental capacities are in decline, and Ralph probably doesn't get the whole message, and when he hands it off to Mary, it loses more information. But if that were true, by the time the message got to him, it should be, "abandon the sewer strategy!"

But since that's exactly what had happened, maybe it had been the other way around. Maybe Zee had wanted them to abandon the sewers and Nathan had somehow conveyed that information to the team leader. Had he talked to Leriche about it? Had he made his opinions known? Maybe it had all happened differently the first time. Maybe the first time they had not abandoned the sewers and somehow that had made them lose the Item. Maybe now Zee had the Item.

Or maybe Nathan had just dropped the ball.

After they'd moved Darcie to a place that was not quite a nursing home, he might have left her for a few days and gone back to the site and climbed down into the sewers and poked around until he found something. Well, if that had ever been an option, it was not an option now. The water was too deep.

In fact, he had few options now. He would take her home. She was not in a total vegetative state. While she didn't seem to know who he was, she could eat and mostly dress herself, and she seemed to be fascinated by Turkish TV. She could break his heart with a sudden childlike squeal of laughter at something she'd seen.

Her doctors thought she might someday walk again. It could have been worse, they told him. David flew in to see his mother. Nathan could tell that the boy, well, the young man now, had been drinking but since he did not disgrace himself, Nathan didn't make a big deal out of it.

In fact, later maybe they could go out and toss down a few together.

That never happened.

So, Nathan had doomed all of humanity. In a little over two hundred years, it would all be over. Or it might all be nonsense.

If he believed Darcie, he could still do something about it. In the coming months and years, he could keep after her until she told him how to do the time traveling bit. Then he could find someone who was born long before he was born, and he could go back in his own time and tell such a person about the Item and the sewer and how they must go back in time and tell someone who was born long before they were born, and so on until they came to a time when a busy bridge on the Euphrates linked Seleucia on the hillside and Apamea on the plain in what was the greater Zeugma metro area. Such a person could just go get the Item and move it to higher ground.

If it were all true, and he went back, he would cook his own brain. Maybe he and Darcie could get adjoining beds and they could chuckle at Turkish TV together forever.

Why couldn't there be some action he could take that would change things in such a way that none of this would have happened in the first place? That was the outcome that most appealed to him—a world where Darcie had never burned her brain traveling back in time to give him information that he had not acted upon anyway.

There was no action he could take.

A couple of days before they left Istanbul, David came back to offer his help, and Nathan could see that the young man was totally sober. His hands shook a little, but he looked a lot better. He seemed to simply be more present somehow.

Darcie was sitting in a chair next the bed of her roommate, an elderly woman who was a lot worse off than Darcie. No one knew if the woman could still hear people talking to her. Darcie talked to her a lot. Darcie was talking to her now.

"What is she saying?" David asked.

That was the question that had been nagging at Nathan all along. He had just not been able to put it into words until now. Of course, Zee would have a Plan B.

Nathan took three great steps across the room just in time to hear Darcie whisper something about the Item in the sewer and how the old woman should pass it on.

WAIT UNTIL NEXT YEAR

Jody Lynn Nye

Eschael spun his gleaming blue sword around in both hands, and brought the sharp edge down upon the skull of a creature that grasped his bare ankle with green-black claws.

"Back into the pit, foul creature!" Eschael shouted, as the slime-covered beast, its head cloven in two, slid down the jagged precipice over the heads of its fellows back into the shadows. Its black blood spattered the hem of his white samite robe, burning holes that healed the next moment as though the garment was a living thing. Eschael reached inside himself for the divine strength to slay the next monster, and the next. The dark enemy seemed to be endless. No sooner had he killed one than another rose over its crushed and bleeding corpse to challenge him. Greasy-feathered harpies tore at his long black hair. Sulphur-scaled winged serpents wound around his limbs, but he slew them all.

Host after host of the heavenly defenders fell as well, gleaming angels torn apart by demons, blessed souls vanquished by deformed monsters reeking of corrupt flesh. Soaring above them, in contrast to the hideousness of his army, rose Lucifer, once beloved of the Most High, as beautiful then as the moment he had been cast forth from Heaven, save that his eyes were cold and joyless.

This Eschael saw by the holy gleam of bright hair, wings, and robes. The only light in the infinity of gray twilight over the battlefield came from the angels and their allies. The presence of the enemy seemed to suck the glory from the substance of good. It dismayed Eschael so much he felt hope sliding away from him. This war could be lost! Evil might triumph. Tears burned down his beautiful cheeks.

He must not despair! Angrily, Eschael sliced through the serpentine neck of a multi-headed creature with smooth, dark red skin. The Most High was the creator of all things, bright and dark. That power would see good triumph over evil. Eschael could not surrender hope, but it was hard to hold on.

Had he, Eschael, too, lost his eternal joy? The war was enough to make the very stones weep. First to fall to the blades and spikes of the unholy were the innocents: birds and beasts and humankind. The Most High was already mustering forces from every corner of creation, yet not soon enough to rescue those tender, helpless souls from destruction. They fought so bravely before they were destroyed. Surely, surely if one defender of good survived this Armageddon, none of them must be forgotten. If it were he, Eschael vowed he would sing every name before the golden throne of the Most High, even if he had to sing it alone. He knew every fellow angel, from the least cherub to the thrones and dominations, would pay the same tribute. How valiant were all those who fought!

Ichor sprayed Eschael's face. He spat it out and stabbed at the giant spider who sought to weave him in its toils. How subtly the evil one had begun his onslaught. It was not a bold and decisive declaration of war against good. No, the signs had begun to appear one at a time.

The Most High's own creations were not unaware of the signs of the coming of the end of days. Indeed, that most precious creation, Man, often joked, in a way Eschael envied, about that which constituted a sign that the end times approached. Most of them were unlikely keys, such as the advent of an honest politician. In spite of their cynicism, a few honest leaders had come and gone, some with little notice or acclaim, and none had opened even one of the small locks that had bound Lucifer in the pit.

But one of the signs at least was true, and it had come to pass under Eschael's very eyes. And, he feared, with his collusion.

Like the Most High, humankind loved games and sports. The act of moving their bodies in skilled motion brought them palpable happiness that could be felt by other creatures, particularly angels, capable of reading the emotions of others as if they were written text. The warlike tendencies of the flesh and blood beings were subsumed into play. Human spectators must have been able to absorb the sensations as well. Eschael loved to sit unseen among the non-participants, feeling the joy, frustration, excitement, anger at the opposing team, anguish at losing, bliss at winning and ever, always, *hope*, most beloved emotion of the Most High. Thus Eschael was able to enjoy the feelings twice, once from the players, and again from the audience.

The team that lived most greatly in hope came from an arena a mere giant's pace away from a great sea of sweet water, the Cubs of Chicago. How they had come to represent one grain of sand on one side of the balance of good versus evil was something only the Most High knew. The key that locked one infinitesimally small corner of the pit had descended to them along a lineage so complex that the recording angels kept scrolls and scrolls depicting it. Hope generated by the Cubs' devotees helped to keep Lucifer bound and away from the ranks of the blessed. Should those hopes be fulfilled, well, a disruption in the balance would cost many lives. To relieve the pressure of those concerted prayers from time to time, the Most High would smile upon the Cubs, but terrible things always ensued elsewhere that the Most High must accept or balance out. The previous victory known in baseball as the World Series championship that the Cubs had won had set of a five-year chain of misfortunes that had culminated in a war that killed thousands of humans across the sea and devastated many nations on Earth. Tears flowed from Eschael's eyes as he recalled guiding souls of the dead from the battlefield to stand before the throne of the Most High where they were assured of their places in heaven.

There would be no such redemption here. Heaven

warred with hell, and destruction here meant oblivion. And it was all Eschael's fault.

He chopped the neck of a deformed black dragon, an echo of Lucifer's favorite disguise. He brought his sword down again, heedless of the spatters of acid blood that burned his hands and feet. The head parted from the body, which collapsed, twisting and hissing. Eschael saw Arvayiel, one of his fellow messenger angels, besieged by a horde of monsters burning like dark suns and flew to his aid, sword raised on high to smite.

Then Eschael heard the call, the sweet song that contained his true name, every long syllable of it. He anguished at turning away from Arvayiel, though obedient as ever and forever to the Most High's summons and orders.

Except for once.

The guilt of his failing wreathed him like smoke as he appeared before the Throne and beheld the glory of the Most High. The presence of the creator of all things was indescribably beautiful, with skin of a purity and gleam that made gold look like dross, hair silkier than clouds, eyes brighter than the sun, and crowned with a wreath of rainbow so vivid it reinvented color. Eschael prostrated himself before the Most High.

For a moment his creator said nothing, only looking at him with infinitely beautiful and kind eyes full of sorrow.

"Rise, beloved," the Most High said. Eschael stood tall. "See around you. This is not the way I wished this to begin. But I allow the wheel to turn as it does.

I allow the angels to blow their trumpets and wield their swords. But this is not the time in which it must happen."

Eschael was full of remorse. It was all his fault. A recording angel appeared before the Most High. He saw the whole map of time revealed to him, and it was all in gold, except for a few entries. One was marked in black. That showed the moment in which Lucifer, beloved bright angel, had defied the Most High and been sent away forever. By comparison, the tiny flaw in the pattern where Eschael's mistake was recorded. The letters were of silver, not sacred gold.

"All things are my things, and all plans are my plans, but these were set into motion too soon." Eschael was ashamed, then he felt buoyed up by the love that flowed to him from The Most High. "These must be expunged," the Most High explained, kindly but firmly. "They can be, but not without price. What wilt thou do to correct them?"

"Anything!" Eschael exclaimed. "I will do anything to correct it."

"Wilt thou, though it cost thee everything? Wilt thou give up heaven?"

"Without hesitation," Eschael asserted, with his whole heart.

The warmth of love flowed around Eschael once more. "As I have written it, so shall it be. I am going to break the Arch of Time, as it is inscribed here. You shall have one chance to put right what is wrong and rewrite those letters in gold. It is not time for the last battle to commence, and this will cause time to flow backwards. I knew that this would happen, just as I knew that a sacrifice would be required to close the gate once again to save all creation from destruction."

Eschael steeled himself, buoyant with love for his Creator.

"I am ready," he declared.

"Thou wilt not see me again," the Most High said, with loving sorrow. "But thou wilt forever be beloved by Me, and thou wilt be in my thoughts and those of all the hosts of heaven."

With hands raised, the Most High called into existence an arch. The wondrously worked uprights and lintels were intricately woven of rainbow, moonlight and gold. Within it, Eschael beheld events of the ages: stars being born and dying; species coming into existence, prospering or failing; storms, volcanic eruptions, floods, ice floes of every color; angels singing; beings of every kind making war, music, and love, all events writing and unwriting themselves on the paper of existence. The arch began to glow. It grew more and more intensely brilliant until Eschael had to shut his eyes against the gleam. Sound came to his ears: human speech, music, the rush of wind and the hum of engines, bird song and animal cries. It coalesced into a roar of voices cheering. Eschael looked at the Most High. He recognized the moment. The Most High reached out with gentle hands and broke the rainbow arch at its peak just wide enough for Eschael to slip through into the green-touched scene within the gorgeous frame.

"Hurry. My blessings are upon you."

The way was shut. Eschael looked behind him, but the rainbow arch and the face of the Most High were lost to him. He could no longer hear the voices of his fellow angels except as a distant echo. Truly alone for the first time in existence, he knew how miserable Lucifer must have felt when he was cast forth from heaven.

He wished he could ask such a question, but his Creator and the recording angels were beyond his reach. He did not know if he could bear to be among his fellows again, knowing they could come and go as they pleased, and he could not. He loved Earth and humankind, but they were not his brotherhood. But he was not Lucifer, Eschael thought resolutely. Eschael was faithful to his vows. He would greet his fellows with love when he met them again. In the meantime, he was on an errand.

Wrigley Field was exactly as he remembered it from that moment so many years before, on that night of the pivotal game of the playoffs. Eschael had sat in the far left field, his joy nearly overwhelming him as he had sat among the excited fans. He made his way to that place again.

Women and children were there, though by far the greatest number were men of ages from first maturity to near dotage. Eschael loved them all with the depth to which he was capable. So beautiful was their enthusiasm. Such anticipation that they shared among them for this game. The Cubs had been at their best this year. A new coach, full of grace, had joined the team. Elvis Banion, who had come to Chicago from the mysterious fields of Arizona, had injected just the kind of enthusiasm that the team needed. Eschael settled himself into the same place, on top of a guard rail. He needed no actual space, but it gave him the feeling of being a human spectator. He envied the Most High's beloved creation, human beings, for occupying a place in such a beautiful creation as this Earth.

The night weather was clement, clear and unseasonably warm, a benison that Eschael had been permitted to bestow upon the city. Angels were given blessings by their creator to spread throughout nature, often when they saw a good opportunity for it to be appreciated. Rainbows were beautiful, and should be seen by as many eyes as possible. In Eschael's view, if only one human viewed it, that was worthwhile, too. He allowed himself to polish up the beauty of the old park, adding an extra shade of healthy green to the ivy on the outfield wall. All who beheld it would feel the blessing.

The warm evening was almost ignored in the growing excitement as the sixth inning began. The Cubs' lineup enjoyed good health and high spirits. So far the dreaded Mets, their long-time foe, had been shut out of any score, and the Cubs had gained three runs in rapid succession. That was the way the ancient green scoreboard read: 3-0. Eschael cheered for the team with the rest of the fans.

"That religious freak is back," one man near him confided to his wife. "Can't you hear him? 'Hosanna' this, 'hosanna' that?"

"He's just happy," the wife replied. "Let him alone."

The man grumbled and signaled the vendor for another beer.

The fans chattered at one another, energy rising about them. They couldn't see the rainbow clouds of their enthusiasm forming, but Eschael could. He reveled in them. This game would be the clincher, as the Chicagoans told one another. They had been undefeated in this playoff series thus far. They only needed to win this game, then the long-awaited World Series was the next step. They could not fail to go all the way this year! Eschael felt a pang of sorrow.

One Met on base. The young Cubs pitcher, Sandford Belkowski, nodded at the catcher. Eschael did not need to see the fingers concealed between the splayed knees to know that the catcher wished him to throw a curve ball. The batter, Idris Ikemani, was very slightly blind in the outside edge of his left eye, and a curve would loop out of his range of vision. The Cub players did not know why Ikemani always missed an outside curve, just that he did. The angel marveled at the skilled observation the humans possessed. While their eyesight was not the equal of hawks or cats or many sea creatures, they made use of the great brain behind it. Intuition was a sense that the Most High had placed within them, and the best of humans used it.

The ball flew from the pitcher's fingers.

"Strike one," shouted the umpire. An honest man of sixty years of age, Cedric Madden, would have had eight years left in his profession, had the end times not have begun. The television sportscaster picked up the call and announced it over the intercom system. Belkowski received the return of the ball from the triumphant catcher, and wound up again.

Ikemani swung mightily, and connected. The ball

flew into the night sky. The fans held their breath, fearful anticipation rising. All the men and boys around Eschael's perch sprang to their feet. The legendary left fielder, Bobby Cameron, six foot three inches tall and long-limbed like a gazelle, leaped after it, but stopped suddenly as soon as he judged its trajectory. The slower wits of the crowd caused them to boo him, a sound that turned into cheers as soon as the ball fell just short of the left field bleachers, an inch or two outside the foul line. Cameron chewed an invisible mouthful of gum, and retreated back to his stance, his dark-skinned face impassive. Madden made the call.

"Foul ball. Strike two."

The excitement in the stands grew. Two men who had never met before in their lives, Maurice LeGossier, a nineteen-year-old African-American university student, and Barrett Lewis, a nervous, overweight Jewish lawyer of fifty-two years, exchanged high fives beside the bleacher rail. How dearly they loved their team. Eschael sat on his perch, dejected. He knew how they longed for the victory he was there to deny them, one they should not have enjoyed in the first place. He wished he could tell each and every human among them the price for that overwhelming delight. But they would not listen. They would not believe him. Miracles were a commonplace in this Chicago, and angels sent by God were as ordinary as hot dogs.

Belkowski wound up. It was a mighty curve ball, with the tiny hop at the end. Ikemani swung and missed.

"*Steee*-rike three! *Yer* out!"

Ikemani's head drooped. He trotted back to his dugout, swinging his bat in one hand. The crowd erupted in cheers. The Cubs must only strike out ten more Mets, and they were on their way to the World Series. The energy was so high it buoyed the team's defense. The next two batters fell swiftly. The Mets retired, defeated, still scoreless.

The sting of a pipe organ split the air, and a local celebrity strode out to stand on home plate with a microphone. As eagerly as angels singing hosannas around the throne of the Most High, every spectator in the stands rose. Eschael stood with them, his clear tenor voice ringing out along with those whose worship he shared.

"*Take* me out to the ball game, *take* me out to the crowd . . ."

The familiar song rolled on his tongue like honey, but Eschael sensed the merest hint of a tang in it, an unpleasant savor that he had not observed before.

". . . For it's *one! Two!* Three strikes, you're out at the olllddd balllllll gaaame!"

All the while they were singing, Eschael was certain something felt wrong. He couldn't put a name to his misgiving, only that more lay here than a simple re-righting of the cosmic balance. He sensed heat rising with the energy in the park, something he had never noticed before. He mused over it through the seventh inning, and part of the eighth.

The Cubs retired scoreless from their at-bat, and took their places in the field. A light wind whipped around the park, carrying the sursurrus of urgency. The first Mets batter fouled twice, then struck out.

Belkowski had wearied; it was time Banion retired him. As Eschael recalled seeing it happen the first time, the Cubs coach signaled for a time out, and a new pitcher, Orshek Armour, trotted out to the mound. Gratefully, Belkowski tossed him the ball.

The second batter, David Winslow, clipped the edge of a ball that rolled between the legs of both the first and second basemen, allowing him to run to first. The fans shifted with dismay. They were so pleased by the shut-out, and didn't want it spoiled.

Jaime Munoz stepped up to the plate. He was the Mets' power hitter. Armour lowered his head over his glove and studied his foe with a practiced eye. He wound up and threw.

Armour's patented curve ball should have gone right around the bat, but Munoz swung around just at the right moment and caught it. The angle wasn't perfect. Instead of arcing out high into center field, it deflected off to the left, as Eschael knew it would. Bobby Cameron got under it and backed hastily toward the far wall, raising his glove for the catch and the second out. It was going deep. Humans swarmed off the bench towards the rail.

"He's going to catch the ball!" cried a voice ringing with the beauty and power of eternity. "He must catch it! Stop My humans from interfering!"

It sounded like an order from the Most High. Automatically Eschael's wings spread as he rose to obey, as he had once before in these precise circumstances.

He stopped suddenly, just before he moved into position behind the left foul pole. He knew the Most High was taking no direct action here, either by word of mouth or deed of hand. It was impossible, now that the Arch of Time had been closed. Eschael realized with a jolt that he had been fooled! But by what? By whom? He flew up to the top of the scoreboard to look for the source.

Cursing, in the same glorious voice, boomed through the stadium. No one else responded to the invective, so only Eschael must be able to hear it. He searched through the stands, and recoiled with hatred.

How could he have missed the beast? In the middle of the center field bleachers sat a servant of the Dark One, a blue-black, dragonlike demon. If the humans around it could have seen, they would have fled screaming, tough Chicagoans or no. Its wide-jawed head whipped around like a pennant in the wind.

"Damn you!" it cried. "How can you be here twice?"

Eschael regarded it with shock. That was the lovely voice that he had heard and, to his shame, obeyed, in the excitement of his first experience of this moment.

At that moment Eschael realized the mistake he had made was not his fault. That was why the Most High had been so patient with him. He was not guilty of disobedience, but of gullibility. Evil imitated good when it pleased. Eschael's actions were proof that anyone could be fooled by his own good heart.

"You will not make me err again, foul creature!" he cried, drawing his sword.

The demon grinned at him, showing six rows of blood red fangs.

"Well, if you won't, I will!" he laughed. Gathering

all six legs under him, he spread four insectoid wings and sped toward the end of left field.

Eschael saw his intention, and flew after him. The Most High had sent him to set the timeline back in order. The Dark One must not be allowed to upset the balance again!

Time compressed around the two of them. The fleeting ball slowed until it crawled on the air, inching towards them. The demon knew he could not trick Eschael into preventing interference a second time. He scrambled to wind himself around the left field bleacher rail, creating a wall that prevented anyone's passage. He spread out pawsful of long claws, and snarled a challenge.

Eschael grasped the creature by its antennae and pulled. The creature held on, shrieking. The rail whined in protest as it bent upward. Eschael ignored the pain as the demon swiped at him. He must get them both out of the way before the ball reached them.

Finally, the snakelike tail slipped off the railing, and the two found themselves catapulting high into the sky until the ballfield was a small, irregularly shaped dot of green. The demon kicked Eschael in the face and dove through his arms, arrowing for the almost invisible particle of white. Eschael slashed with his sword and lopped off one of the demon's wings in flight. Screaming, the horrible creature spiraled down into center field, crashing just behind second base. It scrambled to its feet, claws out and ready. Eschael was upon it in a moment, sword raised.

Unseen to the players, the spectators or the television cameras sweeping the field, the battle continued. Eschael chopped at his foe, digging a furrow between second and third base. Hoping to elude him, the demon dove under the earth just behind the pitcher's mound. Eschael didn't fall for the bait. He followed its progress above ground, flitting after the shadow he could see deep below. If the demon meant to cause mischief it must emerge.

The demon surfaced inside the Cubs' dugout. Eschael started to stab at it, but his enemy popped into the body of one player after another. Eschael could not endanger the humans, and the creature knew it. If the cameras spotted the evil grin each human wore for a split second, viewers might judge that the Cubs were slavering over their inevitable victory, but it was a most unseemly expression.

At last the demon had no more humans in which it could hide. It snatched up a handful of spectators and thrust them at Eschael.

"Let me do my work, or they die!" it shrieked.

Eschael regarded the humans hanging limply in its claws, some spattered with beer or hot dog mustard. He put a vision into their minds that they were still in their seats. He could spare them the fear of knowing they were in the power of a demon from hell.

"If a few die, it will still serve the purpose of the Most High," Eschael called.

The demon snarled. As Eschael had anticipated, the creature had no patience. It threw its captives at him. He caught them all in the sails of his great wings, and set them back in their places.

The delay gave the demon a head start back to left field. The ball still spun slowly, but it was closing in on its moment of destiny.

Eschael made himself as large as the stadium, hoping to protect the ball field inside his substance. The demon, shoved out of the park over the great lake, sped in to attack him. Eschael whirled his sword, trying to anticipate the creature's next move.

It feinted again and again, and was rewarded by a slice from Eschael's glowing blue blade. Yet it made one more cunning thrust. Eschael failed to counter it. The monster's head ducked inside his arm, chewing through the angel's side, seeking to kill some of the fans sitting just above the center field wall. Eschael cried out, dropping partway into the earth, and a torrent of leaves fell off the ivy-covered wall, but the beast's bite missed. The humans were unharmed.

The crowd's yelling returned to Eschael's ears like the boom of the sea. He and the demon exchanged glances. Both of them knew the psychological moment was coming.

They threw one another apart, ichor and blood running, back to the corner of left field, just inside the strike zone. Eschael thrust the demon back with his sword, calling on all the power of the Most High.

"Defend this place and this moment!" he cried.

The demon cackled, setting up his remaining left wing like a screen, keeping back the rush of male fans who surged to the stair rail.

Eschael wrapped himself around the creature, ignoring bites, scratches and cursing. With all the strength that was in him, he lifted the demon up into the night sky as the male fans, unaware that left fielder Bobby Cameron was immediately underneath them, went to catch the ball. To them it was clearly foul.

If it landed in the stands, it would be out of play, but if Bobby Cameron caught it, the shut-out would continue. Four outs to the World Series. They could not lose.

Eschael knew they must, or the world would be destroyed.

A claw went through his wing as the demon sought to escape. Eschael ignored the agony and held on tighter. Compassion filled his heart for the humans below. He knew the Most High felt it as well, but it was a small sacrifice to prevent the bigger disaster. He could see the shape of his former self shimmer and fade into non-existence.

"Wait until next year," the demon snarled, though he sounded dejected. "These fool humans will succeed one day in spite of you. My master will be free!"

"Never!" Eschael whirled his sword around in midair and put the point through his foe, who seemed to have lost all will to exist. Eschael took out his sense of frustration on the creature, and scattered its remains all over Waveland Avenue. He turned his attention back to the field.

Cameron leaped. It was a miraculous leap.

There was no one left to trick Eschael into interposing himself between the ball and the eager hands who sought a souvenir from this historic game. A hundred men rushed forth, their eyes upon the ball. The blameless college student, Maurice LeGossier, was closest.

His was the hand that reached out and deflected the ball away from Cameron's questing glove.

No satisfying smack of the ball hitting the leather pocket. Cameron's glove remained empty. No cry of "Yer out!" No triumphant organ sting. The Met, unimpeded, trotted all the way around the bases, driving in his fellow on second. In one short moment the score changed to three to two. The buoyant energy that had filled the field all evening long drained away like water swirling down a whirlpool, leaving the fans and players speechless and limp. The park fell silent.

Cameron, cheated of his heroic catch, let loose a string of invective on the fans in the stand. The umpires hustled over to argue with him. The ball was fair. No, it was foul. No, it would have been fair. In any case it had not been caught. The runs were allowable.

"Let's look at the video tape," one of them suggested. But it was too late, and everyone there knew it. The beautiful moment was spoiled. The shutout was lost. Then, the thirst for vengeance rose up in the fans, and turned upon the object of their ire, the man who had destroyed the Cubs' game.

Eschael's wings were around the youth in a moment, shielding him from the pummeling blows of the fans. Through the invisible cage of feathers LeGossier stared at his erstwhile fellow celebrants in dismay, sorrow written large upon his honest face at the enormity of the sin he had committed. He was miserable to the depths of his stainless soul. He had never dreamed that the ball was still playable, that Cameron was so close to making the catch of a lifetime.

More people barreled down the stairs toward him. Barrett Lewis looked at the advancing crowds and flipped his own coat over LeGossier's head. Security guards hustled into the stands at that moment. Eschael let them through his guard. One of them started to pull the unprotesting youth down the concrete stairs toward the exit. The booing fans, paying no attention to the lethargic motions of their beloved team on the field, threw beer cups and garbage at the retreating fan. Eschael deflected them all.

"I didn't mean it!" LeGossier protested, as the silent men hurried him down dark stairs and out into the glare of the street. The guards hailed a taxi. "I'm so sorry! I didn't mean it! I love the Cubs!"

"Kid," one of the guards said at last, "don't come back. Don't answer the door for a while, either. You might wanna go somewhere until this blows over a little. It don't matter what you meant, it's what you did." He leaned into the cabbie and handed him fifty dollars. "Take this kid where he wants to go. Get outta here."

LeGossier's head drooped in misery. The car screeched away from the curb and set out along Clark Street. Eschael surrounded the yellow vehicle with his whole substance, preventing anyone from seeing the license number or the faces within.

Eschael felt so sorry for him. LeGossier was an innocent. He didn't even get the benefit of the ball he had touched, since he failed to catch it. Seeing a fortune to be made, another fan in the stands picked it up. To Eschael, the human had the same gleam in his eyes as the demon.

The heavenly voices would sing for LeGossier, all knowing of the sacrifice he had made. Angels know all that the Most High wills them to, whether it takes place in the past or in the future, and all would see how the end times had been avoided, thanks to this one youth's actions.

"I give thee one last gift, directly from My mouth," the Most High had said to Eschael, moments before the Arch of Time had sealed shut behind him, "and thou must pass along and share these words with the unfortunate object of My will: what has happened must happen for the sake of all creation and My world. Thou art not to blame. Thou canst not see the pattern because thou art part of the pattern. Thou art but a tool in the etching of the great design. I love thee and I am grateful to thee."

Eschael whispered those words to the young man as LeGossier stared unseeing through the windows of his rescue chariot. The words of the Most High did not comfort him. Eschael heard what he was thinking. LeGossier knew he had been seen by a dozen television cameras that had beamed his image around the world. The kind offer of a coat to cloak his face was too late to shield him from opprobrium. He was marked. The memory of a disappointed public was long. It saw him as the villain who had robbed their and his beloved team of their assured victory. He feared retribution. Eschael agreed it was likely. He vowed to watch over the youth for the rest of his life.

Even after this game, this day, this season, was long forgotten, LeGossier would be in danger if he dared to come to Wrigley Field in person. The poor young man would henceforth and forevermore be shut out of *his* heaven, as thoroughly as Eschael was shut out of his. Eschael knew just how he felt.

PRESENT PERFECT

Loren Coleman

Over a breakfast of white toast smeared with honey and cold scrambled eggs with ketchup, I spread the morning *Seattle Times* over the vacant end of our dining room table and search for evidence of change. The thick aroma of over-brewed coffee rises from the chipped mug near my elbow. I don't drink coffee. I do read the political columns.

The woman who thinks she's been my wife pauses behind me, bends over and kisses the back of my head on the small bald spot.

"Good morning, my time traveler."

I wish I had never told her.

Pushing the eggs around my plate, I stir up a smear of soft yellows and bloody red. I've never had fresh eggs before these last seven months. I haven't decided yet if I like them. Setting my fork on the blue Formica, I ignore the rest of my breakfast and chisel through the dense reporting. Print media leaves a great deal to be desired.

"Simon is seeking his first Senate seat," I say, scanning the page.

Thumbing back into the first section I follow the article into a bramble of political editorials pieces growing around next year's election. It's my job to help get Gregory Simon elected president in 2024. It will have been my sole purpose for coming back. I have fourteen years.

Carol Williams picks up my fork, balances it on the edge of my plate and then uses a paper towel to wipe the egg smear from her WalMart tabletop. She's a very tidy person with manicured fingernails and waxed eyebrows and raven black hair that she often blow-dries twice to get it just so. It's nearly impossible to get her to iron a shirt, but she does pick out my tie every morning and tightens a perfect Windsor around my neck.

Not the woman I would have chosen for wife, perhaps, but amiable and supportive. Asking for anything more is just being greedy.

Future Perfect never promised me any kind of wife, in fact. But field agents are trained to deal with the situation we find, as we can find ourselves in any situation. Once you unhinge a man (or woman) from the timestream, it's actually a very small expenditure of energy to thrust them back to a determined point. History reforms around us. Memories bloom full-born in friends, relatives, and coworkers. We have a job. We pay taxes.

We begin to effect the changes as laid out in our conditioning.

I snap the first section closed and push it to one

side. Local news has very little appeal for me. Sports is a great place to find change, but those will have nothing whatsoever to do with my mission.

I do a vanity scan through entertainment, to see if anyone I know from Future Perfect has managed to make themselves famous. It's wrong of them, but it happens from time to time.

Nothing.

I ask, "Will you search the net today, find his campaign site, and where we can mail a donation?"

Some days I find it ironic that the high school's computer sciences teacher can't log on during the day. Today it annoys me, and I feel the worry-line creasing between my eyes. Fortunately, Carol works at home, buying and selling antiques over the net. Wonderful idea, eBay. Another three decades of development by time travelers and it will have become the perfect worldwide voting system.

"Can we afford it?" Carol asks.

I set the last section, the business section, aside and use a floral-printed paper towel to clean newspaper ink from my fingertips. I trade the black smears for some yellow egg under my fingernails, and spend a moment cleaning that out as well. "Can we afford not to?"

She sits down with her own coffee and smiles a perfect little smile. "Your mission. I forgot."

"Never leave the future to itself," I said, pushing my chair away with the backs of my legs as I stand. "Rule number one. And for maximum effect, it's best to be early." It's the same idea as compound interest, really.

Carol has heard this before. "Because we're all time travelers."

Not all of us.

The bathroom is larger than our old bedroom, and I spend ten wonderful minutes under the multi-nozzle jets that hammer me into wakefulness. Rinsing the last of the soap from my chest, I shut off the water and step out onto the thick terrycloth mat before reaching for the soft towel on top of a nearby stack. The woman who believes she has been my wife is standing in front of the sink, wearing bra and panties only, brushing her teeth and smiling at me around a wide mouth flecked with white paste. It's my first indication of the day that a change has occurred.

She's African-American.

Nails, manicured. Eyebrows, waxed. Her hair is dark, and thick, and still mussed from bed but I can see how it will be perfectly styled in another twenty minutes. Her wedding ring is the same as Carol's, the same twist of Black Hills gold that matches the one I wear on my third finger. But there is no mistaking that her skin is the color of toffee, and for all my training I pause.

"Everything all right?" she mumbles, spitting out frothy paste.

I resist the urge to wrap my towel around myself. I've never been shy before. "Fine," I say. I hope she doesn't hear the strain in my voice. "Didn't hear you come in."

"You're late."

I nod. School. Classes. Changes. "I'll hurry," I tell

her, rubbing myself down with the thick towel while heading for our bedroom.

She smacks me on the ass as I slip by, making my escape.

Our new house still has that fresh carpet smell. Our bedroom furniture is the same walnut finish that Carol and I picked out after we cleared our first twenty thousand. For one of Future Perfect's field agents, making money is no hard task. The business section from any local paper and an online trading company can set us up quite nicely.

When we have permission.

I do.

In another six months I will have made headlines as one of Seattle's most fortunate teachers, turning a limited savings into a solid six-figure account and becoming a patron of charity as well as Gregory Simon's political campaign. I know I'm only one of several hundred on this particular mission, but each one of us counts very heavily when we're being weighed against the momentum of the timestream. Some encouragement whispered at the right time. Funds donated to the various campaigns, or to be used against rivals. Creating actual scandals to bring down the wrong man. We are the last link in a very long chain that stretches back hundreds of years, bringing about change to sculpt the near-perfect future we left behind. Bringing it closer to a living utopia. At least for those of us with citizenship.

Those of us who matter.

What matters at the moment, though, is to find out who my new wife is and possibly even who I am. Each one of us is like a key sitting in a lock, being turned to create change. But the lock can change as well by the actions of another key. History reforms around us, complete with new identities.

As primary research goes, it's fairly easy. My nylon wallet is right where I leave it every night, on the edge of my dresser stack. Next to it is a modest Phillipe-Patek watch and a gold bracelet bought out of my first ten thousand profits. A Washington State driver's license is in the wallet's first slot under the fold. I am still me. It never hurts to check.

Second slot I carry a copy of my wife's license. It's easy enough to explain. How often do you need that information when filling out a form for a movie rental card, or when dealing with online finances? Her dark complexion photographs better than my pale skin. Carol Williams. Same name. Interesting.

And easy enough, since I have over a year of practice with that name.

"Are you going in today?" she asks, walking in behind me. She wraps strong arms around my chest and hugs me to her. I tense as her cotton bra smooths across my back, then she bites me playfully on the shoulder. "Or taking another of your infamous sick days?"

What shift in the past might cause such a personal change intrigued me. Especially since I wondered how it could possibly affect my mission. Always keep an eye on tomorrow.

"Too much to do," I tell Carol, digging underwear out of my drawer and stepping into them. Socks, shirt, pants. She helps me pick out the right belt to match my shoes, and then selects a tie for me. "Never leave for tomorrow what can be accomplished today." But I'd take a long lunch to hit the cybercafe. By noon I would have researched what other changes had happened other than mixed-race marriages.

"Why not take a break with me today, and time travel back tomorrow to get your work done?"

Had I told her, too? I once tried to explain how action, taken today, propagated through time. Great changes were not made through a single event—like an assassin's bullet or a one-time gamble—but over years, with hundreds of simple decisions. Real time travelers (and here I could have been speaking metaphorically as well as metaphysically) never let opportunities pass them by.

"I do the work today," I told her, "and tomorrow comes that much closer to being perfect."

She pouted, and it is actually quite endearing. She loops my tie around my neck, pulling me to her for a kiss, and then ties a deft Windsor in less than thirty seconds. I wish I knew how women did that.

"You're a good man," she says. "Even if you drive me crazy some days. All right. Go to class and fill young minds with knowledge. Sneak away to your computers. Make us some more money and play your little games. You've earned it, Mr. Williams."

I smile. Impulsively, I reach out and draw her into a hug. Field agent training. Act on your impulses, it adds normalcy. She is still not the wife I would have likely chosen for myself, but again, expecting anything more would be greedy. "Thank you," I tell her. And I mean it.

"Just make sure you say goodbye to the kids this morning."

Kids?

Geoffrey and Kate both love being taken to Forest Lake Park, with its petting zoo and playgrounds and a long grassy hill that kids sled down in winter, roll down in the summer. It's a seasonal ritual I've gotten used to. Today an industrial size sprinkler sprays jets of water out over a large cement wading pool. I hear the screams and laughter of hundreds of kids frolicking around the park.

Some people bring small, portable grills. Others bring picnic lunches. A small snack shack serves sweating hot dogs and buttered corn on the cob and cotton candy. And coffee. Bitter and dark and piping hot. Or cold, highly caffeinated espresso.

I still do not like coffee.

I still worry about my mission.

Staking out my claim to a bench where I keep an eye on five-year-old Geoffrey and his older sister, I use my wireless laptop to scan for new changes. Hotkeys allow me to page through text, follow links, and explore at my whim.

The recent news of Boeing Corporation's first female CEO spins off into a search of women in business, women in politics . . . women in industry! I track that back to World War II, and a campaign led by Rosie the Riveter who just had to be a time traveler out of Future Perfect. Rosie, leading an army of American women into the factories, and giving birth to the idea that a woman's place was not necessarily in the home.

How was Future Perfect handling this latest change? As well as I have, watching Carol take advantage of our wealth to leave off her home business and return to college for a business degree? Well, why shouldn't she? I don't teach any more. We have a maid in twice a week to help with cleaning, and I can cook for myself now. I like eggs. I finally decided. I can fix them scrambled, poached, and hard boiled. When I stop to think about it, I find that fried hard with salt and a dash of Tabasco over them make for a good breakfast.

Sometimes changes sneak up on us when we aren't looking.

Sometimes we sneak up on the changes. When we look far enough ahead.

Gregory Simon is already being talked about as a future presidential candidate. One electoral vote from Washington State (in an election where he was not even running) suddenly splashed him up on the political map.

Future Perfect's doing, I'm sure. It's a trick they've used before, to prime another candidate for the 1980s (the single vote also coming from Washington State). His presidency set down the first building block of a one-world economy. The elector accomplished all that on a two-year mission. Nice work if you can get it.

They're talking again about overhauling the electoral college. It will never have happened. Even with ePoll on the near horizon, we're not about to put ultimate power directly in the hands of the people.

A wet little boy who believes he has always been my son plops himself down on the bench next to me. "Da. Katie won't push me on swings."

Geoffrey has forgotten his towel over by the pool and he's shivering, even in the warm July sunshine. Wood chips stick to his feet. I've learned, and brought an extra towel. Brushing it over him, I sop up most of the water from his hair, his face. Geoffrey has very fine eyebrows and large brown eyes. Some days I regret not remembering his actual birth. He must have been a very beautiful baby boy.

"You know how to swing," I tell him, smiling. "Kick back, kick forward."

Geoffrey thinks about that a moment, and I take the time to pull up my accounts on the wireless system. He shakes his head and some water I missed splashes tiny droplets onto the laptop's screen. "What you doing?"

I'm considering how useful it might be to transfer a large donation to a progressive candidate running for the governor of Michigan. I don't know much about him except that he's black, a state senator, and he's running against the man who we believe will be Simon's opposition in 2024. I'm wondering if I can derail the opposition to Simon this early. But I do not tell Geoffrey this.

"I'm time traveling," I say. Sometimes it feels good to admit it.

His frowns are very comical. And very familiar. He has the same crease in between his eyebrows that I've seen in the mirror many many mornings. "Will you be gone long?"

"I don't even have to leave this bench."

"Push me on the swings?" he asks.

Katie is playing follow-the-leader with a group of older girls. It wouldn't be fair to pull her away. But I cannot leave the future to itself. "Next time?" I ask, and I hear the disappointment in my own words. I don't get an infinite supply of next times.

"Means no." Geoffrey shrugs, also disappointed but not about to let it get to him for long. He hops down from the bench, studies the playground quite seriously, and then bolts for the wading pool again. "Bye, Da."

With a few violent taps on the feathertouch keys I transfer the funds. I think about digging a bit more into this candidate's background. I don't think he's Future Perfect. I doubt he will have amounted to much by the time Gregory runs. I have six more years.

I go play with my son.

I want to know which time traveler had the bright idea to bring punk music back from our future. I have it narrowed down between the Dead Clerks and Blue Lizard Tango. Obviously the 1970s weren't ready for it, with our music of self-empowerment being twisted around into a rage-against-the-man ideal which has hung in there for five decades.

And now I have a daughter with purple hair and a ring through her eyebrow.

Kate (not Katie, not anymore) sits in the back seat of our new SUV next to her brother, wireless 'phones nested in her ears and the volume up so loud that the backwash of violent sound annoys Geoffrey. And me. The large vehicle smells of popcorn, from last night's trip to the cinema, and sweatsocks. Kate plays soccer. I know without looking that she left her cleats and socks behind the seats again. Like her choice in music, it's one more minor act of rebellion which adds up over time to point out that the girl who has been my daughter will soon have arrived at that place where her stubbornness blooms into full force teenage independence. I will not be here to see it.

Carol doesn't mind the music or the sweatsocks. Then again, when she has her head into a spreadsheet, nothing else matters. Sitting in the passenger seat, the woman who has been my wife and mother to my children tucks her way through page after page on her palmtop, worried that her new designer clothing start-up chain will take a serious hit after Gregory Simon is elected. It's a legitimate worry, with the small business freeze that will have happened by 2026. It's caused a number of debates between us.

She's supporting the governor of Michigan, the one I never thought would amount to anything. Our votes are going to cancel. It's going to be a close race.

"He also is a big proponent behind the new economical vehicle proposal," Carol points out. We're five minutes away from the polls, but she can't help it. We both know our minds are made up. We both know that we are right. "These SUVs aren't helping the energy crisis."

I know that SUVs only have another twelve years before legislation is passed to ban them from civilian ownership. I maintain, however, that the minds behind Future Perfect never had to play soccer dad for a weekend with five teenage girls to pick up from the after-game pizza party. A roomy interior preserves sanity.

The most important day of my mission has arrived. I'm about to cast my physical vote for a better future, after which my work is over and I'm called back for my next assignment. Yet here I am, arguing against centuries of effort on our part.

Geoffrey's junior high plays host to our polling district. The last year of out-of-home voting. I pull into the parking lot with a twinge of nostalgia, knowing that I'll miss these yearly election-day trips of the entire family. Parking the monstrous vehicle, I signal for Katie to at least turn her music down to merely outrageous levels. "Best behavior," I ask them. "This is a serious day." None of them know how serious.

Carol puts away her palmtop with its amber-glowing screen, slips out and opens Geoffrey's door for him. "Never leave the future to itself," she says, as she has every year.

Geoffrey jumps down, takes his mother's hand. "Because we're all time travelers."

I bite down on my first response. Not all of us, is what I thought to say. But it isn't fair to the people who have been my family over the years. I've missed out on quite a bit of their existence, and they've all made their own decisions at times, but none of them have ever been anything but supportive.

Asking anything more would be greedy.

Kate surprises me by looping her arm through mine as we walk into the high school gymnasium, street shoes squeaking on the polished wood floor. "Thanks for the movie last night," she says.

"Knew you would like it."

Of course I knew. Not because the movie was still big in the future (it wasn't). Watching Katie grow up, the day to day changes adding up, I can see the patterns and the differences my little actions over the years have made. It's very much like time travel. I keep striving for perfection.

The kids move off to wait on the bleachers, parking themselves together, even though I know that as soon as Carol and I duck into polling booths they will find their friends and forget about the politics and the news events of the past few years in favor for fashion trends and gossip. That's okay. They have their entire lives ahead of them to effect change.

Don't they?

It's a very sobering thought. One I wrestle with as Carol reaches up and straightens my tie. "Good luck," she offers me, very serious of a sudden. Does she remember how I used to follow Simon's early career?

Does she know that in fourteen years, she has never failed to set out my tie for me? Not once? It's an impressive feat, actually. Amazing what adds up to be important over time.

I step up to the computer station, protected from rude eyes by cloth partitions to either side, and tap the screen to bring up ePoll. My user number registers, and my personal ballot appears. Right at the top is the only choice that has mattered to me for fourteen years. Gregory Simon on the left-hand side of the ballot. His opponent on the right. I pause, and the certainty I've been trying to maintain all afternoon fades away.

Fourteen years of having my ties laid out for me, and watching children grow up. Encouraging Carol to get her bachelor's and then a master's degree. Dealing with all the little changes and doing everything I could to affect the future when everyday was already perfect. I'm not sure at what point I had decided that. It was in there somewhere among the morning kisses and play dates and soccer games. Between pulling out slivers and washing grass stains out of knees.

I was even developing a taste for coffee.

I wasn't ready to give that up.

I've worked for Future Perfect for fourteen years. Today is for me. I imprint my thumb over the box next to Simon's opponent before I talk myself out of it. It's out of my hands now.

Outside the booth, Carol waits. She tucks her hand into the crook in my arm. Together we collect the children. "How did it go?" Kate asks, smiling. She's always found this whole trip amusing. Never serious.

"I'm not sure," I tell her. "We'll have to wait and see." The news is on at home, and my computer is tallying up votes as they are reported across the country. But maybe, "Pizza? And a movie rental?"

"All of us?" Carol asks, a question in her eyes.

I nod. "All of us. The future can take care of itself for one night, right?"

Because we're all time travelers.

BLACK ARMBANDS

Brenda Cooper

February 3rd, 2003

L ola wore an old tie-dyed shirt she'd rescued from
the back of her closet. Her bright green raincoat
hid most of it, and she clutched her latte with both
hands as she walked beside me to the Seattle Center
grounds. We hurried under the monorail and past the
bright blue and yellow Experience Music Project. The
Space Needle touched the clouds over our heads.
Many other people walked beside us, everyone
streaming the same direction.

Five old women—really old women—with canes
and long skirts and straw hats decorated with flowers
struggled to hold up a purple quilt (a real quilt, not
some clever cardboard sign) with the words "Grannies
against War" sewn on with scraps of off-white and
fuchsia and yellow fabric that matched their dresses.
The women were beautiful, like old trees. They
laughed and chatted with passers-by, and read other
people's cardboard signs, nodding approval and en-

couragement. Lola broke into a smile, squeezed my hand, and whispered, "I want to be like them in twenty years."

I leaned down close to her ear and whispered back, "Thirty years. You don't have enough wrinkles yet."

She cocked an eyebrow and thrust her hip playfully into mine. I put my left arm around her and pulled her close. She smelled of coffee and cinnamon scones.

Seattle Center felt like a rainy block party. The grannies warmed my heart, and so did most of the crowd. Lola and I, in our mid-fifties, were just above the average age of the crowd. A fifteen-foot-long papier-mache peace pipe glided past our heads, held up by three young women. We passed a sign proclaiming "Lake Forest Park: Neighborhoods for Peace" and stopped for a moment, watching suburban parents herd laughing kids in red and yellow raincoats. A golden retriever and a boxer with red and white no-war signs taped onto doggie coats on their backs snarled at each other.

The lawn was about seventy percent covered from where we stood, with people slowly filling it from all sides. Their colorful signs and rain parkas looked like a vast flower garden, a bright spot in the gray spring morning. I breathed deeply, glad this wasn't as hard as I'd feared.

The crowd was still thin enough to move through easily. We walked past five Seattle police on horseback. Their horses' teeth scraped on metal bits, and their hooves squished restlessly on the damp grass. The uniformed men were silent. They had rifles.

Lola must have felt me shiver. She leaned into my

arm and said, "It's okay. There won't be any violence here—this isn't like the WTO protests."

I almost told her not to be so sure yet, but we literally bumped into a tall thin man with a wispy smile and gray hair past his shoulders selling peace buttons. "We'll take two," Lola said.

My fingers shook so much that counting coins seemed impossible. "Keep the change," I said, and Lola smiled again, as if being here lit her from the inside. She pinned my button on, and I looked down at her and asked, "Why are you so happy here? We're protesting."

"It reminds me of the sixties. I was at Berkeley."

At least she wasn't at Kent State. She was the right age. A song erupted from the podium and Lola pulled me over toward the concrete steps above the bowl of the amphitheatre. The air smelled like sage and cigarettes and patchouli incense and I caught a passing whiff of marijuana.

We were almost at the steps when I saw the boy. He was maybe twenty, with curly brown hair to his shoulders, a red headband, and a black armband. He carried a big purple flag with a white peace sign on it and stood waving the huge flag in eye-catching dips and swirls.

The old nausea hit me so hard I fell. The grass was wet, and I was on my hands and knees, mud between my fingers. I couldn't undo Kent State, couldn't take it away, couldn't heal anybody or even myself, except by forgetting. It was the armband that made me remember as much as the flag. They wore them that day, black ones just like this boy's. We were his age.

I held myself up on hands and knees, arms shaking, knowing I'd fall again if I stood, not wanting to lie all the way down on the wet grass. Light rain fell on my back.

Then Lola's hand was on the nape of my neck and someone laid out a rain poncho and two other people helped me turn and sit on the plastic. I buried my face in my hands, not wanting to see the boy with the flag.

When I opened my eyes he had moved on. Lola sat next to me, the cool rain wetting her cheeks and forehead, clinging to her lips like dew. She didn't ask me anything, which might be why I told her. I hugged my knees in close and made myself look out over the crowd, trying to spot the boy with the peace sign. I couldn't see him. "I was at Kent State."

Lola drew in a breath and her hand tightened on mine. "Were any of your friends hurt?"

"I was in the National Guard."

I watched her eyes closely. Concern turned to puzzlement, and then, briefly, to horror. She covered the revulsion, dropping a mask of neutrality over her face, but her eyes held no light.

April 15th, 2022

"Lola and I stayed together for two more years," I said, "but it was never the same as our first three years. We still went to coffeehouses and read each other stories, and we walked along the waterfront in summer, holding hands, and we never talked about Kent State. Deep inside, I know that's why I lost her.

It was like a knife between me and the world, and once Lola knew about it, it cut between us."

Doctor Nin gazed out her office window, a slight frown on her thin brown face. She listened, but she couldn't possibly understand. She was in her mid-thirties, half my age, not even born in 1970. She looked severe: dark brown hair pulled back in a short ponytail, light brown skin, a black sweater.

I scuffed my feet on the floor and pushed myself upright in the uncomfortable plastic chair. "You see, Doctor, a man can do a thing in just a moment that taints the rest of his life. A single bad decision can ruin a life. That happened to some of my friends in 'Nam. Even though I never went there, I got tainted by the same war. It was our own people, kids, whom we killed." My voice was steady, but I could hear the sadness in it. I think she must have, too, because she turned to face me directly, her eyes serious.

"Have you wondered why you're here, why we chose you for this study?"

I'd wondered about it. "I figure it's for history. I'm close to my own death, and so maybe you want to save my story." I didn't tell her what she knew already. Medicare didn't pay enough to keep me in medicines, and this study covered all of my medical costs as long as I was in it. That was why I chose them, not why they chose me.

Her next question took me by surprise. "What do you know about quantum time travel?"

"I don't understand it any more than I understand quarks. I remodeled houses for a living until I retired."

She laughed a little, and sipped on her water. "I don't understand it much either. No one does. But I understand what it means—it's tied up with the many worlds theory and amounts to real time travel, although limited to observation."

"I know that much." Then I caught up to what she might mean, and I sat up straighter. "So, I can go back and undo Kent State?"

"No matter what we do, our history doesn't appear to change. We don't know if other histories change, or if all histories exist." She licked her lips. "You must understand, this is an experiment in psychology. We'll send you back, with your consent, and let you see it all over again. It provides perspective on experiences. We've done it with over fifty people, and more than half woke up feeling much better afterwards. You win—you get to see what really happened and maybe forgive yourself. And we win; we learn about history by interviewing you. What you can tell us now is obscured by time and there are no videos of the event."

"So why send me?"

"Only someone with resonance to a particular moment can go back. Getting back is tied to emotional energy—I can probably send you back to Kent State, but I doubt I could send you to any day two weeks before. You don't remember that time, or care about it."

I didn't want to go. Not unless I could change something. My hands shook in my lap. I sat back and tried to look less affected than I felt. "I want to save those kids. You're telling me there's no way I can do that?"

"Our history doesn't change. Those four students

will be dead. Many worlds suggest that many possibilities exist, but you must agree not to change anything or we won't send you back."

"Do I go back physically? Really? Will I *be* there?"

"We don't know exactly what happens. Based on memories from other travelers, you merge with your old self for a time, as long as a day, and as far as we can tell, you remember this time too. When you wake up here, you'll have relived something important to you."

I coughed, a long fit, then drew air in big gasps. I needed the Medicare. "How does it work?"

"We close you in what we call a quantum Schroedinger's tank. We open the tank, and either you will have gotten back successfully, with a clear memory of the experience, or you won't have. The math requires a quantum computer to do it." She stood now, looking down at me, with no trace of sympathy in her voice or her eyes. She didn't appear to like me.

Maybe she did understand Kent State.

The oddest question cropped up. What if she wanted me to go back and change something, but she had to tell me not to? Maybe we were being watched. Or maybe I was feeling paranoid. I hadn't dated anyone for long since Lola. I still missed her.

The room Dr. Nin took me to the next day was a spare institutional beige. It held two chairs, a counter like a medical examining room, and a big oblong box.

Dr Nin told me to climb into the box. Then an assistant, a little slip of a woman with Hispanic features and a soft voice, taped electrodes to my skull and poked a thick IV needle into my arm. She taped a tiny flat black box, some kind of monitor, to the back of my knee. It itched.

My hands sweated. I wished I had never agreed. I didn't want to see the self that was in the Guard, the one that fired a gun at kids just because he was told to. I never knew if I actually killed or wounded anybody; they didn't do ballistics tests. I didn't want to find out.

It was quiet inside the box, which was bigger than the sensory deprivation tanks from the seventies, maybe four times as big my body. I felt the space around me more than the box, and a faint breeze blew warm air against my left cheek.

I counted breaths, twenty. Suddenly there was a twist—I don't know how else to describe it, like the box and me and the air and the breeze moved to the right and down—

May 4th, 1970

—and brightness stabs the perfect blackness for a moment, like I just took dark sunglasses off.

The light stops and I can see normally.

It's almost a clear day. The sky is a little hazy. I smell rubber and sweat and my vision is impaired, then I remember I'm looking through a gas mask. The fire is out in the ROTC building behind me, but as shred of charred smoky scent is still strong enough to seep into the fetid gas mask.

I'm confused for a minute. Dizzy, and my knees are

wobbly. I feel—disoriented; only it's n̶o̶t̶ ̶m̶e̶, ̶i̶t̶'̶s̶ ̶t̶h̶e̶
younger self.

The guard, all thirteen of us in Company G̶ ̶(̶I̶ ̶d̶i̶d̶n̶'̶t̶
have to count; I remember the number) are m̶o̶v̶i̶n̶g̶.
The other companies move around us.

I glance down at my watch. It's 12:03. We will fire
at 12:24. The chronology is burned in from repetition;
news stories, television documentaries, eventually
websites. I don't tell my body to move, to look, or to
breathe. I'm a passenger. I want time to settle in, but
there isn't any. This is my chance.

I can hear his thoughts. <This is crazy. They're burning down America. We have to stop them.>

I feel his anger, mixed up with fear. Funny, I don't
remember either. I remember the way I felt afterwards, the exhilaration, the adrenaline, the shock that
followed the rush. The guilt that followed the shock,
and stayed. I had forgotten the fear and the anger that
I started with.

I was able to look at my watch, but whose thought
was that? The gun is in my left hand, ready for me to
grab the butt with my right and aim it. I think about
lifting my right hand just an inch.

Nothing happens.

<Something's wrong.>

OK. So my hand didn't move, but I had an effect.

I think *move your right hand up*, and the hand
comes up for a second and then drops.

<What's happening?>

I've gained attention. His (our) body is sweating
and the sweat smells of fear.

All right. I'm older. I know a few things. Like you don't force someone who's scared.

I think, *You're about to do something bad.*

The Guard in front of us stops, we stop. We're on the top of Blanket Hill, and the students are gathered below us. I remember Seattle, and Lola, and the huge crowd. This crowd looks small. I can see the lawn clearly; there is more grass than students. They have signs and some of the young men give us the finger.

<They hate America. We have to stop them.>

Suddenly, I feel wet grass beneath my left knee and the rifle is up. Fear grips me, then I realize it's too early, remember this is just the tear gas. Canisters whistle through the air over my head, bounce, roll. Smoke billows out in long streamers and most of the kids stumble away, hands over their mouths and eyes. One of them darts straight into the white smoke, yellow shirt pulled up over his mouth, and throws a canister back at us. Another one, all in black, does the same thing. I don't know why. We're wearing gas masks.

We follow them as they run from us. I try something else. *They're scared.* We stumble. *They're like you. They're scared.*

<I'm not scared. Who're you?>

Part of you, an older part. You're about to help kill four of those kids. You don't want to do it.

<Maybe it will take death to make them stop.>

The whole contingent of Guard is up and moving. I can feel the muscles in our arm, quivering, taut, holding the M-1 with a bayonet fixed out in front of us. We go down the hill and up another one, herding the demonstrators. There are just over a hundred Guard, and a few hundred of them. They don't have weapons. We're moving them toward a football practice field, passing through the last remnants of tear gas. A thin blonde girl looks like a doe caught in headlights, then she turns and walks slowly in front of us, acting unconcerned. Two boys near her walk backwards, looking at us all the way, saluting us with middle fingers, but backing up all the same. They are yelling something, but I can't tell what they're saying. The group in front of us is smaller than it was a few minutes ago, bunched up. Some of the curious have moved away.

We stop, and one of the boys bends down and picks up a rock. He throws it at us, but we're too far away for it to matter. The rock lands fifty feet from us.

Two Guard throw rocks, and they miss.

They're scared. They won't hurt you. I desperately try to wrench control away, but the body doesn't listen.

<They should be scared of the Viet Cong. They should go and help. We don't need flowers.>

I laugh, remembering the flowers, the way they felt like an affront, and the earnestness of the bedraggled girl who gave them to us yesterday, the day before Kent State.

<It wasn't funny.>

I laugh harder, and the laughter is sweet release. Suddenly there is less separation. I feel his (my!) humiliation and anger and fear, and I bleed away cynicism and the dreadful knowledge of what will happen. I bleed memories in. I realize how intense, how young he feels, and that I didn't need to hate someone so young.

The relief, the forgiveness, is like a river, strong, demanding attention, but there's no time to swim in emotions. Not yet.

Look at your watch.

Surprisingly, a twist of our wrist shows the watch briefly. It's just past 12:20. Four minutes left.

More rocks are thrown. Confusion reigns for a moment, students and Guard moving with no real purpose, unsure what to do next. We're bleeding time away. The demonstrators are fenced in on three sides and we're on the fourth side. They can't disperse. I wonder which of these kids we will shoot soon, and our stomach rises with nausea at my thought, as if forgiveness gave me some resonance with this body.

Someone barks an order I don't hear, and the whole group of us Guard turn and walk away, and children follow, taunting us. A boy holds a black flag with a white peace sign painted on it, jabbing it towards us, like a weapon. Some of the demonstrators have stopped in the parking lot, but the tenacious ones are not afraid and they keep coming, maybe thirty yards from us. Each step seems to take a long time. I know what I want to do but don't know if I have that much control.

We're at the foot of Blanket Hill again. A few of the students are closer, maybe twenty yards now, but no one tries to stop us; they just want to yell at us. They want us to hear, but I still don't know what they're saying. One of them pumps his fist up and down in the air. The one holding the flag jabs it at us. Both of them wear black armbands.

I experiment. *Stop*.

We stop for a moment, then keep going, as if the habit of formation is too hard to break. I try to remember everything I can about the moments after the shooting. I remember the horror and the guilt. I pound him with memories.

We're halfway up Blanket Hill now. Moments left. Maybe ten steps.

Stop!

We stop. Some students start to walk away. I see the parking lot, and right now it seems far away.

I hear a command behind us. "Ready!"

Run!

An intake of breath, the feeling of something fragile breaking, maybe his control, sensing my knowledge, my age, my years. Giving in. Whatever happens, it is a change in me as much as him, a recognition of each other. I am no longer a passenger, and that is his will.

I run. Right at the students. I turn to face the Guard and point my rifle up at the sky. "Don't shoot!" I yell. Knowing they might have enough adrenaline to shoot me. A row of Guard is kneeling. The guns are pointed at me.

"They're children. Don't kill them!" I throw the M-1 down, standing over it, making sure none of the demonstrators can rush me.

And a wall of Guard moves down to subdue me. No one shoots.

No one shoots.

Thank you.

I'm pulled to standing, and the Guard, my comrades, surround me. Their features are masked, but their stances vary from angry to relieved to concerned. The students are silent.

<I'll bet I'm in trouble now.>

I send him my relief. *No, not really. You may be embarrassed, and maybe they'll throw you out, but it's doubtful they'll court-martial you.* I wish I could send him the perspective of someone three times older than he is. I almost wish I could stay and see if he uses this new chance, if I've given him enough memories to make something of himself. *This was the right choice.*

I surrender to him. The next choices are his.

May 5th, 2022

I woke filled with euphoria, able to feel the warm breeze against my left cheek again. The box lid lifted slowly, and two sets of hands reached in to help me sit up. It was easy to sit up, as if I had woken naturally from a long deep sleep. My breathing was clear and my chest no longer rattled. As I climbed out of the box and stumbled onto the floor, someone handed me a robe. I twisted it around myself, blinking in amazement at the white walls. They were beige yesterday. Dr. Nin sat in a comfortable navy blue chair with her legs crossed, wearing a light green suit. The color looked great on her, accenting her cheekbones. She smiled easily at me. "Welcome back."

Two people I'd never seen, the ones that helped me out of the box, took seats. One was a young man, shy of thirty, and the other was an older blonde woman who had clearly once been beautiful. She gestured at an empty seat and I sat down, although I felt like I had the energy to walk around the block.

The new colors bothered me, they were bright and cheerful, but wrong. The paint was chipped by the doorjambs. "Thank you. What day is it?"

"May 5th. You slept normally through the night, and now it's 8:00 AM." Dr. Nin handed me a cup of coffee. "Here, this should help you out. It's from Zaire."

Something was wrong with what she just said. I took a sip of the coffee, which tasted strong and smelled rich and earthy, and I realized what was wrong. "I thought Zaire changed its name?"

Dr. Nin drew her brows together and frowned lightly. "Not that I know of. Sometimes travelers are a little disoriented when they wake up."

By coming back to the right time and the wrong place? I realized that I had changed the past, changed my past, too. That explained the clearer breathing, the extra energy I felt. I looked around for more signs of change, and they existed everywhere, subtle things. The young man wore glasses, which almost no one did anymore. The cut of his shirt was subtly off, almost feminine. Filmy blue curtains hung over the window.

A thousand questions ran through my head, but I was suddenly afraid to ask them. The other Dr. Nin was so sure that history doesn't change, and I don't want to alarm this version of her, not yet. I needed to know more about this world, to understand what I'd done. Pictures of Kent State with the Guard pointing rifles at me danced behind my eyes and I smiled, sure it would be okay.

I dressed in the clothes they handed me: blue jeans, which I never wore, and a soft light green sweater. They fit so perfectly they must have been mine. It felt odd to put on his clothes, and I wondered briefly if he was waking in the more sterile version of this room, but the thought was too much for me and I sat down again heavily, needing to focus on small things.

They interviewed me for about an hour, and I acted tired and a little queasy, which wasn't too far off. I answered their questions the way I remembered Kent State now. Thankfully, they didn't ask anything about the years in between.

Finally, Dr. Nin looked over at me and said, "You're tired. Patrice is waiting for you. Come back tomorrow and we'll do a longer session."

Patrice? I stood and walked out the door that used to lead to the lobby.

It still did. The lobby was navy and gold, not gray and tan, but otherwise it looked very much the same. A pretty dark-haired woman waited just past the door. She looked up at me, and a huge smile opened across her face. "Dad? Are you OK?"

"Yeah, I'm fine." My heart filled at the idea of a daughter, and I thought about the younger version of me that I left back there, no longer a murderer. It made me feel wonderful, and curious, and alive, but cautious. I felt as if I'd stolen something, as if I didn't belong here. I smiled at Patrice, wishing I knew her, and follow her out the door.

There were a lot of people walking, and it took me

a few moments to notice that there were only a few cars, all small. Patrice led me onto a bus, and I followed her, watching her. She moved well, confident, her hair swinging with her bouncy walk. She wore a wedding ring on her left hand.

On the bus, I continued to feign being exhausted. Even though the memory of a different life was too much to hide from family, I wasn't ready to deal with it yet. Thankfully, Patrice hugged me goodbye just after we stepped inside an unfamiliar home in a block of unfamiliar homes on an unfamiliar street. "Bye, Daddy. Got to go to work. See you in a few hours." A puzzled look flashed across her face, perhaps at something I hadn't said to her.

There was no one else in the house. Wood and plastic must have both gone out of fashion; this furniture was all metal and glass and fabric, but oddly elegant and comfortable. A few hours seemed very short, so I looked around for a news source.

Novels with unfamiliar names sat neatly ordered by genre in a metal bookcase, but they all appeared to be detective books, or suspense, or science fiction. No history.

One shelf of the bookcase was empty expect for a family picture. I recognized myself, and a small dark-haired woman who looked like Patrice, and a girl that must be Patrice at about twelve. The background of the photograph was a desert somewhere, maybe Arizona. We all looked happy.

It took me a few moments to figure out that the glass surface of a desk was actually a monitor screen that responded to my hands. I used computers to play games in my old life, so I could use the net, protect myself from viruses, etc.

I expected to have to guess at a password, but the computer responded instantly. The screen looked little different from what I was used to. It brightened immediately as I touched it and displayed icons for news and weather and mail and search.

I touched the search icon tentatively, and a screen came up with a blank boxes and checks to limit searched by date or number of responses.

A search for "Kent State May 4, 1970" turned up almost nothing. A line in a long entry about protests that led to the Second American Revolution.

I click on highlighted words and spend hours putting pieces together. The protests continued for a while after 1970, but no deaths were recorded in 1970 or 1971. Instead, laws were passed forbidding assembly, free-speech rights were rescinded, and the government poured enough money into Vietnam and Cambodia to nearly go broke. More even than we had. We didn't win in this history either, but more people died. A search for "Watergate" turned up information about the hotel. But by 1980, the new oppressive government was thrown out in massive riots. Just over seven hundred thousand people died.

I paced, disturbed, walking back and all the long length of the hall, not wanting to open any doors or look out any windows. My footsteps echoed.

The passage of time forced me back to the computer. Post-revolution, we'd done quite well. No Gulf War. No war on Iraq (I smiled; Lola would be pleased). Different wars, but not for twenty years. This America appeared safe and prosperous and wealthy.

Seven hundred thousand.

I didn't have the courage to look up the four dead students from Ohio and see if they died in the Second American Revolution.

A man can do a thing in just a moment that taints the rest of his life.

GODSPEED

Christina F. York

January 28, 1986

"Mayday! Mayday! This is Air Force One. There's been an explosion; we're missing part of the left wing. We are going down."

Muffled by the headphones the president had tuned to the cockpit, the pilot's voice cracked with stress. Strapped into his seat, surrounded by his Secret Service detail, President John Glenn knew the end was near.

In the midst of the crisis, he was still struck by the irony. A decorated combat pilot, veteran of two wars, the first man to orbit the Earth, and he was about to die in what should be the safest passenger aircraft in the world. Annie, who had supported him through all the dangerous undertakings, would be widowed by an accident that should never happen.

Time slowed, stretching like summer taffy. Each second felt like minutes, as the presidential jet continued its plunge through the banked clouds, hurtling toward the unseen ground below.

Around him, people moved in slow motion. Shouted orders became a deep hum, as voices slowed, then stopped. The plane slowed, and time stood still.

Glenn glanced quickly around, looking for any sign of movement. Everyone was frozen in place, in the dim cabin lights. Everyone but him.

He had to move.

Obeying the reflexes that had saved him so many times before, he tore off the passenger restraints, and started toward the cockpit.

From behind him, a flash of golden light bathed the dim cabin. For an instant, it reminded him of the firefly-like lights he had seen on his first space flight. Then the light faded, leaving the cabin in shadows.

"That won't save you this time, Colonel."

He whirled around, toward the sound of the voice. There was a man, a stranger, behind him. Glenn blinked, trying to focus on the man, but he couldn't see him clearly. The cabin light was low, and it was as though he was shrouded in fog, *inside* the plane.

"Who are you?" Glenn demanded.

"Don't you know?"

"I can't see you. How could I know?" He wasn't afraid, but this stranger was damned annoying, and he had much more important things to do than stand around arguing with some guy in a fog bank. He could save this plane, if he could just get to the controls in time. He knew he could.

"Yeah, you can save them," the man said, as though Glenn had spoken his thoughts aloud. "But not in the way you think."

"Who *are* you?"

"Who I am isn't important. You can call me your guardian, if you need a label. It's who you are that matters." He gestured toward the empty seat. "Might as well sit back down, Colonel. No one is going anywhere for a while yet."

The fog slipped lower, as the guardian settled into a seat across the aisle from the empty seat.

"I know who I am. I'm the President of the United States. And I have my people to protect."

"Sit down." It was a command this time, in exactly the tone to activate the retired colonel's military training.

He sat, assuming the rigid military posture that had been a part of him for so long.

"At ease, Colonel." The guardian waved a hand—he thought it was a hand—at him. "I told you, we aren't going anywhere."

It was true, the plane wasn't going anywhere, though it should have augered in by now. Instead, it hung inside a cloud, defying the law of gravity.

"What do you want?"

"Like my name, what *I* want isn't important. The question is, what do you want?"

Over the years, Glenn had learned the hard lesson of waiting out a question he did not want to answer. He sat ramrod-straight, and stared at the shifting cloud. The heater fans hummed, sending warm air swirling through the cabin, but the cloud around the guardian remained undisturbed.

After a moment, the guardian continued.

"Haven't you ever wondered how you managed to survive all the missions, all the dangers, you've faced over the years? You flew combat in two wars. You flew untested planes. You survived that first orbital Mercury flight, when everyone thought you might burn up on reentry. Did you think you were just *lucky*?"

February 20, 1962

Mission Control was hushed, as the 11th scheduled launch approached. After months of delays and re-schedules, they were finally going to send a man into orbit. Finally, with multiple orbits, they would be back in the space race. Unless the launch got scrubbed again.

From the capsule, Glenn was patched through to his Annie, at home in Arlington. Hearing her voice made his chest tight.

He tried to reassure her. "Hey, honey, don't be scared. Remember, I'm just going down to the corner store to get a pack of gum."

"Don't be long," she answered.

His voice caught, as he said, "I love you." He was glad no one could see his eyes at that moment.

Glenn heard Flight Director Chris Kraft call a hold, with less than ten minutes to go. It was the second in under thirty minutes. The Bermuda tracking station was having trouble with their radar.

They had come so close this time. He was in the capsule, ready to launch. Would today be just another delay?

The silent seconds ticked by. For two long minutes, everyone waited for a decision.

Finally John Hodge in Bermuda said, "We're go."

The countdown resumed.

Familiar voices went through the procedures they had drilled on for months. Today it was for real. He waited, listening, hardly daring to believe it would finally happen.

At eighteeen seconds the countdown went to automatic. For the first time, he *knew* he was going to fly into space.

Seconds later, the engines roared to life, the holddown clamps released, and the giant rocket slowly lifted off the pad.

Later, someone would play the film of his launch, and he would hear the one thing he couldn't from the capsule. In the launch blockhouse, Capsule Communications— Capcom—was Scott Carpenter. As the rockets fired, he said, "Godspeed, John Glenn."

The flight of Friendship 7 was etched in Glenn's memory. The glory of the first sunset, the sudden blinding brilliance of sunrise. The fireflies, a swirling cloud of glowing golden lights around the cabin, which no one had ever explained to his satisfaction.

There were other memories. Problems with the automatic altitude control. His irritation when flight control wouldn't voice their fears about the heat shield. The searing heat of reentry, not knowing whether the heat shield was intact. Wondering if the capsule would withstand the next minute. The elation when the chute blossomed over him.

Everything had worked the way it was supposed to. Or was there more to it?

The plane remained frozen in midair, as the guardian waited for an answer. Glenn shook his head. He was grateful for the faith that sustained him in times of peril, and for his good fortune. But he had never questioned its source.

"The big guy *likes* you, man! Haven't you figured that out by now? Think about it. The flight controller says 'Godspeed, John Glenn,' that pack stays in place, and you drop into the ocean, pretty as you please."

"I didn't even hear him," Glenn replied.

"It doesn't matter whether you heard him or not. He said it. That wasn't the last time, either. Every time something went wrong, every time you were in danger, somebody remembered the magic words, and you came back safe. It was a ritual with your regular ground crew, something the chief mechanic repeated on every Air Force One flight.

"Every time until today."

They had left the ground ahead of schedule, before the arrival of the regular crew. They were anxious to reach the Space Center in Florida, where the stunned NASA engineers and astronauts were trying to make sense of this morning's horrifying explosion.

As Air Force One climbed away from Andrews Air Force Base, Glenn had watched the capital pass out of sight behind them. He was one of the staunchest supporters of the space program, and he worried about the opposition the program would face when he returned.

Then he dismissed consideration of the long-term problems, and focused on the next few hours. The grieving families of the victims would be waiting in Florida, waiting for comfort from their president.

It was ironic that he would be the one. It could so easily have been another president, offering the meager comfort to Annie, and his family. He knew, perhaps more than anyone, that it could never be enough.

He hoped he could make them understand how important the program was, to the country and to the individuals who had given their lives for it. He believed in a life of service, and the brave men and women of *Challenger* had believed, too.

He prayed that their families shared that belief, as Annie and Dave and Lyn did his.

"Do you mean—?" Glenn hesitated, hope rising within him.

"You can't change what happened this morning," the guardian answered. "Disaster is going to bring down *Challenger*, no matter what you decide, Colonel. But you can change what's coming. Not this year, and maybe not the next, but soon.

"They'll send up another shuttle, and lose another crew. *Discovery*. A little thing, really. An access hatch blows off at launch, and damages an engine. But, like I said, the big guy likes you. He'll bring you home safe.

"But if you're not there, that disaster will end manned spaceflight."

The thought sickened Glenn. The work, the sacrifices, the lives given up for the program. It couldn't end this way.

"What can I do?"

"Go back."

"Back? Back to where?" He looked around. There wasn't anywhere to go, except down—to meet the ground and end in a ball of flame.

"Not *where*. *When*. Go back and take a different path. Not the one that leads to the White House, but the one that dead-ends in the Senate."

March 16, 1984

Super Tuesday hadn't been very super for the Senator from Ohio. Beaten in primaries and caucuses across the country, he faced the inevitable with his usual re-markable calm.

This wasn't his first disappointment, nor, perhaps, his greatest. Alan Shepard had beat him into space. He had been forced out of the 1964 Senate race by an injury. He had lost the 1970 Senate race to Metzenbaum.

He didn't lead a charmed life, not by a long shot. But he had gained more than he had lost. He still had Annie, his kids, and his honor. He wouldn't trade any of them for anything, including the White House.

When his Senate staff assembled, he played a popu-lar song for them. They listened, as Kenny Rogers sang about the gambler, "You've got to know when to fold 'em."

With his head high and his shoulders back, he main-tained his dignity in the face of defeat. He announced his withdrawal from the race at a press conference in a Senate caucus room, declaring, "Although my campaign for the presidency will end, my campaign for a better America will continue."

Glenn was confused by the memory that wasn't his. He had done well on Super Tuesday, giving him the boost that earned him the nomination and the White House.

"That isn't what happened."

"It could."

Glenn stared at the guardian. They were about to smash into the ground at terminal velocity, and this guy was telling him he could go back in time and change things?

He had never had a hallucination in his life, even when he had truly gone where no man had before. But maybe he wasn't able to accept the end of his life, and this apparition was his way of blocking it out.

"You're not crazy," the guardian said, once again hearing Glenn's unspoken thoughts. "This is real, and the choice is yours.

"Go back. Make a difference. Ride the rocket again. You're the biggest hero NASA's got; they'll find a way to let you go. And when someone says 'Godspeed, John Glenn'—and they will—you'll all come back down as smooth as can be. You can save that crew, Colonel. The space program will have a hero again, even if no one knows exactly what it cost you."

"There's got to be a catch . . ."

"You won't be in the White House. You *will* have political trouble, and you'll never get farther than the Senate. That enough of a catch for you?"

"But I will always know I *could* have."

"Nope. Doesn't work that way. Once you go back, this never happened. You won't be able to tell anyone, because you won't remember."

"Or you can go up to that cockpit and try to bring this plane down safely. You're missing half a wing, and even *you* can't overcome that, but you're free to try." The fog swirled, as though the guardian had shrugged inside his cloud. "Who knows? You might make it, if you can suspend a few laws of physics."

For a moment, he dared to hope. Maybe he could overcome the damage. But the program, the research and exploration that he had given his life to, that he believed in, would be doomed. And six good people, people who shared his love and dedication to the space program, would die.

January 28, 1986

The images of the exploding shuttle were indelibly etched in the minds of every citizen. The scene had been replayed endlessly, as a stunned nation watched, unable to fully accept the disaster in the clear Florida sky.

Within minutes, questions were being asked both in Mission Control and around the world. How could this happen? What was the cause?

Who was to blame?

The future of manned space flight hung on the answers to those questions. For now, no more Americans would fly in space.

A delegation from the nation's capital was quickly

assembled, and shuttled to Andrews Air Force Base, where they would depart for Florida.

A detail of Marines watched as Air Force Two took off, carrying the Vice President to Cape Canaveral. Aboard the plane was one of their own.

As the jet turned south, one young Marine said softly, "Godspeed, John Glenn."

"Is that where I'll be, if I go back?"

"Yeah. Same airspace, different plane, different companions. And a different future."

Compared to the loss of manned flight, personal ambition was a petty concern. There were things he could change, and things he couldn't. He hoped he had the wisdom to know the difference.

January 16, 1998

DANIEL GOLDIN, Chief Administrator, NASA: "When someone who has risked their life countless times for a space program and for our country comes to you and says, 'I'm willing to take the risk of space flight and serve my country again, because I think we could do more to benefit the lives of older Americans, can I go;' you don't say no. I am extremely proud to announce that John Glenn of Ohio, the first American to orbit the Earth, will get his long-awaited and much deserved second flight."

Glenn could feel a lump in his throat when he considered the possibility of being allowed to fly again. It was a dream he had given up long ago, an ambition for a younger man.

"Will they really let me go?"

"They will need you, more than any of you will know."

Hope bubbled in his chest. The prospect made him light-headed with joy. "And I can make a difference?"

The cloud moved slowly, as though the guardian was shaking his head. His voice was somber when he replied. "Yes, you can make a difference, for that mission. There will be others, ones you can't change. One person can only do so much, you know, no matter how much the big guy likes him.

"But you can save *Discovery*, and you can save the people on this flight."

Glenn took a look around. His Secret Service detail had been with him since the campaign. He knew their wives and children.

He knew the press secretary and two speech writers were working in the conference room, even though he couldn't see them. One of the speech writers had just moved her ailing mother into her home, where she could care for her.

For each of those people, he could make a difference. If he could believe what the guardian was telling him.

"It's the truth," the guardian said. "Or at least a possible truth. If you choose that path."

October, 1998

The T-38 rolled to a stop on the tarmac at Cape Canaveral. Beside it were four identical planes. Although he was sitting in the second seat, John Glenn was once again flying a jet plane, and preparing for a flight aboard the shuttle *Discovery*.

The guardian seemed to grow impatient, his tone sharp as he asked again, "What do you want, Colonel? Do you need to see more?"

Glenn hesitated. Hope swelled within him, a dream rekindled by the images the guardian had shown him. Was that hope clouding his judgment? Perhaps he could do more to protect the program from the White House than he could from the flight deck of the shuttle.

He wished he could talk to Annie. For forty-three years she had been the best advisor, the strongest supporter, he had ever had.

"This is your decision, Colonel."

October 29, 1998

The day dawned bright and clear. It was as if Mother Nature herself had given her blessing for the launch. But it takes more than good weather to make a safe flight.

The countdown droned on, each second ticking over as each member of the huge team performed their duties.

Standing on the pad, the flight crew looked up at the rocket that would carry them into space. They were tiny orange specks against the massive machine, a few hundred pounds of bone and flesh facing a four-and-a-half-million-pound behemoth with a million moving parts.

With five minutes to go, the countdown stopped.

Two small planes had entered the airspace near the Cape, and would have to be removed.

Finally, the last few minutes ticked away, and the engines lit.

In Mission Control Scott Carpenter repeated the magic words.

"Godspeed, John Glenn."

Glenn considered his choices. The cloud stirred impatiently.

"You said no one could help me decide," Glenn said, his voice slow. There was one thing he had noticed. "But you have not addressed me once as 'President,' only as 'Colonel.'"

The guardian was suddenly still, impatience turning to wariness. As Glenn suspected, the observation had been not only accurate, but significant. He had his answer to the last unspoken question.

"Send me back." As soon as the words left his mouth, he knew, all the way to his bones, he had made the right decision.

The cloud stirred, and Glenn thought he saw the guardian nod. "You got it."

The light faded around him. He was dropping, weightless, through time and space. As the darkness overtook him, he looked back. The guardian's cloud had become a swirl of tiny fireflies, just like the ones he had seen surrounding *Friendship 7* on his first flight.

The cloud passed through the bulkhead, swarming around the plane as they emerged into the darkness. Before they vanished completely, he heard the guardian say softly, "Godspeed, John Glenn."

Reboot

Annie Reed

"Are you going to miss it? Being a hero?"

I heard snickers and groans, pretty typical for a crowded classroom full of nine-year-olds. I've been in enough of them over the years to know. These days the desks are all molded plastic, clean-lined, ergonomic, not the knee-scraping wood and metal-framed contraptions I grew up with. The cafeteria smell's gone, too; now it's the smell of too many bodies crowded together in too small a space. Everything's more crowded these days.

The girl who'd asked me the question, a pretty thing with braids in her auburn hair and shaved patches the size of my thumb on the sides of her skull—the newest thing in fashion, my granddaughter tells me—blushed a bit but managed to keep looking at me.

"Children!" That was the teacher, a harried woman whose face—lined around her mouth, weary shadows underneath her eyes—looked every one of her middle-aged sixty or so years.

"That's okay, that's okay," I said. I held my hands

up in a shushing gesture and the room quieted down. I smiled at the girl with the braids and naked strips of pink scalp. "It's a legitimate question. Not the first time I've been asked, so don't go getting embarrassed, no matter what these guys think." I winked at her and she smiled back. I still had some of my old charm. At least it still seemed to work on nervous nine-year-old girls.

"So are you?" she asked again.

Now it was my turn to blush a little. No matter how old I got, hero worship was something I'd never been comfortable with.

"Well, see . . . I don't think of myself as a hero. Not at all. I'm just a working man like everybody else. Sometimes I go talk to nice folks like you, and sometimes I go someplace in another time. It's all just part of the job."

"But aren't you going to miss it? Going to other times?" This came from a boy farther back in the crowded classroom. He was thin—pretty much everybody's thin these days, but I'm old enough to remember when a lot of people weren't so I tend to notice—and had a rainbow-colored shock of hair over his left ear and forest green spiral body art covering his head where the rest of his hair should have been.

There were fewer giggles this time.

"Of course I'm going to miss it, but I've been working hard for the last seventy years or so. I think it's about time I did some traveling in this time zone, see the world, enjoy my granddaughter and her children."

That was my canned response. In truth I was going to miss the hell out of this job. I wasn't ready to retire.

REBOOT 181

I went to work like everybody else, did what I was told; then before I knew it, enough years had gone by that now I was about to retire whether I wanted to or not. Nothing personal. It's in the program. It's your time.

Just didn't feel like my time.

I answered a few more questions from the kids, standard stuff like—

Who's the most famous person you ever met in the past? (Nobody as far as I know. Most of what we do is observe and record, no interaction, but there were a few trips I'm kinda fuzzy about, so who knows?)

What's the most exciting thing you do? (These days, waking up without a backache is pretty damn exciting, but I couldn't tell nine-year-olds that. I made up a story about outrunning the bulls in Pamplona, and that seemed to get everybody laughing. Could just be the idea of me with my old man's body outrunning anything, much less a bull.)

Do you ever change anything on purpose? (The stock answer is no, we don't change anything, just observe. But I wouldn't actually know. Just like everybody else, I flow with time; any changes made in the past become something that's always been a part of my present.)

Eventually the classroom lights dimmed a bit and a warning tone signaled the end of class. The children gathered their datapads, their few paper books, and filed into the crowded hallway. I slid off the corner of the teacher's desk and rubbed my sore rear end. The teacher walked up to me, holding out her hand. Her grip was firm, her skin rough.

"That was wonderful, Mr. Russell. You're very good with children."

"I've had a lot of practice." More and more over the years. I was the most recognizable person who worked in the program. Langford Russell, the first man to go backwards in time.

The first guinea pig for the program, more like it.

I found another guinea pig waiting for me in the crowded hallway outside the classroom. Tall and thin and a good fifty years younger than me, William Gibb was a prime example of why I was sent to talk to a bunch of nine-year-olds. The program's always needed new blood. There's a lot of past to observe and record. I talked to William's class more than a decade ago, and he was impressed enough that when he turned eighteen, he joined and became a time traveler like me.

I just wasn't expecting to see him here today. It occurred to me that maybe he'd been sent to observe what I said to the class. Make sure the old coot didn't let anything slip he shouldn't. I didn't much like that idea.

"Don't you have better things to do than babysit a relic like me?" I asked.

"What?"

William's voice was softly accented. He could sound British or Irish or even Australian when he wanted. It was a good talent to have when you're supposed to blend in. Me, these days I just look like everybody's harmless grandfather. Put me in the right clothes, and I blend in damn well.

"Oh, no, nothing like that," William said with a shy

smile. "I looked up your schedule, knew you'd be here. There's something I wanted to talk to you about."

A sea of children flowed around us, laughing and chatting and shouting to each other. So many of them crowded in the hallway, I could barely hear myself think much less carry on a coherent conversation.

"Outside," I said.

William nodded. Together we wound our way through the maze of hallways to the relative quiet outside the school. Not that it wasn't noisy outside, too. The world was a pretty full place these days. People crowded the sidewalks, packed in cars on congested streets, worked in smaller and smaller cubicles only to go home to the tiny apartments they shared with family or friends or even just acquaintances. Privacy was fast becoming a rare commodity. It's another reason I enjoyed all my trips to the past. I wondered sometimes if the people who lived back then appreciated all the wide open spaces. I know I sure did.

We managed to find a vacant spot on a bench at a bus stop about a half block away from the school. A city bus was just pulling away, its exhaust belching smelly black smoke. We'd have a few minutes before the next group of commuters started to congregate. I sat down at one end of the bench and William sat next to me.

"What's so important you had to track me down out here? It couldn't wait for my retirement party?"

Some people at work were throwing me a surprise party that afternoon. I wasn't supposed to know about it, but it's hard to keep something like that a secret, even for people who are trained to keep their mouths shut.

William quirked an eyebrow at me in amusement. "Figured you might know about that. And, no, I didn't think this could wait."

A woman walked by with two toddlers in tow. William waited until she passed before he said anything else.

"Do you ever get back and not remember what you did?" he asked.

I nodded. "Sure, sometimes." In the early days of the program the trips back through time always gave me God-awful stomach cramps and a splitting headache. After some trips I was sick for days. If all I got now was a little amnesia on occasion, I counted myself lucky.

"That's happened a few times in a row to me lately," he said. "I got worried, so I went to the program doctor to make sure I hadn't caught anything." We were well inoculated against anything we might run into in the past, so I never really gave it a second thought. "I got a look at my chart. They were testing me for things I've never heard of, which I suppose is not surprising given some of the places I've been. But there was one word on the chart I was sure I'd seen before, couldn't remember where at the time. Cancer." He turned to me, a strange expression on his face. "Have you ever heard of it?"

I tried to remember a sickness called cancer. Couldn't. "Sure that wasn't just your birth sign?" Some people still believe in astrology. Wouldn't put it past the program to have that in our charts. They seem to know everything else about us.

"I was born in February."

He took a pack of cigarettes from his jacket pocket, offered me one, but I shook my head. Never saw the appeal of smoking myself. Some people said it calmed their nerves. I wondered if that's why William smoked. His hand, as he raised the cigarette to his lips, trembled a little.

"I probably should have let the whole thing drop," he said. "They gave me a clean bill of health. Fit as the proverbial fiddle. Then I woke up last night and remembered where I'd heard the word before. It was on a news report on the tube one time when I went back, something about the rising death toll from cancer after above-ground nuclear testing."

Watching television in the past was against program rules. I always thought it was a stupid rule since we were sent back to observe, and the people of the last century or so seemed as hooked on television as people today were hooked on the entertainment net. Observing the people of the past should mean observing their habits too. But the program said no, and like the good little guinea pig I was, I never watched. William had.

"They're gonna kick your ass if they find out," I said.

"Yes, well, more than my ass is in for some serious kicking, I'm afraid." He took another drag on his cigarette. "I couldn't understand why I had no memory of cancer, so I hacked the program this morning to find out."

I'd heard rumors about people who tried over the years to get inside the program. Never heard if anyone succeeded. The program's security people dealt pretty swiftly with anyone who tried. No wonder William was nervous. "Kid, you're in some serious trouble."

"We're all in serious trouble, Lang. All of us. Cancer is just one of a host of diseases that have been eradicated. Not only wiped from our bodies, but the memory of them has been wiped from our minds. Like they never existed at all. I eliminated something called 'Acquired Immune Deficiency Syndrome.' Johnny Crompton, a man I trained with, eliminated hepatitis. And you . . . you eliminated cancer." He took one last drag from his cigarette and crushed it underneath the heel of his boot. "These things used to give people lung cancer. Millions of them died from it. And no one in this time has ever heard of it, including us. Why not?"

I had eliminated a disease that used to kill millions? How the hell did I do that? And why was William acting like it was the worst thing in the world?

"Why do I get the feeling that's not all you found out?" I kept my voice low so only he could hear me.

He looked over his shoulder, probably looking for program security. For the first time I noticed a scab behind his right ear, half-hidden by his long, curly hair. He'd removed the chip implanted under his skin, the one that lets the program find us and pull us back through time. Maybe that wasn't all the chip did. Without really thinking about it, I fingered the patch of skin behind my own right ear, feeling the hard nub of the chip underneath my skin.

"You were the first one who went back to the past. How did the program work then?"

I started to tell him that it was just a job. I'd answered an employment ad, gone on an interview, had a battery of physical tests administered by stern-faced men and women in white lab coats, and been hired. The first test run had been little more than a ten-second trip back in time and then a yank back to the present to see if time travel actually worked.

Only . . . had it been more than that? Or maybe less?

"They didn't celebrate," I said. "I was the first man they sent back in time, and when I got back after that first trip, they didn't celebrate. They just ran more tests on me. It was like business as usual."

"Maybe that's because you're not the first person they've sent back."

What? "You mean they sent some poor slob before me and it didn't work and they never even told me?"

"No. I mean the technology isn't new. Just new to us."

Sometimes the world does a curious little shift that has nothing to do with time travel. You can be sitting minding your own business, and all of a sudden the world goes a little grayer, life tastes duller, or shadows suddenly have more depth, like something's just come into focus, and you feel displaced from surroundings that are as familiar to you as the skin on your hands. I felt that shift when I got the call that my wife had been killed—all the bright colors seemed to leach out of the world in a single instant.

I felt that way now, listening to William. If it had

been any other person, I would have thought this was some elaborate prank played on the guy who's retiring. But I knew this kid was serious. I heard it in the tremor in his voice, saw it in the thin sheen of sweat that had broken out on his upper lip.

"What else did you find?" I asked.

"Most of the time all we do is observe and record. But sometimes we're instructed to leave things, or to touch certain people in certain ways. Those are the missions we can't remember when we get back. Lang, I've . . ." His face flushed and he glanced away from me. "According to what I could find, I've had sex with people in the past . . . women . . . men . . . I've even hurt some of them. I saw myself doing it like some mindless fool, and I can't remember any of it."

I blanched. In the fifty-two years I'd been married, I never once strayed. The mere idea that I could have betrayed my wife in the past and not remembered . . .

"Did I . . . ?" I couldn't even say it.

William shook his head. "No, not that I could find. The program is huge, and I didn't have time to look everywhere. I wanted to find out why we were instructed to do these . . . *things*," he almost spat the word out, "that went against all our training. I dug deeper. And I found things . . . references to past experiments, population quotas, re-education programs. Even those talks you give now. All that dates from the time you entered the program. Nothing's been updated, been changed. It's almost like the program is following a formula. Something developed somewhere else."

"Somewhere else. You mean another planet?" A part of me couldn't believe I said that out loud.

"Maybe. I'm not sure. But you said the first time you went back, it was like business as usual. Maybe that's what it was. Business as usual. Just in a different location."

"You're crazy," I said, but there was no real conviction in my voice.

"I know that's how it sounds, but think. Disease has been systematically eliminated. We live much longer than even our parents—all of us remember that much, anyway. Yet we're all still compelled to have children. We're taught that in school. Even I want children of my own someday. We're filling up the planet, overwhelming our resources. The program is obviously orchestrating at least part of this, but why? I couldn't find that out. I hit a security wall, and then my implant started to buzz and I knew I had to get it out. By the time I was done with that, security had shut me down and I was out of the system with no way to get back in."

My own head was buzzing, but it had nothing to do with the implanted chip behind my ear. "Why are you telling me all this?"

"Because you were the start of it. Because I was able to do one last thing before I was kicked out of the system." He took a long, shuddery breath. "I created one more mission for you. To go back one week before you were hired. Do what you've been trained to do. Observe. Maybe I'm wrong. Maybe there's nothing sinister to all this. I don't think I am."

William took a slip of paper out of his pocket. "These are the codes I used to get into the program. Where you're going, they won't know I've already used them, they won't have any reason to change them."

I took the slip of paper, stuffed it in my own jacket pocket without looking at it. The sun was still shining through the layer of haze that always seemed to blanket the city, but I felt cold, cold and numb.

"If I find out you're right . . ." I had to stop and clear my throat. "If I find out there is something sinister going on, what am I supposed to do about it?"

William looked at me for a long moment. He was scared, I could see it in his eyes, but he was angry too. I could see that in the line between his brows, in the tense set of his mouth.

"If I'm right, we've been played for fools. Not just those of us in the program. All of us. All of this—" he gestured at the mass of people moving around us, "—is not supposed to be this way. How much has technology advanced over your lifetime? We live longer, but except for time travel, how far have we advanced? I think maybe that's been orchestrated too. It isn't natural."

He stopped only long enough to light another cigarette. "I was sent to Australia once. Couldn't quite figure out why. Here I was, out in the middle of bush country, flat and dry and desolate as far as the eye could see. At least it looked that way at first. There's this fence, you see. Bisected the entire bloody continent. I thought maybe that's what I was supposed to observe, so I walked closer. Saw tire tracks all along the side of the fence. Saw gates here and there. Pretty soon a truck full of hunters pulled up to a gate on one side, four men spilled out, opened the gate, and then they went hunting on the other side. My side. What I thought was desolate wasteland was home to more rabbits than I ever saw in my life. Pretty easy targets, those rabbits. There were so many of them.

"I still remembered the rabbits after I got back, so I found out what I could about that fence." William started talking faster now, like he was running out of time. "Those rabbits were brought to Australia for sport, Lang. They had no natural predators there and the rabbit population exploded. All these diseases we've eliminated, I think they're man's natural predators, keeps the population in check. Without them our population has exploded. It's all been planned."

"We're being raised for sport, is that what you're telling me?" I couldn't keep the anger out of my voice. I didn't know who I was angry at exactly, but a slow burn had settled in my belly.

"I don't know, but I don't like the possibility. If that is what you find, is that the kind of world you want for your grandchildren, your great-grandchildren?"

William stood abruptly. "I can't stay here any longer. I know they're going to catch me eventually, but I want to give you enough time to be gone first."

"If I do this thing, if I find what you think I'm going to find and I change it, you know there's a possibility—"

"That I will never have existed." He squeezed my

shoulder briefly. "Do what you have to do. I don't much fancy the idea of someone opening a gate someday and using me for target practice."

Neither do I.

Neither do I.

I've been many places in the seventy-odd years I have worked in the program. My own past wasn't one of them.

It was disorienting at first, a clash of memory with reality, like going back to the first school you attended and discovering that it was much smaller than the impressive institution of your memory.

Program headquarters were located in a massive building in what was then a new industrial park on the south edge of the city. Even in the early days of the program, it employed hundreds of people. I remembered it as a hive of activity, organized chaos, the codes and security measures and electric cart people-movers more complex and incomprehensible to my young eyes than any airport terminal. Now, after all this time working in the program, the security measures weren't intimidating.

Except I couldn't use my own security identification to get in the building. Dammit.

The mission William had created for me was a simple one. The pretty technician who had strapped me into the displacement chamber hadn't batted an eyelash as she scanned my instructions. "Should be an easy trip for you, for your last one," she'd said. Then she leaned in close to my ear. "Don't worry. I'll have you back in time for your party. Wouldn't want you to miss that."

With a wink at me, she'd started the displacement program. I felt the tingle on my skin, a tightening in my bowels, that feeling of abrupt movement without moving, like when an airplane suddenly loses altitude, and then I was in another time. Bright sunlight, no smog; the smell of fresh-cut lawn from the landscaping in between the buildings, and the pleasant cooing of a pair of doves perched in the eaves of the building next to where I materialized. Without security clearance.

"Seems you didn't think of quite everything," I muttered. I patted my shirt pocket where I'd put the paper with the program codes William had given me. I had changed into a plaid flannel button-down shirt and jeans, clothes I hadn't worn in years. They felt comfortable somehow, like crawling into bed under your favorite blanket.

Maybe I could bluff my way in. I knew enough about the program, after all, to at least make up an authentic-sounding story.

I went in through the front doors with a group of people wearing white lab coats and a couple of men, one middle-aged (for the time) and one in his twenties, both dressed in jeans like me. Inside the front doors a receptionist sat behind an impressive black granite half-wall. Off to her left was the real entrance to the program, a locked glass door embedded in a wall of glass. A security card and fingerprint scanner opened the door. The security guard leaning up against the half-wall in front of the receptionist's desk insured only one person at a time went through the security door.

I took a deep breath and prepared to make my spiel.

"You guys here for the interviews?" the receptionist asked. I realized she was talking to the two guys in jeans. And me. A small sign mounted in a clear plastic holder on the short wall said "Janitorial staff interviews, 9:00 AM" and gave today's date.

I looked at my watch. It was five to nine. Maybe William had thought of more than I gave him credit for.

I nodded along with the other two guys.

"I'll take you through," the security guard said. "I'll need your driver's licenses or other identification, something with your picture on it."

That wasn't a problem for me. I had a driver's license with my picture and a phony name just in case I ever needed it. Of course, it wasn't entered in the system. Not yet. Not for about another week or so, anyway. I just hoped the security guard was only taking ID's to make sure we behaved inside and not to do a background check.

We handed our licenses over and the guard stuck them in his back pocket. He opened the door and led us down a short hallway to a conference room. Three other men sat inside.

"Stay here," the guard said. "No wandering, understand?"

Everyone nodded. As the guard turned to go, I walked over to him. I kept my face turned away from the camera I knew was hidden in the light sconce on the back wall of the room.

"Got a bathroom handy?" I asked. I played up on my age a bit. "If this is going to take a while, I probably should take care of that first."

The guard looked at me like I was crazy for applying for a job at my age, but he was professional enough not to say anything. In those days people could still sue for age discrimination.

"Sure, just make it quick, okay?" He let me out of the conference room and pointed to the bathroom I knew was down the hall. "Three doors down. And no—"

"Wandering," I said, and I gave him a grateful grin. "Got it."

I walked down the hall, taking my time, shuffling like my joints hurt more than they did. The guard gave up on me, apparently satisfied I was no threat. By the time I got to the bathroom, the hallway behind me was deserted. I walked inside, locked myself in a stall, and pulled out my own security card. My picture, my real name, but the only place the security card was actually scanned was the front door. The rest of the time I just had to wear it like a badge and act like I knew where I was going. That I could do. Of course, the guard would eventually discover his elderly job applicant had flown the coop and come looking for me. I could always try to palm the card and claim confusion if I got caught, but I hoped it wouldn't come to that. I hoped to be finished before that.

Outside the bathroom, I checked the hallway. Still clear. I turned down the hall in the opposite direction from the conference room, and made my way deeper into program headquarters. I passed a few people in the hallways and got a couple of raised eyebrows over my lack of a white lab coat. After a glance at my security card, they just kept on walking.

All I needed was a terminal where I could log on using the codes William had given me. I found what I needed on the second floor. An office, no name on the door. I opened it, prepared to give my old-guy-lost spiel, but it was empty. I shut the door behind me, sat down at the desk, unfolded the piece of paper, and logged into the program.

It was all there, just like William said. Files for every mission I would ever go on, all planned in advance. Steps for re-education of the population to emphasize home and family. Plans for the systematic elimination of every major disease and illness known to man, most of which I'd never heard of. Or didn't remember, since they existed in this time. I found the mission I had—would?—gone on that eliminated cancer. I didn't understand the science behind it, but it had worked. Cancer was unknown in my time.

It was enough to convince me there was a plan. I just didn't know what it was.

I entered the rest of the codes William had written on the paper. The terminal in front of me went blank, blinked with a bright light twice, and then the screen came alive with color. And words. At least I thought they were words, but written in a language I'd never seen before.

Behind me the door banged open hard enough it slammed into the wall. "What are you . . . ?"

I turned to find the security guard closely followed by one of the white lab coat people I'd walked in the front door with this morning. A woman, her face stern behind silver-rimmed, owl-eye-shaped glasses.

"Back away from the terminal."

The security guard had his gun out and pointed at me. I'd never looked down the barrel of a gun before. The damn hole at the end of the barrel looked huge. I could almost see my red blood splattered on the blank white walls of the office. My old guy spiel dried up on my lips. I did what I was told, got up and backed away from the terminal, my hands raised slightly in the air.

Lab coat woman looked at the terminal and uttered an oath. The security guard glanced at it—if I'd been the age I was in this time I might have tried to overpower him when he looked away, but right now I was too intimidated by the gun and too handcuffed by my years.

"Leave us," the woman said. She pressed a button on the terminal and the monitor went black.

"You sure?" The guard didn't sound convinced.

"You're not going anywhere, are you, Langford?" she asked.

I blinked at her. From where she was standing I didn't think she could read my name on the security card, but then I realized that her glasses didn't distort her eyes, didn't make them look bigger or smaller. The glasses were just for show. Part of a costume, just like her white lab coat.

"You know him?"

She smiled, but with no real humor. "I've known him for years now. You can go. He won't be causing any more problems."

The guard holstered his gun and left, shutting the door behind himself. I'd never been so glad to see anyone leave in my life. At least that I remembered.

But then again, the way the woman was looking at me, like I was a bug on her clean kitchen counter, I might have been better off with the guard and his gun.

"I'm surprised," she said. "This isn't like you. You've always been such a good worker for us, never a complaint. I've heard retirement doesn't agree with some people. Perhaps that's the problem. You've become bored. But no . . . wait . . . " She seemed to look at something I couldn't see. "You haven't quite retired yet, have you? And you met with William today. Clever boy. Or, at least, he was."

A chill ran through me, and a sick weight settled in the pit of my stomach.

"How do you know me?" I managed to ask, though my voice came out a harsh croak.

She shook her head. "When you know how to travel through time, time is no longer linear. I've lived far longer than you. I have all my memories, from all times. And I can access all the information the program has stored in its infinite memory."

"But you were surprised to see me here."

"Yes, well . . . one has to anticipate a problem before one can see how to prevent it. We just never anticipated a problem with you. Or William, for that matter. Pity we can't access your dreams; it would make this all so much easier."

We. As in "them." As in different from us.

"William was right, wasn't he?" I didn't need to ask. I already knew the answer.

"Very intuitive, that boy." I realized another reason for her glasses. They hid the predator's gleam in her eyes. "I hope you're not going to ask me what I'm going to do with you. It should be obvious that for you, retirement will mean something else entirely now."

I could have protested that I was a hero, people would notice if I went missing, but I knew that wasn't true. I was only a hero because the program made me one. It could just as easily erase me from everyone's memory, and the hero would vanish without a trace.

I felt deep anguish then, almost a physical pain, at the thought that my granddaughter and her children would never remember that I even existed.

My granddaughter . . . my great-grandchildren . . . I couldn't let them live in a world the program controlled. Not knowing what I did.

I lunged for the terminal. There was one more command to enter; William had written the key sequence after the last passcode.

The woman was fast, surprisingly fast. Inhumanly fast. She slammed her body against mine, knocked me to the floor. My knee came down hard on the linoleum tile and I saw stars, but I managed to roll to my side, kept my momentum heading forward. Toward the terminal. I just had to press two keys.

I never got the chance. Just as I was reaching out with my hand, the woman hit me with the desk chair. I heard the bones in my neck snap and I fell like a stone in a boneless heap.

I lay there, unmoving, and thought about rabbits behind an unending wire fence the color of her glasses.

The woman's shoes moved into my field of vision. "Pity," she said. "At least you put up something of a fight. I rather enjoyed that."

A shrill noise sounded in the room. Shoes moved out of my range of vision. I heard frantic clicking on keys, a muttered curse, and then rough hands were on the back of my head, over the chip. I felt a wetness there but no pain.

"What have you done?" She lowered her face to mine. Hers was livid with fury, and I realized William was more clever than either of us had realized. One of the codes he'd given me was a fail-safe, tied to my chip. "It's crashing! The program is crashing!"

If I still had control over my body, I would have laughed at her. As it was, my vision was failing, blackness creeping in around the edges. It was enough to see her shoes retreating as she ran from the room.

No more program. We had destroyed it, William and I, at a point in time before I made my first trip back. What this would mean I had no idea. Would I still exist a week from today, find another job instead of the one that led me here? Would my children still be born, my granddaughter, her children? William? Would the world go on as if the program never existed? Maybe. I hoped so. I believed in the fairness of the universe. It was all I had.

Blackness continued to creep in, but with it I saw a long line of silver fence, miles and miles of it, almost as if I was flying above it. And as I passed, the fence dissolved, and the rabbits ran free.

ME, MYSELF, AND AY

Susan Sizemore

"What have you done?"
Horemheb awoke with the horrified words he'd spoken ringing in his ears. He'd put the memory of them aside for years, but now they rose up out of the dark place where he'd hidden them to haunt what he knew to be the last hours of his life.

There was too much light in the room. Too many people hovering, staring, waiting. Prayers buzzed in his ears. And the wailing of women in the background was a false, shrill irritant.

Had he died as a soldier defending his land and his king, it would have been an easy, honorable matter, involving only pain. Dying *as* king was a far more complicated matter. Not only did he have to deal with old age, infirmity, and pain, there was also ceremony, symbolism and significance to his passing from the land of the living to the land of the dead. His death had *importance*, so they wouldn't leave him in peace for a moment.

If he'd known the end would come with such com-

plications, he might have let that Hittite swordsman
cleave him in two the last time he'd taken the field.
But then, the barbarians would have poured into the
delta and the land beyond, even as far as the sun
maddened city of the Heretic king.

But Horemheb had driven the barbarians back, and
returned to keep guard of the lands. It was not within
Horemheb's nature to die simply out of frustration
with the way things were at home. No, he'd returned,
and let events lead him to this public dying.

Public or not, the memory of that night rose up and
struck him despite the supposed protection of priests
in gilded god masks gathered around his bed, all of
them solemnly chanting spells and prayers for his protection. Why were they not protecting him from
memory?

"What have you done?"

*He had known something was wrong when a walk
through the gardens and halls of the palace showed too
few guards for his liking. This was no way to protect
the king. Especially a king that the priests did not love
and the people did not trust. The army obeyed Horemheb, but the guards of the palace could be bought—
and had been bought this night. Horemheb was certain
of it as he moved with greater and greater speed
through the dark, empty halls of the king's own house.*

*By the time he reached the child's room he was cer-
tain of what was happening. He only prayed he was in
time to stop it, though he hated the thought of who he
knew he would have to punish.*

*"Ay," he whispered even before he pushed open the
painted cedar door to Tutankhamun's bedroom. "Ay,"*

he said, even before he saw the bent figure in the shadows beside the bed. "What have you done?"

It was not just the king lying too still on the bed. The boy was family to both of them. He was Horemheb's wife's nephew. He was husband to Ay's granddaughter.

"He was a good boy," Ay said. The old man turned toward Horemheb. He stepped from shadows into the glow of lamplight. Tears ran down his wrinkled cheeks. "A good boy."

"Is he—?"

"Do not ask foolish questions, soldier. You know the shape of death."

Horemheb took up an alabaster lamp and moved forward. When he held it up a golden sheen illuminated the small, twisted figure lying face down on the bed. Yes, he recognized that stillness, the lack of soul within the vessel. There was blood on the back of the boy's shaved skull, and blood on the gold head of Ay's walking stick.

"Why did you—?"

"It needed to be done. How could I not do it myself? To have trusted the job to some underling would have been unfeeling—sacrilegious. Though I felt no god pass from the living land when I struck. Not like the evil that oozed from the Heretic's body." Ay sighed, looking down at Tutankhamun's body. "I'm glad he had none of that taint in him."

Horemheb remembered the Heretic's death, in the courtyard of his Aten temple, midday on another blindingly bright, scorching day. The king's great wife had arranged the assassination herself, and stood back, watching, with Ay and the priests of banished Amun at her side. The Heretic, tall, misshapen, his skin brown as mudbrick from all the years of standing in the light of the sun, did not looked surprised when Horemheb's soldiers surrounded him, and Horemheb drew his own gold-hilted sword to accomplish the deed.

Some of the brightness went out of the world the moment the Heretic breathed his last; the sky turned from searing yellow-white to merely hot blue. A hint of coolness coming up from the river threaded through the heated desert wind. The whole world suddenly felt—better. Not right yet, but promise entered the living world with the death of the one who had sent the gods away.

Killing Akhenaten had been the right thing to do.

But this—

"If he was not tainted why did you kill him?"

"For the lands, of course. Why else slay a child I loved." Ay turned to face Horemheb, and let his cane fall to the floor. It landed with a rattle, and rolled beneath the bed. Ay stood with his legs wide apart to keep his balance without the aid of the stick. "He was sixteen," Ay went on. "Not really a child, though we all think of him that way."

It was true; Tutankhamun was very small for his age, his limbs skinny, his head too large for his narrow shoulders, and his neck so stiff he could barely turn his head. The reality of his appearance was not a match at all for the beautiful paintings and statues that were shown to the people as the image of their king.

Tutankhamun was sickly, but those who brought him to the throne had always hoped he would grow out of his weakness. The priests had claimed to work every spell and powerful prayer they knew for his recovery. But Horemheb suspected that the followers of Amun had not really tried very hard to bring aid to the Heretic's heir.

Horemheb had known the boy was flawed, but he had not been willing to give up on him. Ay, it seemed, had made his own choice.

"If he had given my granddaughter living children . . . if only there had been a son . . ." Ay sighed. He glanced down once more at the boy he'd killed. "It broke your heart when each little girl came stillborn into the world. It broke the gods' hearts more, the peoples' hearts even more. It broke my heart the most. If you could have given me a living great-grandson, it would not have come to this. I hate that it has come to this."

Horemheb hated it as well. There should have been a child by now. Tutankhamun and his sister-wife Ankhesenamun had been trying to have children since the boy was twelve. Ankhesenamun was nearing twenty, and had had only disappointment, and great physical and mental anguish in her attempts to become a mother to a future king. She had grown to hate Tutankhamun's touching her. Horemheb knew she frequently complained of her lot to Ay, her grandfather.

The deed was done, and Horemheb felt no anger at the killer. He did think that Ay should have given the boy more time, but understood why he did not. The Two Lands needed to heal, they needed strength. They needed a proper king to perform all the rituals that kept the land safe.

"Who will rule now?" he asked Ay.

"*You,*" the old man answered.

Horemheb went cold with shock. He took a step back, and held his hands up before him. "No," he declared. "*This is not my wish. This is not my place.*"

So they buried the boy hastily, with borrowed grave goods, and Ay took the throne. But he ruled with a guilty conscience, and frequent nightmares. He often told Horemheb he wished he could take the deed back. It became Horemheb's dearest wish as well, for after four years, Ay died, and Horemheb had no choice but to become Lord of the Two Lands himself. He did the best he could to bring order to the lands, to restore *ma'at.* But he had no son who lived. He'd hand-picked an old friend, a fine general, to rule after him. But . . .

We should have given the boy more time.

Is that what you truly wish?

Horemheb focused his fading attention on the priest in the Horus mask that had asked the question. It took what seemed like a very long while to realize that the falcon-headed man was no priest, but the god himself standing beside Horemheb's deathbed. He was surprised for a moment to see a god, but then he remembered that he was king, and gods talked to kings. Kings became gods, after all. He and Horus were to be one and the same in the afterlife.

Am I talking to myself, then, Lord of the Sky?

Not quite yet, the god answered.

You are between the lands of life and death.

This second voice spoke with a deep, rough growl, and Horemheb saw that it was the jackal-headed guide to the afterlife.

You've floated here unable to step forward or back

for too long, Anubis went on. *You'll soon unbalance the scales of* ma'at *if you can't make up your mind.*

I have to be the one who chooses to die?

You are both god and king. Your choices have meaning for the living and the dead.

You are perhaps too troubled to take your proper place with us, Horus said. *What would you do to return the scales of* ma'at *to balance?*

Do not ask, my brother, Anubis warned. Then the jackal god sighed. *We know what he would do. We know the danger.*

Ma'at *must be served,* Horus answered. *The gods cannot fear justice and truth.* The hand of the god touched Horemheb's forehead; cool, cleansing fire flowed through him. *Do what you must,* Horus urged. *Do what you can. For the sake of three kings, do what you think is right.*

Three kings. Horemheb remembered the boy's vulnerability. He remembered Ay's perpetual sadness after the boy's death. He remembered his own complicity, the remorse that followed him to this moment between life and death where the world had a chance to be put in balance again.

He had always wondered what he could have done. And now, because he was among the gods, he knew.

The House of Silence was hardly a tomb, despite its daunting name. In fact, Horemheb found the place bustling and busy. It was an older palace, full of older women, tucked away in the middle of a wide, rich garden. The women who dwelled in the House of Silence were the minor wives of dead kings.

As he was conducted through courtyards and passages to the rooms of the lady he sought, Horemheb learned that these castoffs from the royal household were not spending their declining days in indolence, wistfully dreaming of past glories as he expected they would be. No, indeed. The House of Silence was full of the clatter of looms turning out fine linen. The gardeners were busy cultivating vegetable crops. The fishponds were teeming. And it was the old ladies themselves who supervised all this busy, profitable work.

He had dreaded coming to this place, but found he liked the atmosphere. By the time he was shown into Lady Ahset's rooms he knew how to present his proposal to the elderly lady who had been minor wife to the king's grandfather, Amenophis III.

She met with him in a small courtyard just off her bedchamber. He took a seat opposite her, beneath a wide blue and yellow striped sunshade, and they took a long, assessing look at each other.

"I've heard of you, general," she said. "Not young, but not yet old. An uncomfortable courtier, I think. You've come to engage me in some plot."

"An old woman with gold on her wrists and neck, but without the vanity of makeup to try to hide her age," he answered. "You were a rival of the great wife Tiye," he answered. "Long absent from the intrigues of the harem. And you miss them."

She laughed, showing that she still had most of her teeth. "I was never a rival to Queen Tiye," she said. "It was the king who loved her too much to allow any

rivals. It was by being her friend that I found my way
to the king's bed."

"You found your way there often enough to present
him with a child."

Ahset made a dismissive gesture. "A daughter. He
had sons by Tiye."

"But both those sons are dead now. And the son
of one of those sons is on the throne. Time moves
on," Horemheb said. "Royal daughters can be valuable when the king is young, and in need of wives."

They looked at each other thoughtfully for a while.

Finally, Horemheb said, "Your daughter has a
daughter, does she not? Her father is the Nomarch
Merikare?"

"I think you have more knowledge of my family
than anyone else in the court. And why is this?" she
asked. "What more do you want to know? And what
is it you want with the girl?"

"Is she a girl?" he asked. "What is her age? Is she
unmarried? If so, would her grandmother bring her to
the capital so that she might be introduced to the
court?"

"She is old enough to bear children," Ahset said,
well aware of what Horemheb wanted with her granddaughter. There was a gleam in her eyes that told him
the old woman was ready to strike a bargain.

"Then I have business with her," he said. "The
granddaughter of a king has value. There is work for
her to do."

Ahset laughed. "Yes. In this house we appreciate
the value of work."

He lowered his voice, even though they were alone. "Tutankhamun is sickly. His wife is jealous of her place. But his councilors grow ever more impatient for him to have a son. It will be dangerous for the king if he does not produce an heir soon. If we present this girl of royal lineage to him, we must be certain that she is fertile. Nothing must be left to chance."

"Ah," she said, and nothing more, but the old woman nodded. She understood perfectly well what was necessary.

Then she gave him wine and cakes, and they spoke of the linen trade. He made a bargain with her trade in cloth, and this gave him an excuse to return to the House of Silence several times in the next three months.

Early in those months, Ahset had her granddaughter brought to the palace. The girl's name was Muyet, and she was a beauty. When the moment was right Horemheb had his wife invite Muyet into their household.

The next step was bring her to the king's attention.

Horemheb first brought the girl to a feast, dressed in the thinnest linen made by her grandmother's weavers. It was a feast that the great royal wife did not attend. Horemheb made sure that the king saw the girl. Ay saw her as well, and by the end of the evening there was a thoughtful look on the old vizier's face as he glanced thoughtfully from the king to Muyet, and back again.

Horemheb was not sure that Ay liked what he saw, but he obviously recognized the possibilities. Perhaps the sight of Muyet got the old man to thinking about the logical solution to the problem of the king's having an heir. Ay was fiercely loyal to his granddaughter— she was the great royal wife, she was one of the reasons he stayed in power. But Horemheb was betting on Ay's loyalty to the kingdom to accept the possibility that Muyet offered. The girl carried the blood of the royal line, blood she could pass to an heir.

Horemheb and Ay did not discuss the matter, but Ay did see to it that the great royal wife was engaged elsewhere when Muyet was brought back to court a few days later. This time the king and the girl were left alone in a garden. Muyet was bright enough to seize the chance she'd been given. Not long after she was declared a secondary wife, and she was with child. The child was born early, but healthy, and he was a son.

Ay could have prevented this usurping of his granddaughter's place, but he did not. If he suspected that the child was not fathered by Tutankhamun he never showed it.

Ankhesenamun remained great royal wife, and for the first two years after the heir was born she swung between being heartbroken at losing favor, and relieved at not having to share her half-brother's bed again. This daughter of the Heretic and Nefertiti had never been particularly stable. And it was known that the love of her father's god Aten still burned inside her despite the official restoration of Amun and the other gods.

It was through religion that she found a way to once more influence Tutankhamun. While his son grew stronger by the day, the king grew weaker. At first in secret, then openly, Ankhesenamun preached the benefits of worshipping the sun to the sickly king. She took him out into the light, and that did seem to help his weakness. She found magicians and priests, followers of the sun god that had gone into hiding, and built a small temple for them in her own palace.

And some of these priests and magicians found their way into the household of the heir, and began to teach him of the Aten, the sun god that they claimed was the only god. The king did not forbid these priests teaching his son, those he wisely did not officially approve it either.

The priests of Amun and the other gods were outraged, especially when the Aten priests began going out among the people to speak of the Aten. This was a new thing, a change in the way Aten was worshipped, a change in the way all gods were worshipped, really. In the time of the Heretic, the belief was that only the king could intercede with Aten for the people. The king was always the only one who stood face to face before the gods for the people, but the Heretic had forbidden any prayers or sacrifices to the Aten by anyone *but* him. The people were forbidden from prayer to any god, but they were allowed to pray to the king. The king alone prayed to Aten.

This new outgrowth of the heresy abandoned the Heretic's claim to be the only intercessor, and began to instill the belief that anyone could stand in the light of the sun and pray. It was turned into a religion of the people, a religion without temples. It was against *ma'at*, yet people began to believe in the god they had

hated when the Heretic had imposed Aten wo....p
on them.

All this happened slowly, subtly, with the conniving
of Ankhesenamun, and the compliance of the king.
Ay kept quiet, later telling Horemheb that renewed
interest in Aten helped keep a balance against the
power of the priests of Amun. Horemheb was off
fighting the Hittites to protect the borders, and much
was kept from him. In fact, he was kept away longer
than he wanted, and not called home until the king
himself ordered it. The reason for Horemheb's return
was to be honored at a ceremony awarding him Gold
of Honor for his many years of service.

Tutankhamun was obviously dying when Horemheb
returned to court. The king's spine was bent to the
point where his head rested on his chest. His limbs
were mere sticks now. His voice was a feeble whisper
punctuated by rasping coughs.

The boy that stood tall and straight beside him was
nearly twelve. Fortunately, he looked much like his
mother, and there was a resemblance to his great
grandfather, Amenophis, after whom he was named.
Horemheb could not help but smile at the handsome
boy he never dared think of as his son. It was the boy
who presented him with the golden bracelets that were
a gift from the king.

Horemheb's smile froze, and his pride in the moment deadened when he saw the many-rayed sun sym-
bol of the Aten that decorated the bracelets. He had
no choice but to put the bracelets on, but his hands
were so stiff with shock that he fumbled them into

place. They were uncomfortable anyway, like grasping hands on his wrists.

After the ceremony he sought out Ay, and Ay told him everything about the growing Aten worship over the last several years. When the old man was finished, Horemheb wished he had never come home. He felt as if everything he had done for the lands was for nothing; as if he had made all the wrong choices; as though he had made the wrong prayer to the gods, but the gods had answered it anyway.

But he had saved the king's life. He was certain that if he had not introduced Muyet and her child into the mixture of court intrigue, someone surely would have replaced the boy king with someone who could breed. Well, the king was no longer a boy, he was dying, and the world was no more in balance than when the Heretic had ruled.

"I should have left well enough alone," Horemheb declared.

"I have been leaving things alone," Ay answered. "Mostly. I'm too old to care very much anymore."

And so they parted. Horemheb went home, heavy of heart, feeling his age, and all the wounds he'd taken in battles in war and politics. The first thing he did when he reached his house was take off the heavy golden bracelets.

The first thing he saw was the rash already growing, marking a circle on his wrists where the bracelets had been. The rash grew quickly, and fever came with it.

He did not know if the poisoning had been ordered by Ankhesenamun, the priests of Aten, or perhaps even the king himself. Horemheb could only guess at the reasons. Perhaps in revenge for the death of Akhenaten so many years ago. Perhaps because the king was dying, and wanted to remove every perceived threat against his son's ascension.

Whatever the reason for it, the poison did its work. Within a few days, Horemheb breathed his last.

As he entered the land of the dead, Anubis was waiting for him. *I knew it was a mistake to let you have your wish,* the jackal god snarled. *But you only get one chance. It's too late to go back and do it over again now.*

The Valley of the Kings, 3267 AE

Howard Carter, archaeologist and Egyptologist, had worked and wished for this day all his life. He tried not to let the excitement that burned in him show as he stood before the recently uncovered door of the last royal tomb to be excavated. He was, after all, a scholar, and the head of a scientific expedition. It would simply not *do* to show that he was giddy as a schoolboy, surrounded as he was by superstitious native workers, and with his patron, Lord Carnarvon, standing so closely beside him.

This was the holy of holies, Carter was certain of it. After years of digging he had found the tomb of Tutankhamun, father of the pharaoh that had changed the world. He would be the first to look inside this long sought-after tomb. He would prove that everything in the scriptures had really happened, and happened when and where holy writ claimed. Right here in Egypt.

Oh, the era of the pharaohs was long gone. This land had seen many conquerors, and power had shifted away from the land of the Nile long ago. But the Idea remained, even though those who had founded the faith had been forgotten for thousands of years. Scientists and grave robbers had been excavating the sites of Egypt since the middle of the last century, enlightening the world.

Carter had spent his life as one of those diggers. His goal had always been to find this tomb, to prove the existence of this legendary king. And now he had finally found the site.

He stepped back for a moment to let the workers finish breaking a hole in the heavy limestone doorway blocking the entrance. Then he took up a candle, took a deep breath, and stepped forward to peer through the small opening.

"What do you see?" Carnarvon asked anxiously from behind him.

A long time passed before Carter could bring himself to speak.

"Nothing."

Carter knew his voice held no emotions, but under his breath he swore to the Sun, and the Son of the Sun who'd eluded him. Carter fingered the gold sun disc amulet he faithfully wore around his neck. Grave robbers, or more likely, heretics, must have desecrated it long ago.

What had Howard Carter seen within Tutankhamun's tomb?

"Absolutely nothing."

Super Lamb Banana

Sarah A. Hoyt

John Lennon thought he was going to be mugged.

And it shouldn't happen here. He was at Liverpool docks, where the tourists were as thick on the ground as muck in a back alley. He thought he'd be safer here than near his rent-subsidized flat. But these days there was nowhere safe.

John peered with near-sighted anxiety at the man approaching through the foggy evening. He looked taller than John and big and approached with the sort of purposeful confidence only criminals had.

Turning away, John tried to use his cane to steady himself on the cobblestones that the fog turned slippery.

The steps got closer.

Tap, tap, tap, John pushed his cane against the cobblestones, balancing himself, desperately trying to move faster, to—

The water slap-slapped against the moorings of Albert Dock. The bracken smell of river water surrounded him. Somewhere, far away, the noise of women laughing and glasses tinkling echoed, so faintly that it might as well have come from another world. Probably at the Liverpool Tate Gallery. Or the Beatles Museum.

But out here, John was alone with his pursuer.

John had nothing that anyone could want. He wore an old turtleneck and threadbare jeans and, in his pocket, kept his return bus ticket back to his flat. None of which would be worth much, even at a street market.

But it didn't matter. The mugger might lose his temper. He might kill John for kicks. Or for nothing.

John tried to walk faster. His heart sped up and his breath came in short puffs.

The steps behind him neared, relentless. John tried to run.

His feet went out from under him, as the too-worn shoe lost purchase on the slick cobblestone. He gave a faint cry and struggled to hold himself upright with his cane. Somehow he could not set it firmly on the pavement.

The ground rushed up to meet him. He hit on the side of his face. His bad hip sent a vibrating pain through his body that made him curl in a ball and keen.

Behind him, the steps turned into a run. Jackals always got excited when prey fell.

John tried to get up, scrabbling to his aching knees. The breeze was cold where his jeans had torn against the stone. In front of him, a blurred yellow glare like a boulder painted an unholy color offered a grip to help him get up. He couldn't quite see what the thing was, since his glasses were badly out of date. But he reached out, anyway, and scrabbled with his hands at smooth cement, trying to find a handhold.

"Sir, are you all right?" a man's voice asked. Strong hands, on John's shoulders pulled him up, helped him balance against the yellow thing.

John rested against it, panting, the sweat from his exertions cooling fast on his body.

"Mr. Lennon, did you hurt yourself?"

Dizzy, his head aching, his skin abraded, John turned to look at the man. Was this the same person who'd followed him through the fog?

He sounded like a Yank. And, up close, he had that well-scrubbed, clean-shaven look that so many Yanks had these days—always giving the impression they were overgrown schoolboys. Couldn't look less like a mugger.

"I'm fine," John said. "Perfectly fine." The last word faltered, as he realized that the man had called him by his name. The man had recognized—John.

Which—considering how difficult John found it to recognize himself when he looked in his mirror and saw his domed, balding head, his rheumy eyes, his sagging chin—must rate as some sort of a miracle.

The Yank seized hold of John's hand and shook it up and down with much unnecessary vigor. "I'm Richard Sforzi," he said. "I'm so glad to meet you at last. I was hoping you'd be coming to the reception at the Beatles Museum."

He stopped, doubtless because he couldn't fail to notice how John's eyes had narrowed at the mention of the Beatles.

John *knew* that when anyone said he was a great fan of John's, he actually meant he was a great fan of the Beatles. He'd probably flown all the way across the Atlantic to go to the reception at the Beatles Museum—which celebrated the fact that Paul had given the museum his gold-plated Rolls Royce, or perhaps the gold-plated thong underwear of his young wife.

John felt his lip curl into a snarl, and controlled it by an effort of will. These fans—his or not—were often good for a pint of beer, or—rarely—two fingers of something stronger. Really rarely they would have other, illegal substances they were willing to share.

John forced a slightly daft smile upon his lips, and looked at the man with what he hoped was an encouraging gaze. "So, a great fan of the Beatles, are you?" he asked. "I was going to the museum me'self. To have a gander at what not that McCartney has donated now. Good old Paul McCartney, that, always finding ways to make money out of the three notes he knows, no?"

"I always thought you were a much better musician than McCartney." Sforzi swallowed. He grabbed John around the wrist and spoke in a great rush. "You probably still are, er . . . if you're still playing . . . The only reason I came England was that I hoped to meet you, and the Beatles Museum seemed like a place to find you."

It was, of course. Not just because it allowed John to get away from his lonely flat for a few hours. Not just because there would be free food, and there was always the hope of a fan to touch for a drink or a handout.

No. Most of all, Lennon came to these things for the same reason one's tongue dwells upon an aching tooth. Because sometimes the pain is too great to do anything else.

There was a time he'd been as well known, as famous, and as wealthy as Paul. Where had he gone wrong?

He looked through the fog, towards the subterranean entrance to the Beatles Museum—marked by an iron arch. It was all so long ago. And so few people remembered him. Really remembered him. They remembered the Beatles. That was all they remembered. John had sunk from their consciousness.

"Well, I was thinking," Richard Sforzi said. "I'm not very interested in the museum, now that I've met you. If you'd let me take you out for tea and some cakes, or—" He looked around, with a stranger's helpful certainty that a tea room will materialize in front of him, and spoke with the Yanks' assurance that there was nothing a Brit ever needed more than a cup of tea.

"Make it a pint or two and you've got a deal," John said. "My cane fell down, somewhere." He held onto the big yellow bulk behind him.

This close up, he identified it as Super Lamb Banana—a sculpture erected back in the eighties to—the artist said—symbolize the perils of genetic engineering. It had the front of a lamb, the end of a banana and an idiotic expression on its near featureless face. For some reason, it always reminded Lennon of Paul McCartney. Perhaps it was the air of great self-satisfaction.

John let go of the statue, as Sforzi handed him his cane.

He smiled as Sforzi said, "The Super Lamb Banana. I couldn't believe it when I heard about it. It's the sort of empty-headed, feel-good commercial art that takes up too much space in the real world."

It was going to be a fine evening.

The pub was the kind of upper-class pub—all shadowy nooks and heavy oak tables, and a roaring fireplace located so it could be seen from almost anywhere— where no man would dream of meeting his mates or having a friendly game of darts.

These days, it was a world closed to John—a place of money and privilege where he simply could not enter. So he relished his moment back in, remembering those days—now like a dream—when he could have bought the place twice over.

Sforzi navigated amid the tiny, candlelit tables with the assurance of a man to whom this type of place was all too common and sat down at a white-cloth draped table.

When the slick and blonde waitress approached, Lennon ordered two fingers of single-malt—amber and cold in the thick-walled glass. Sforzi ordered something thick and bright green.

"Absinthe," he told John. "Though they don't make it with wormwood any more. No madness . . ."

Sforzi started speaking. John just sat there, con-

tented to have his drink and stare at the roaring flames
in the fireplace. He concentrated on appearing to listen, but he knew there was not much point. Fans always raved, and Yanks were the worst of all.

There was that woman, three years ago, who'd told
John that if only he'd married her, instead of marrying
Yoko, everything would have been fine. Forgetting, of
course, that John had once been in love with Yoko
and that the fan-woman didn't have even a tenth of
Yoko's personality.

At first Sforzi's conversation seemed headed in a
similar—if less romantic—direction. What John would
have filed under *how great you could have been, if
only*—

Did the fans really think that these things had never
occurred to him? That he didn't run through his memories in the night, trying to figure out where all his
fame and all his power could have gone?

But then he heard, "in most worlds, of course, you
did not make it so big, you know. But I'm sure there
must be one. If you change just one thing and manage
to make that world real, it could make you the biggest
ever—bigger than Jesus, you know, as you said."

John blinked at the man. "Worlds?" he asked.

"Yeah, I was telling you," Sforzi looked around,
like a spy who fears being followed. Having satisfied
himself that no one was listening in, Sforzi turned back
to John. By the light of the candle, his blue eyes shone
unnaturally bright. "I work for NASA," he said. "On
a secret project. You see, every time that you make a
decision . . . every time one of us makes a decision,
it generates another universe . . . another world. All

these worlds, going on forever, compressed together like pages in a book, but never touching."

John lifted his eyebrows. Ah, it was not a madman but his near cousin. A science fiction chappie. John himself had watched "Star Trek" religiously once upon a time. He understood this. At least the bloke was not saying John should have married him and not Yoko.

"Parallel worlds," John said, firmly, to show he understood. Also to prevent the conversation from getting stranger. "I understand that. Now, if there were a way to find a better one, eh?"

Sforzi's eyes shone brighter. He leaned forward across the table. "There is," he said. "There is." He looked weirdly Mephistophelian with the candle lighting him from behind, as he hesitated. "At least, there is a way of going back in time to the fork in the road and taking a different one from the one that's led you here—and if you find the right fork . . ."

"Time travel?" John asked.

"It's actually a quantum uncertainty mech—" Sforzi stopped, waved his hand expansively. "Close enough. Yes. Time travel."

"So I can go back to my younger self and—" John said, helpfully. The man was insane, of course, but it was an entertaining form of insanity.

"Warn him. Tell him what to do, what not to do. And then he can . . . change."

"Why would my younger self believe me?" he asked. "I don't even look like myself any more."

"Well," Sforzi scratched his head. "Well . . . is there

something you could give him? Something that could prove you are . . . he?"

"My journals," Lennon said, happy to solve this hypothetical puzzle.

"Journals?"

"I've written them since I was fourteen or so," he said. "So if I were to meet myself anytime after that, he'd see that the first journals were his. Also, he would know where my life went wrong without my needing to tell him all of it."

"You don't have the journals with you, right? I could take you back in time right now. Car is outside."

"Car?" Lennon had been so carried away with the fictional puzzle, he'd forgotten this man believed it. But a car? He expected them to travel back in a car?

Sforzi shrugged. "I built the quantum device into it. Makes it easier. Just a rental car. I'll remove the device when I return it."

"Ah . . ."

"Why don't I take you to your flat now, and we get your journals and go back in time?"

Why not? Because Sforzi was delusional? Because John had no time for this?

But John had all the time in the world, and even if he got nothing more out of this adventure, the lark allowed him to spend a longer time in Sforzi's brand-new BMW with its leather upholstery. It would be a few moments away from the squalor John's life had become.

He'd gotten the journals—twenty red-cover notebooks in a box. John had become slapdash in journal-keeping after he and Yoko had been deported by American immigration authorities back in the seventies. He wrote almost every week. Well, sometimes every month. Definitely at least once a year.

There wasn't much to write about. Yoko hadn't been able to endure England for very long, and it seemed like only a few minutes before she filed for divorce and left for Paris with most of John's money and copyrights.

Not that John begrudged them to her. He'd always admired the way she looked out for herself. And besides, she'd left him plenty to live on until he issued the next big album.

But then, there had been parties—he was free, after all—and drinking and . . . other stuff, and somehow the album never got made, and, by degrees, so slowly he hardly knew how, he'd found himself living alone and forgotten in a bloody state-subsidized flat. And the world had gone on. Twenty-year-olds didn't even know his name.

"Well," Sforzi said. "Do you know where you want to go?"

"Yes," John said. He'd thought about it, all the while he was making his rickety way down the eight flights of stairs from his flat to ground level. The elevator was on the blink again. He knew where he wanted to go, on the off-chance this worked. "I know exactly where I want to go. I want to go back and never get involved with Super Lamb Banana."

"Super—"

"McCartney. Paul. We'll see how far he goes without me, shall we? We'll see how Super Lamb Banana does without the real artist to make it all seem important. We'll see about his albums and his concerts then."

He held the cardboard box on his skinny, withered legs and thought maybe, maybe another world existed in which John had a chance to be the artist he should have been without Paul grinning around him, fuzzy, undefined, and vaguely benevolent—like Super Lamb Banana.

And then, John wouldn't need drugs and alcohol to dull the pain of his stolen art. And he could have kept on. He would still be wealthy. He would be famous. He would be the greatest artist in the world.

Seventeen-year-old John Lennon stood outside the Quarry Bank school. School was over for the day.

He wore his Teddy Boy tight pants and flamboyant jacket, but he felt as if he was quite a different creature from the teenage boy who had left the school yesterday. Yesterday, when the old man had handed him a box full of tattered diaries.

At first he'd thought the old man was a bum. Then he'd noticed a certain air of family resemblance—the sharp nose, the angular chin; he'd thought it was his father, come to reclaim him after all this time.

But, while anger and bewilderment and relief all rose in John together, rendering him mute at seeing this long-lost father, the stranger spoke. He said he was not Freddie. He was John himself, come from the future.

John had spent the night awake, reading those diaries—at first euphoric as the diaries "predicted" that he would be one of the greatest musicians of all time. But then the tone of the journals had changed. John had become bewildered by the constant betrayals by friends and lovers. And then shocked at his abandonment, his disappearing from the public mind.

The old man—his future self?—had scribbled a note at the end of the journals, telling John to steer clear of Super Lamb Banana. Super Lamb? Banana?

John had no idea what that meant. But he did understand the other things the old man had told him, "McCartney is no good for you. McCartney will only live off your art."

From the diaries written in the last years of the band, John understood that Paul McCartney had taken over John's music, that he'd overpowered John's greatest creativity and cheapened John's art. Made John irrelevant.

John frowned. And Paul seemed so nice, too. In fact, John had just about decided he would let Paul join the Quarrymen. Well, forget that. John would take the Quarrymen to glory all on his own.

He saw Paul walking towards him down the sunlit street, a smile on his face. Right. Time to stop that friendship before it went anywhere.

John Lennon straightened his tie self-consciously. He'd been retired from his teaching job for twenty years now, and he'd grown unaccustomed to his tie. But businessmen always wore ties. And suits. And John was meeting with an important movie producer, after all. A man who wanted to make a movie about the Quarrymen.

Bloody time, too. Rock-and-roll had been an important form of music, even if now defunct. Though it
had come from the Americas and had petered out
without reaching most Europeans, those it had
reached, it had marked deeply. It was about time
someone realized what a great thing the Quarrymen
and other groups like them had been and how their
experimental sound could have changed the world.
Perhaps even introduced a new way of thinking to a
generation—broken the bonds of puritan morality that
still encased British society.

John had heard that in America sometimes men
went to work without their ties, but that would be
unthinkable anywhere in Europe.

Which is how John spotted the Yank who was supposed to meet him. He got out of his BMW, looking
florid and well-scrubbed, wearing a grey suit of the
best cut and a shirt open at the collar. No tie.

John stood near the absurdly yellow sculpture of
Super Lamb Banana. Built in the eighties, it seemed
to Lennon to embody all that was phony about the
commercial art that surrounded him now. If only he'd
got a chance. If more people had appreciated rock
music. If it could have reached the masses.

"Hello," the man said. "I'm Richard Sforzi."

"I'm John Lennon," John said, stepping forward.

"Oh, Mr. Lennon," the man said. "I know."

"Of course I remember the old man when I was in
school," John said, leaning across the table. "He was
the reason I never took in that chappy . . . Paul
McCartney. Fellow went on to make himself a pretty

good album or two, I think. Made some money, dropped out of music, emigrated. I heard he's a building magnate somewhere in Canada."

The American waited, on the other side of the table, staring—as if there were something obvious that John should be realizing.

"You mean, his story was real?" John asked. "That he . . . That I . . . Time travel?"

"If you didn't think it was real, why did you turn Paul down, when he tried to join the Quarrymen?"

John shrugged. "Well, back then I thought it was real. I thought—" He shrugged again. "But then . . . nothing happened that the diaries talked about. No flower power. Nothing. I mean, the yan—the people in your country got pretty wild there for a while, but it seemed it never reached the children of the middle class, and it all . . . " He shrugged again, unable to convey the impossibility of sons and daughters of the middle class prancing about in velvets and silks, with flowers in their hair, experimenting with different substances and different ideas. Oh, they'd all dressed a little wildly in their youth, but then they'd settled down to careers. They'd settled in. Even John, when he'd got his job as an art teacher—

"Don't you miss playing?" the Yank asked. "Don't you think you could have been much greater in music? Much, much greater?"

"Do you still have the diaries?" Sforzi asked.

"Somewhere, back at my flat," John said. He'd never married. Every time a girl got close enough, he thought they might turn out like the two wives mentioned in those disturbing diaries. He lived alone in a neat little flat that contained everything he'd ever acquired—carefully catalogued and itemized. "I think under the desk in the parlor."

"Well, why don't you go and read them and tell me where you'd like to go to try the next fork in the road to greatness."

"Travel back in time?" John asked. "Really?"

"You've done it before," Sforzi said.

"But I don't remember that," John protested. "I mean, I don't remember being the person to go back. So . . . how come you . . ."

Sforzi shook his head, as if forced to explain something elementary. "Because you grew up in this reality. I didn't go back. I just came here. To see if it had worked out."

"Oh."

"I have the car right outside," Sforzi said. "Waiting for you."

John didn't know why he believed the man. Or rather, he did. Too well. The man had left the impressions of his fingers on John's glass, when he'd bought John a drink after school. And John had looked at those prints, and his own. They were the same.

Then the man had given John diaries, the earlier ones of which were exact replicas of the little red notebooks in John's room at Aunt Mimi's house—Mendips in Menlove Road.

So, either the impossible had happened or John had traveled back in time to warn himself. He was not to stick with the Quarrymen. The Quarrymen would never go anywhere.

Oh, the man had given John a sheaf of diaries, too, but John had yet to get past the first two diaries—those that described the events in the next year or so. The diaries seemed to talk of a fictional future in which John and the Quarrymen changed their name to The Beatles—why not the rockroaches? Or perhaps the loco-usts?—and went on to change music and the world.

But though that diary and the part of the second John had read sounded so hopeful, he knew how it would all end. He'd heard the older John talk about it. The Quarrymen—and thus, probably the Beatles—would go nowhere. It was time John found a better way to express his art. A way to change the world and make himself known.

He'd stashed the diaries away in his room at Mendips. And he would drop the foolishness of music, he decided. He would stick with art, stay with it. He could do great things in art.

John Lennon thought he was about to get mugged when the man came at him out of the fog. John was just walking from the Liverpool Tate to the car park and was just walking past Super Lamb Banana, when he saw the man come at him, full of confidence and certainty, like a man who has a purpose in life.

Most of the time, this sort of purpose is to mug someone.

John stood, trembling in his cashmere turtleneck, his hands deep the pockets of his well-cut pants—his artist uniform. To run or not to run. Well, he had only a few pounds on him, and a handful of cards all easily canceled and reissued. He put a hand out, to hold on to the Super Lamb Banana, which stared idiotically next to him.

The man walked briskly towards John, and stopped a few steps away, looking as little like a mugger as it was possible for a man to look. He looked well-scrubbed and eager, like an overgrown boy scout. "Mr. Lennon," he said, and Lennon placed the look and the accent together. A Yank?

The man waited a moment, as though he felt that Lennon should know him. Lennon didn't, of course, and the man registered that minimal let-down that people did when their favorite artist did not recognize them at first sight.

He rallied admirably, though, smiling wide and extending a clean, square-fingertipped hand. "Richard Sforzi, Mr. Lennon. I'm one of your greatest fans."

Lennon nodded and refused to show any surprise, though so far as he knew all his fans were British. He made a decent living and all, and his art—canvases suffused with light from which emerged creatures as strange and distorted as everything had looked when Lennon had refused to wear glasses, back in adolescence—sold very well to a cultured elite, appreciative of the outre.

But he'd never made much inroad into other countries. Other countries were more conservative than Britain. Since WWII there had been a tendency to conformity worldwide. A closing of the ranks against the strange. And John's originality wasn't appreciated. In fact, this was something that nagged at him, as he rounded his mid-sixties.

He shook the man's hand. "You're an American dealer, then?"

But the man had grinned, a strange, crooked grin as though he felt guilty for something for which he could not apologize. "I'm an American, though my work . . ."

"You're an artist?" John asked, impatient, sure that this was only a fledgling come asking for advice or help.

The man shook his head. "No, not at all. Look." He hesitated. "I think I can help you. Make your art have more impact, make you better-known, make you the influence you were supposed be in the world at large."

Well, that was more like it, John thought, as he put his hand in his jacket pocket and absent-mindedly jiggled the keys there to the tune of "Three Blind Mice." Maybe this was one of those mad Yanks that made their money in sugar beets and then spent it all in promoting a baseball team. This one wanted to promote John's art.

John gave a look over the man's impeccably tailored grey suit, his well-cut hair. He thought very few muggers dressed that well. And John was not a well-known enough artist to attract a kidnapper.

"Would you come with me and have a drink?" Richard Sforzi said. "I'll explain it all to you."

John shrugged. "Right, why don't we walk?"

The man was probably not a kidnapper, but there was no point being stupid.

"You're bloody mad," John said, as he sat back, with the whiskey in his hand. "I mean, of course I remem-

ber the man. And he said . . . well, let's see—that he
was from the future. Let's say he was. And that you're
the one who helped him time-travel. What are you
saying? That I still haven't got it right?"

He twirled his glass around, with minimal move-
ments of the wrist, imparting a swirling motion to the
amber liquid within. "Why would you think that? My
art is well-liked. Critics say it burst upon the British
art scene like a breath of fresh air. I sell enough to
support myself and Cynthia. And our boy . . . well,
he's married now. But I raised him decently. Nice little
house. I never had any real problems making ends
meet." He gave the man across the table an appraising
glance. "So, even if you're telling me the truth . . . why
should I trade this success I have on the off chance
of something bigger? The chap—myself, I guess—who
gave me those diaries didn't look like much of anything. I'd say I've improved considerably upon his
fate. Why should you think I can do better?"

Richard Sforzi looked anxious and exasperated, all
the while attempting to look endearing. He looked, in
fact, like a little boy in need of going to the loo while
his busy mother drags him on a shopping trip.
"But . . . haven't you read the diaries," he said.

"Oh, the beginning. Till it became clear the Quarrymen would go nowhere," he said.

Richard Sforzi leaned across the table, "But they
did," he said. "They did go somewhere. Not the
Quarrymen, really, but the other group that came
from them. The Beatles. They—"

"Beatles? That's an idiotic name for a group."

Sforzi just shook his head. "The Beatles," he said,

putting great emphasis on the word. "Changed the world of music. The world of everything. Their music, at first innocuous enough to penetrate into middle-class homes, attracted fans from every walk of life. And then, when they got experimental, their entire generation followed them. They created a freer world, a more creative world than ever been before. They changed the world in their image."

John grimaced. "You make it sound like a messianic religion."

"It was. In a way. You—I mean, him . . . I mean, you in another alternate world, said in an interview that the Beatles were bigger than Jesus. And for just a moment it looked that way. You were certainly bigger than any other man in recent memory. I just thought you could have been bigger. I still think . . ."

"Right," John said, and tossed back his drink in a single gulp. "Listen, I really have to get back. Cynthia is expecting me. It was fascinating to—"

He got up and started to walk out of the expensive little pub. But Sforzi grabbed at his arm. "No. Listen. You may go if you want. But promise me one thing. Promise me you'll go home and read those diaries. You still have those diaries, right? Why don't you go and read them? Just so you see how much bigger you were in that world? That first world. How your art, your . . . critical acclaim pale beside the kind of revolution you helped start once . . ."

"I can't really promise—" John started.

"Come on. Are you afraid of finding how short you've fallen of your potential?"

"No. You see, the grandchildren—"

"You still do have the diaries, right?"

"I'm sure they're in the attic, somewhere."

"Why don't you read them, tonight?" Sforzi asked. "I'll be here tomorrow," Sforzi said. "If you should find you want to travel back in time and change *anything*."

John frowned and, without dignifying that with an answer, he turned around and walked back to the car park. But by the time he got to his car he was already thinking—his art was good, but he'd never set the world on fire. He'd always felt deep within that there was something he was supposed to do. Something big he was supposed to accomplish.

He wondered if that feeling came because some part of his subconscious mind knew how much bigger he could have been if only . . .

There had been an ache within him all along and the stranger's words had ignited it into excruciating pain. He could imagine greatness that even he had never dared dream of. And it was all lost.

That night, after Cynthia lay asleep, he'd crept up to the attic and found the diaries, together with the collection of biographies of famous people that he'd brought there from Aunt Mimi's when she'd died and he'd sold Mendips. Now, sitting on the dusty floor of the attic, by the increasingly weaker beam of a flashlight, he read diary after diary.

How great a man he'd been, in that other reality. But then . . . why had he looked so much like a retired school teacher? And if he'd been all that famous, all that wealthy—if he'd had fame and power to change the way an entire generation perceived the world, why had he tried to go back in time and warn himself?

John read on. Little by little, it started to make sense. The bad relationships, the betrayals, the substances required to dull the pain. He read, half-cringing, about his deportation from the States for drug use. The deportation he'd never thought to fight because he really, secretly, wanted to go back to England and this was the only way Yoko would allow it. Of course, she had divorced him soon after the deportation. But the end of his marriage hadn't freed him. Instead, it had started his slow spiral into penury and irrelevance.

If only he could have held on. If only he could have continued. If only he could have remained at his peak forever.

But how? How could he ensure that?

He was willing to suffer for his art. He was willing to endure the friendship gone sour, the love gone bad. But was there anything he could do to stay famous and influential forever?

By morning, he thought he had it. From the tension between his pride in his art and the nagging certainty he could have been much better, a huge plan blossomed. A crazy, risky plan.

He kissed Cynthia after breakfast, as he had every day of their marriage. A dutiful kiss, not meaning much.

Afterwards, instead of going to his studio in the back of the garden, he walked out of his tidy little suburban home to his car. He would not be coming back. Sometimes a sacrifice was required to achieve something really great.

John Lennon followed Yoko Ono out of their limousine and into the Dakota.

He'd been working all evening on their last joint album, *Double Fantasy*. After this he was going to tape something all his own—to reclaim his solo career. And it would be great. It would be the culmination of all his plans

He was glad that the man who'd met him—so many years ago outside his public school—had told him that marrying Yoko would be worth it in publicity, even if sometimes she would seem strange. And he'd told John that it was important to make sure he didn't get deported. Because Yoko couldn't stand to live in England. And if she divorced him, she'd take him to the cleaners.

In fact, he'd outlined an entire life plan for John, till John knew everything he was supposed to do, down to the last minutia of promoting this album. The other John, the older John, had said he'd worked it all out with the inventor of time travel. He'd worked to make sure John got what he wanted. At last. He would remain forever great.

Now, on this cold autumn morning, John walked half-bent over, carrying in his hands the tapes for Yoko's session, and he followed his wife towards the building where they'd lived for so long.

He barely saw the little man that approached from

the right. He half-registered by the corner of his eye that it was a pudgy young man, well scrubbed and neat, like an old boy scout.

He had barely registered the object in the man's hand as a gun, when the bullet ripped into his chest.

John staggered, as burning pain and a blazing cold tore into him. He tried to speak, but the words wouldn't come. Another bullet. Another. Time seemed very slow. He couldn't escape.

With a sort of distancing numbness, he was aware of his body's tripping, staggering away from the gunman, stumbling through the glass doors onto the floor of the foyer and falling. He thought of saving the tapes, but his hands couldn't hold them.

He fell on the floor of the foyer and heard the doorman yell hysterically. "Shot." "Hurt." "Emergency." Those words emerged, clear, from others John could not understand.

Far away sirens wailed.

John felt cold. Very cold. Someone threw a blanket over him.

Idiots. That would do nothing.

He tried to take a breath, but the air had nowhere to go, and blood oozed in his mouth. He inhaled it, drowning in blood. Curiously, he wasn't in pain. It all felt very distant.

He was aware of Yoko, and the doormen, and other people, touching, lifting him. But it didn't matter. This did. Because for the first time—in pain and shock—John could see the implications, the ramifications, the exquisite detail of the plan the older John had formed and got this John to follow, unawares.

Everything, from fighting extradition back in the seventies and staying in the States—where crazed murders of celebrities were so much more likely—to the right interview given in the right tone to inflame the fanatic who'd think John had sold out. It had been a gamble, all designed to achieve this end. And it had paid off.

John would die before he could destroy his power, his influence, the memory of his art.

He coughed once.

"It will be all right," someone said, from nearby.

John tried to nod. It would be all right. His art would live, after him, untouched and all the stronger for his having died so suddenly. Everything he had done would acquire even greater meaning. He'd remain true to himself. He'd never become irrelevant or embarrassing like Super Lamb Banana.

He fell into the darkness and there found peace at last.

AND WISDOM TO KNOW
THE DIFFERENCE

Kristine Kathryn Rusch

Marie places her hand on the gleaming silver railing. The time machine looks large and out of place in the empty shop. The window is soaped, clouding the view of the street and the pizza parlor that has faced this building for more than fifty years.

The men are wearing suits, despite the fact that the air-conditioning doesn't work. Perhaps it never worked: there is a fan overhead, and the side windows do open. Counters have been pushed against the wooden slat walls, and dust bunnies litter the scuffed floor.

Marie tugs on the small silver cross she wears around her neck. She is used to this machine—has studied it, has even worked on parts of it—for nearly a decade. But now that it's here, in Dallas, she feels her first moment of doubt.

The men don't entirely understand the process. She's not going to explain it to them. She had enough trouble convincing them to rent this building and move the machine down here. They don't understand that traveling through time and space is not possible; the science fiction culture, from commercials to movies, has convinced them otherwise.

They insisted on watching, all five of them: Mr. Farley from the national headquarters, his advisor and his press aide, plus the state leader Conners, and his Dallas counterpart. She's been introduced, but all she remembers are clammy handshakes and insincere wishes of luck.

They're not interested in her; they just want their results.

And she's going to get those results. She volunteered, for reasons all her own.

"Let's not take all day, Miss North," Farley says, and his voice, with its flat, Midwestern accent, sounds almost alien to her, accustomed as she's become to the East Coast richness of her colleagues' accents at FuturePast.

One of the R&D guys, who is standing in the shadows near the shop's locked door, raises his hand as if he wishes to remind Farley that in this case, today's time does not matter. Marie shakes her head ever so slightly, warning the R&D guy off, then gets on the machine's main platform which the techs lovingly call the cockpit.

She grips both sides of the railing, sees the digital numbers flash in front of her. The machine's power vibrates the steel beneath her feet. She's done this countless times—gone five minutes, ten minutes, two days into the past, but never so far back and never on anything paid for by outsiders.

The vibration shakes her so hard she feels dizzy,

and for a moment, she wonders if the power flow is flawed; after all, they had to set up a special grid just to handle all the energy the machine needs.

But she knows better. The MIT guys and her R&D people have tested and retested the building's power system. It can withstand the jolt of the machine.

Her mouth is dry. She has to set up the program, then start it, which'll add another five minutes onto the procedure—five minutes that'll annoy Farley and his boys. They've paid nearly ten million dollars—tax-free money in the form of donations to the time programs at MIT and FuturePast for this single afternoon's work. The MIT guys have set aside their qualms for a large chunk of that pie, and FuturePast never had any qualms in the first place.

Neither did she, not until she mounted the platform a few seconds ago.

The machine feels different. She's slightly dizzy. The hair rises on the back of her neck, and then there's a flash of light, almost as if she were struck by lightning.

It's not the machine: she hasn't programmed it yet.

She tries to shake the feeling away, but it grows and her vision splits as if she is looking at the world through a prism. Each facet presents something different, and too many of the facets are black.

She starts to speak, to alert the men, and then she realizes that if they think she's ill, they might not let her go on this trip, and this trip belongs to her.

The prismatic vision grows, and it feels like time has stopped. Her hands clutch the railings—the only solid thing in her world besides the shaking platform. The visions in front of her—and they seem like they are right before her—are touchable: she can dive into them, live them, if only for a moment.

The realization makes her feel omnipotent. She pushes that thought away—it's blasphemous—and refines it in her own scientific manner. Yes, the vision is prismatic, but it is also familiar. She has visited more than one place at a time before; for example, when she sits in her favorite chair back in Boston, seeing the harbor out the window as the television blares a baseball game in front of her, and she dips into the book in her hand. She's paying attention to all three, living all three, while ignoring the true reality: the chair against her body, the stale air of her apartment, the lonely Saturday afternoon she's whiling away.

She cannot ignore these prismatic visions. Three seem most prominent. They beckon to her, and she has to dive into them. The scientist in her—the woman in her—will regret the loss of the opportunity if she does not.

She reaches to the first one, the closest one, its blues and yellows and faded whites somehow soothing, like a place she has known and yet forgotten.

Her mind elongates—a visitor trapped in a glass shell, watching a scene below her, and yet living the scene as well. She is both observer and observed. One moment she is on the platform, the next she is in the first vision.

She holds the baby close, his little legs still curled against his tiny body. His sleeper is warm and smells of baby powder. His wispy black hair feels as fine as silk, and he snuggles against her neck as she pats her swollen arthritic fingers against his back.

Her daughter Anne stands near the kitchen counter, her body still puffy from pregnancy; Marie suspects that Anne will never lose the weight, just like Marie never lost hers, something Dan reminds her about all the time.

Marie holds the baby over the chipped porcelain sink, treasuring the few seconds she has as a grandmother, stolen from the hours that Dan is at work. She wishes she could have been there for the birth, but Anne wouldn't allow it; Dan doesn't know about the baby—he'll never know, if Anne has her way.

Marie cradles the baby, the tiny life, so precious, so soft. Anne extends her hands, wanting him back.

"Daddy'll be home soon," Anne says, and the fear in her voice speaks louder than anything else.

Marie kisses the soft head, then hands the boy back. He turns his face toward her, blue eyes catching hers but not really seeing, in the way of the very newly born.

A bruise is starting to form on his soft, pink cheek. She runs a finger over it, frowns at her daughter.

"What is that?" Marie asks.

But Anne doesn't even look like most mothers would. Instead she turns away, grabs her coat and the baby's blanket as she heads for the door.

Her silence says it all. Marie wants to grab her grandson, pull him away from her daughter, her child—and her husband's child—but she cannot. She is trapped in this small house with this man she has sworn her life to, and a daughter who has learned all the wrong lessons. . . .

Marie blinks, startled to find herself on the shuddering platform, in a future—a life?—in which she divorced Dan and has no children. But she can still feel the baby—a grandson, how marvelous—cradled against her shoulder, and the familiar loathing rises within her.

God forgives.

God forgives, but she doesn't.

She puts a hand on her stomach, remembering the house now—his grandfather's house, which they had inherited, all tight walls and cracked floors—a metaphor, she used to say, for the life they lived.

She blinks again. The prismatic vision is back: turning, turning, turning, searching for a facet with light. All is darkness. Dark, dark, dark—

And then she enters the second vision, only this time she doesn't recognize the space. It is mean, meager, a single room with a torn curtain . . .

. . . and the stale smell of cigarettes. Her cigarettes. She taps a Benson and Hedges out of the pack. Her hands shake as she tries to light it; her nerves aren't what they used to be.

She shuts the lighter, tosses it on the presswood counter, then puts her hands against the edges and raises herself up. Her shattered pelvis healed wrong, and the pain along her spine is acute. The doctors told her she was lucky; she could have been paralyzed. Instead, she lost the baby, lost the use of her left leg, and the freedom of movement that came with a fully intact body.

Each step is a reminder of that moment, sitting in a pool of her own blood, her fingers grasping for the drawer in the end table beside the bed, the semi-

automatic, her index finger against the trigger, pulling it once, twice, three times. . . .

Sometimes she thinks she shouldn't have shot Dan, not so many times. Sometimes she thinks once, in the knee, maybe the groin, so he'd know a lifetime of pain too.

But her old cellmate used to say that was prison talking. Prison, which Marie actually misses. She has spent most of her life there, getting three squares, surviving. Not like this single room, with its TV and silence, waiting for each day to end so that she could go to her once-a-week meeting with a parole officer who treats her like a murderer instead of a woman who killed her husband in self-defense.

She gasps, breathing the humid Texas air, her heart pounding. No. Never. She left instead of letting him hit her. After the first time he hit her when she was pregnant.

She left.

Her hand still rests on her stomach, fingers clutching the skin through the cotton blouse R&D made her wear. What is wrong with her? How come no one else has noticed? Has time really stopped?

She cannot tell because she still can't see properly. More darkness, and then one last—a simple ray of light, the only one she can see in thousands and thousands of facets. The third vision.

But this time she stays distant because this time she's—or someone almost like her—is not there. Another closed-off room, this one familiar—her mother's kitchen—only it stinks of urine and burned coffee and sour milk. In the background, the radio plays some rock-and-roll tune, something from her mother's long-lost misspent youth.

Marie knows it's her mother's kitchen not just from the shape of the room, but from the Serenity Prayer plaque that has hung above the sink for as long as she can remember:

> *God grant me serenity to accept the things I cannot change, courage to change the things I can, and wisdom to know the difference.*

Marie rounds the corner into the tiny living room, or rather, whatever is guiding her vision leads her around that corner. A hospital bed dominates the room, hiding the television. The old brown couch is gone, and only an armchair remains.

Her mother leans over the bed, holding a baby bottle in her right hand. She is cooing at something in the hospital bed. It takes Marie a moment to realize that the thing is human, that it is actually female, with features—puffy from lack of use rather than fat—that look like Anne's from the first vision. Only it is Anne without control of her eyes, with drool around her chapped mouth, with no intelligence in her face.

"Mother?" Marie says, but her mother can't hear her—this wizened, exhausted-looking woman who struggles to get an adult infant to take a bottle.

Marie wants to ask what happened, but suddenly she knows. She knows: that dark day she feared was coming, the future day that had sent her to the women's clinic two months into her pregnancy, the one that made her change her life, happened here. Only in this reality, in this place, Marie did not survive. And, really, neither did Anne. Not her brain, shattered in Dan's attack, just her body, maybe not even her soul . . .

Marie backs away, nearly falls off the platform. Someone places a hand against the small of her back.

"You okay, dahlin?"

Accent. Texas. Dallas. Conners. Marie blinks. She's in her reality now, divorced, slender, gray-haired, a scientist on a mission, the most important one, really.

She clutches her necklace, the edges of the cross biting into her hand, thinks: Saul on the road to Damascus, laid flat by a vision. Not several visions. One.

No one else had visions. Except the saints, some of them, but that's superstition and she's not Catholic.

Catholics don't follow the true faith.

"Miss North?" Farley says to her. "You didn't answer Mr. Conners. Not having second thoughts, are you?"

She looks at him, sees his chubby face, small eyes hidden by large glasses. She went to him. This is her idea, always has been her idea. Just because Family Triumphant offered to pay—

The anger returns her to herself. She is divorced, yes, a sinner, yes, but Jesus Christ Her Lord and Savior has forgiven her, and she is on a divine mission, one sent from God.

"I'm fine," she says, glad her voice has not betrayed her. "And I'm ready."

"Then let's get this show on the road." Farley sounds just like her ex-husband, Dan. Dan's too real to her, after those visions, the memories so fresh. The day she told him she was pregnant and he punched her in the stomach—

Of course the memories are fresh. They're why she is here. Faith teaches that forgiveness requires righteous acts. Just because she was afraid, because she did not believe, she went to the women's clinic, put her feet in stirrups, and let them take her child.

And then she never went home, moving to a new life, a secular life until, like Saul on the road to Damascus, she had a vision of her own future, empty and hopeless without the presence of God.

"Miss North?" Farley says again, and even though he is asking a question, he is really giving an order.

She steps up to the edge of the platform, and stops in the cockpit, looking at the digital controls that she has pressed a dozen times. Her hands shake as she types in the date—January of 1970—the time, just before lunch—and the time and date of the return.

Her hands shake, like they did when they cradled her grandson and lit her cigarette, like her mother's did when she held that baby bottle.

Marie shivers, and then presses start.

Time travel has no drama, not like everyone imagined it would. No whirling lights, no changing colors. One minute you're here, the next you're there, almost like falling asleep in a parked car only to awaken several miles away, the car parked again in a different, unfamiliar spot.

Marie arrives in the storage room of Kessler's Five and Dime, the smell of cheap plastic and bubblegum so strong that it almost chokes her. So far so good.

The map of the store was accurate, at least, and now she has a bit of a chance.

She slips through the door, past walls that no longer exist fifty years in the future, and into the main part of the store. The cheap plastic smell is stronger here, almost sweet. A radio plays near the cash register, but there is no piped-in music. People—men in ties and cheap suits, women in dresses with heels—shop, picking up items, studying them, setting them down. A few teenagers in blue jeans saunter through, but everyone else gives them a wide berth.

Marie's clothing places her outside the norm. She is too old for the jeans and the cotton blouse, but she ducks her head and heads down an aisle filled with plastic-wrapped rain bonnets and combs and hair tonics.

When she reaches the front door, she slips out into the blazing Texas sunshine. In the moment that it takes her eyes to adjust, she has the odd feeling that Dallas never changes—all concrete and steel and dilapidated buildings, no matter what decade, what century, a person is in.

Then that feeling recedes as the light fades to normal. The cars that drive past her are twice the size and half the height of the cars she's used to. More people walk on the sidewalks, and no one rides a bicycle.

The pizza place across the street looks clean and new, but has somehow lost the charm that it has in her future. As she stares at the front door, she sees a short woman with shoulder-length hair, heavily sprayed and flipped outward, clutch her purse to her side as she pushes the door open. Another woman follows her, hair short, brown, her stride less confident.

Sarah Weddington and Linda Coffee, two lawyers, getting ready for the meeting that will make them famous.

Marie crosses the street, her right hand clenched into a fist. The vision still haunts her—all that blackness. Was she dead in those realities? Were those separate realities? Separate pasts in which she had no future, or her family had no future, or in which she had no life at all?

She stops a half a door away from the pizza parlor, watching for one more woman. This woman is easy to spot as she rounds the corner, her blue jeans filthy and frayed, her shirt too small, revealing the ever-so-slight mound of her early pregnancy.

Her name is Norma McCorvey. She is a single mother whose first child has been taken away from her because she is unfit. She looks unfit now; her hair stringy, her skin sickly pale.

Norma McCorvey is the answer to Weddington and Coffee's dreams—a woman who cannot support herself because she is pregnant, a woman who cannot afford good medical care, and who cannot raise children properly; a woman who cannot afford to leave Texas to go to Europe for a legal abortion and who does not have the funds for an illegal one either.

Norma McCorvey's main virtue is timing—she is the right client in the right place at the right time. Much later, and her case, if it had gone to the Supreme Court, might not have had such a sympathetic hearing. Without Norma McCorvey, there is no *Roe v. Wade*—

the case Sarah Weddington said only guaranteed a woman's right to choose but which Family Triumphant claims is the legalization of murder—because Norma McCorvey is better known as Jane Roe.

Marie puts her hand over her own stomach, a reflexive habit ever since she had found God.

The visions could not have come from God. Surely God would not interfere in an event like this, with a vessel as impure as she is.

The Bible records another giver of visions, someone who is less trustworthy, who tries to pluck the righteous from their path.

"Get thee behind me, Satan," Marie whispers, then she squares her shoulders and hurries toward Jane Roe.

The mission is so easy; all Marie has to do is intercept this woman, prevent the meeting with the lawyers, stop the case.

So easy, and Marie does it with a smile, with a hand on Jane Roe's arm, and a promise of some comfort in a nearby church, a discussion of God and His purpose for each and every one of his creatures.

But as Marie walks a pregnant woman down the dusty Dallas street, the hair on the back of Marie's neck rises like it does when there is lightning in the air. For a moment, Marie feels that omnipotence around her, threatening her, making her doubt herself.

But she pushes it away—and as she does, she gets a sense of herself as if she is not part of herself—a thin woman who cannot see her accomplishments, her successes, only the bitterness and loss which she claims gives justification to her small and meager life.

She keeps her hand on Jane Roe's arm, moving by rote to the church Family Triumphant assures her is there. And as Marie walks, she realizes she does not feel serene or courageous or even wise.

Instead she feels like she had felt that afternoon on her kitchen floor, her stomach aching from Dan's punch, knowing she is standing at a crossroads, terrified that she is making the wrong choice.

To Lasso a Divine Wind

Mike Moscoe

General Hsin-tu sat on the old leather camp stool and stared at the tiny brazier. It provided small warmth against the cold winter wind of Ta-tu. It was not intended to. This room of the great khan's palace had been stripped of wall hangings, of carpets, of richness. This room was for a defeated general.

Two guards eyed him. Tomorrow Hsin-tu would go before the Great Khan to receive his reward. The Mighty Khubilai, who was elsewhere in the palace carousing and getting falling down drunk, might decree in his hungover wisdom that Hsin-tu would retire to a small patch of grass in the north. Or he might have him beheaded, or choked with dung.

Maybe even choked to death with his own dung. The general had noticed the glances the slaves gave him as they removed his chamber pot. The rewards were great for a victorious Mongol general. So was the punishment for defeat.

Time passed; the brazier was not replenished. One guard began to snore softly where he stood. The de-

257

feated general found sleep as evasive as those pox-
ridden warriors of Zipangu had been with their long
swords and shaved heads.

"What would you do differently?" The words came
like a clap of thunder. Hsin looked up; the guard who
was awake repeated his question softly. The words
were so familiar. They had haunted Hsin-tu for every
moment since wind and sea turned against him and
spun a stand-off battle into disaster. But in all that
time, none had dared speak the words aloud. Not
even him.

Hsin-tu fixed the impudent guard with hard, determined eyes and said the only thing he could. "I would
win no matter what the price."

"Easy to say. Harder to do," the guard said, almost
off-handedly. "Let us see," he said . . . and Hsin-
tu slept.

Even before opening his eyes, Hsin-tu knew he was
no longer at the Great Capital. The world moved
around him, not in the proper way it does a man on
a horse, not even the steady way it does for an old
man on a camel. No, the world swayed under heaven
in the sickening way of a ship.

Hsin opened his eyes. He lay in bed in his cabin on
his great flagship surrounded by all things familiar. On
the walls hung rich silks the great storm had drenched
in salt water. On a table close at hand was the porcelain vase that had shattered into more pieces than a
monk could count. *What kind of demon's work is this!*

He rose from his bed. Nothing was required of him

as silent servants appeared, cared for his morning needs and dressed him in silk and gold. As they worked, he struggled to break this wild pony of flying thoughts, bucking and knocking around in his head. A crack general, he ordered his senses to accept what they saw, heard, felt, even as his thoughts shied first one way, then another, refusing to be saddled with belief that any power—whether good or bad—any power at all under heaven could turn back a season, make glass after glass of sand fall up to refill an hour, a day, a month. Around him, servants completed their duties as they had done many times before, showing no notice that the general they served was older, defeated . . . and likely no wiser. Finished, they bowed out leaving him to the solitude a twitch of his finger ordered.

His stomach was the last to be broken to his will. He would not let it embarrass him, not even before servants he could order thrown overboard with their hands tied. His gut roiled like a tempest tossed sea, but it obeyed. He stayed still until he was sure that it would not rebel.

Finally in control, Hsin-tu strode up the stairs to the main deck. The wind blew from the south, the air was heavy with heat and unspent rain. Around Hsin, men turned to obey him. A wave of his small finger and all men looked to their duty.

As he had before, General Hsin paced off the length of the *Great Pyramid of Heads*, up the right side, then down the left. The sailors had learned to remove their piles of cordage, stacks of sailor things, so that nothing blocked the general's passage. Now he circled the deck, his eyes straight ahead, taking in the impossible sights around him.

His flagship lay, as it had the past summer, in the harbor of Iki. Around him swung at anchor the combined fleets of Koryu and Sung China. Ships he'd last seen dismasted and floundering were as taunt and solid as sailors could make them. When he reached the stern of his proud flagship, he halted. Resting his hands on the solid oak rail, he forced in great droughts of stinking sea air. Raising his eyes to the sun, he made a solemn vow to all things holy under heaven. *I accept what my eyes tell me. Today, it is only middling summer. Defeat is not yet at hand!*

Not yet at hand, but not far away, either.

The khan's guard had asked what he would do different. Hsin had shot him the easy answer. Now he tasted the full burden that came with the flippant reply. "Easy to say."

Hsin turned and again paced the deck around. This time he let his anger free, a hungry tiger seeking to gorge on the hearts of those who had wounded him. *We lost because of those other dung-eating fools Khubilai saddled me with in shared command. Those two are the ones who failed!* Hang that Admiral Hong Tagu from Koryu, nominated to the khan by an empty bell of a man who styled himself emperor of his own land. Hong spoke a flood of advice, hiding any good words he might have in a torrent that left Hsin with little patience and awash in dross from which he could extract no gold. Sung general Fan Wen-hu was no better. An early turncoat from the lazy south, the man had no honor. Fan covered his emptiness by cawing incessantly about the ancient written wisdom that assured him the sun would rise in the east. The first thing Hsin should do with both was to give each a block of gold and cast them into the depths of the sea.

That would be so easy.

What had the guard said? It was easy to say he'd do whatever it took to win. Hard to do it.

It would be easy to take out his rage on the others. But would the Koryu sailors handle their ships any better if Hsin gave the orders? Would those defeated Sung pikemen fight better if a true Mongol rode behind them with whips?

For a final circle around the deck, Hsin-tu walked slowly, forcing himself to admit that he was the Mongol here. He commanded; yet he had failed to form up this menagerie into a battle force that could defeat the Zipangu warriors as the Great Khan ordered. How dearly Hsin wanted those shaved head Zipangu riders sprawled out like an old stallion, with a spit up their ass, properly sacrificed and roasted.

Yes, it was one thing to know that the path he trod led only to defeat. It was another thing entirely to find the path that led to the victory that eluded him two months ago.

The general turned and nodded to an officer who had been following him silently. "Summon Admiral Hong and General Fan to me. And tell Hong to bring his maps and a few of those captains of his who know these waters."

"It will be done, Great General," the officer said and dashed away to see that it was. When last he strode this deck, Hsin had been so sure he knew how to win the coming battle that he found other's words mere distractions. This morning he tasted deeply of his own ignorance. That was a hard change to make.

So now, how to learn that which had stayed hidden from him before?

The ship's glass turned only once before a rowing boat brought Admiral Hong alongside. Hsin greeted him, accepted his bows and asked him to enjoy the morning air with him. Fan arrived a quarter glass later; his army of Confucian advisors and astrologers following him up the stairway. *The man did not take a piss without advisors telling him it was an auspicious time.*

"Have you decided how we will defeat these tent merchants?" the Sung general said as he bowed low.

"I will decide," Hsin said, returning a nod appropriate for a turncoat general of a defeated emperor. "But now," he said, turning to include the Koryu admiral in his gaze, "let the three of us adjourn to my cabin. I have ordered tea."

General Fan's advisors began to talk among themselves, but he waved them to silence. The ship captains Hong had brought bowed with their self-satisfied smirks, but one among them ran below with a handful of maps. Hsin lead the two into his cabin, dismissed the servant who hovered over the tea and offered his guests campstools beside the table that now was covered in maps. Fan offered to pour tea, and did so with good ceremony. For a long time, the three of them sipped in silence.

"It was not wise of the Zipangu to behead the envoys the Great Khan sent them," Hsin finally said.

"True folly," Fan agreed, "and yet, we are blind as we stand off their coast. For I have heard it said that a Mongol embassy is also a Mongol eye. And what it sees, it reports back to the Great Khan." The Sung general bowed low. "I say that in praise of the Great Khan's wisdom, for it is written that to know your enemy is to have him half defeated."

Hsin let nothing of the contempt he felt for Fan show on his face. He had roared at the man's impudence when last he shared those words. That was why Hsin had brought them here alone. In this cabin they could say things with none to overhear, no audience that might require that honor be served, and serving honor led Hsin only to defeat and a cold brazier.

Here, alone, Hsin ignored Fan's insolence. Indeed, he could admit to himself that Mongol embassies were exactly that, the eyes of the Great Khan. A long line of sacked and burned cities proved the value of those eyes. No doubt the emperor of Zipangu had noticed, probably with Sung help.

"To defeat Zipangu, it would be good to know more about their warriors. Good to know who stands hard-faced against us, who might see the wisdom of being the first to join the victorious Mongols," Hsin said, nodding to Fan but concentrating on Admiral Hong.

The man of Koryu ran a hand across the map, as was his custom before beginning a flood of words. "The Zipangu are an island people," he said, eyeing Hsin as if he did not truly believe he had been asked to speak. But before he said more, he paused for a long minute, as if weighing his words and tossing aside those of less use. "Their pirates raided Koryu for a long time before the Mongols came and made us too strong to attack," he said, bowing to Hsin.

"Ah, yes," the Mongol general nodded. "But the Great Khan brought with his strength, also customs officers with hands out for payments for this and that shipped between Zipangu and Koryu. It seems to me that the captain of a small ship might know ways of avoiding such vexing officials. And such captains might know much about the realm of Zipangu that lays at our feet." Thus he gave voice to a thought he would never have shared openly when last he sat with these two men.

"They might," Admiral Hong said, sipping at his tea. "No doubt you have heard of the strange custom in Zipangu. They have an emperor, but a general tells him what to say. Indeed, I have heard that there are two great imperial houses and this general decides from which of them will come forth a new emperor when the old one dies or is ordered to abdicate."

Hsin nodded. Yes, he had heard of this unthinkable path, but he would not have spoken of it, not when his own defeat was just as unthinkable.

"We heard such strange things even in Hangchow," the Sung General said. "There were stories that one of the families chafe under this military intervention in their lives. I believe they sit at Kyoto."

"And where is this Kyoto?" Hsin asked, too intrigued by the possibilities this offered him to mind admitting ignorance before his two co-commanders. Hong pointed to the center of a long island north of Kyushu. Hsin stroked his beard as he studied this new situation.

"When you let thirsty horses drink from the same stream twice, there is more mud than water," he finally said.

"And mud is what we have eaten," Hong said, nodding to soften the harshness of his words, "when we land our forces on the same beaches we used but seven years ago. And there is one more thing an ever-victorious Mongol general may wish to think about," the Koryu admiral went on. "Some ships of Koryu ply their trade among these Zipangu islands. Of late they have often been commandeered to carry warriors from all three northern islands to this southern island. Not only have the wall the Zipangu had build across our landing beaches been hard to take, but there are many more warriors upon those walls than ever we saw seven years ago. They are strong and many."

"But no one can be strong everywhere, Na," Hsin said to the Sung general.

"That is the written wisdom," Fan agreed. "Nor does any enemy present but one face. May I ask, Admiral Hong, do your sailors ever fall among pirates here in Zipangu waters?"

"One man's pirate is another man's trader," the admiral said. "And if you sail with a well-armed crew, even a pirate may see more profit in trade."

"Might some of your captains know Zipangu captains who would like to talk to the well armed before they break their teeth on Chinese, I mean, Mongol steel." Fan actually smiled at his failure to chose his words carefully.

Hsin waved the matter away with his small finger. It was Zipangu blood he wanted now. "Admiral, if we can talk to a few of your captains, and maybe some captains from these local waters, I would like to know if there are any landless who would take land for their pay. Any sailors who would welcome an end to taxes on the trade between here and there."

"If I may be dismissed, my general of the green sea, this admiral of the blue sea has much to do this day." Hong rose. "Let us meet again tonight, for some of these men sail better by stars than by the sun."

"Then let us see what stars may guide our fate," Hsin said, also standing.

General Fan eyed him as he stood. "I like the wisdom I see in your face, my general. Are you sure you have not read one or two of the books I sent to you as gift?"

"Not all war knowledge is to be found in scrolls," Hsin said, showing him the door. "But our fight is with the Zipangu that the Great Khan has sent us against. Not with each other over what may or may not be the source of our wisdom."

The others bowed themselves from his visage. Only when he was alone did he go to his bed, bury his face in a silk quilt . . . and rip it to shreds with his teeth. He wept the bitter tears he had held back before these lesser men. Letting them talk, listening to this or that thing that they knew and he did not was as foul to him as eating dung. Almost he would rather spit their words out. Almost.

Surely this must be better than hearing Khubilai Khan laugh in his cups as Hsin suffocated in his own excrement. Surely, it must be.

The bitter cup drained, Hsin summoned servants to

bathe him, dress him again, and remake his bed. He visited his war stallion Black Lightning below decks. The horse nickered at the sugar Hsin gave it. "You are growing fat," he warned his horse. "We must get you to land where you can catch the wind in your teeth, trample foe beneath your hoofs. I need to feel a head or two split under my sword."

That night Admiral Hong brought his captains and the Zipangu criminals to meet General Hsin. They were insolent types, barely able to bow properly and their faces were set in sneers. Still they came and they talked. "Yes, in Kyoto there are those who chafe under the swaggering Hojos. Gladly would they see the entire Kamakura Bakufu headless in the dust, cut down, root and stem, to the fourth generation." *Now that is a group with the proper sentiments*, Hsin thought.

"The Inland Sea is deep. Your vessels, even this lumbering whale, could pass the rocks," another offered. "We have heard you Mongols love your horses. Along the Inland Sea are coastal plains that would offer them plenty of room to run."

"And your rice fields?" Hsin asked.

The criminals looked at each other, then one shook his head. "The farmers now plant a second crop in the autumn. Wheat for noodles. Those fields would not slow your horses and," he shrugged, "who knows, they might feed them well."

"You talk much, but set no price to your words," Hsin said.

Now a man with gold teeth who had said nothing before stepped forward. "It is not these words that

you will pay us for. Rather tell us what you offer and
we will tell you how to slip your ships between the
rocks. Pay us nothing, and your mighty army will be
nothing but fish food."

"And your asking price?" Hsin said, disgusted to
be haggling with merchants, but the Great Khans had
learned when to buy with gold and when to pay in
steel.

The man with teeth of gold glanced around at his
comrades. "Land, fifty *mou* per man who fights at
your side. Gold as well, as much as we may take on
the battlefield. The cities and towns we will leave to
you. You have the machines to bring down the high
stone walls. We do not."

Hsin mulled the offer for a moment before sidestep-
ping it. "You must be hungry. Join my servants on
deck and feast. We will talk again when the moon
rises."

The criminals showed they did know how to bow
properly as they backed their way out, the Koryu captains at their sides. Hsin waited until the noise of them
was long gone and servants had opened windows so
even the loathsome stink of them had passed as well.
Then he turned to his co-commanders.

"This Honshu sounds like it offers better ground
for Mongols to fight on," Hsin said.

"Will you give all the land away to these pirates?"
Fan said.

"Your troops have been offered no land?" Hsin
asked.

"Not so much as the ground to bury them in."

"Would they fight better for the promise of three hundred mou and the peasants to farm it for them?"

"That would certainly excite them more than what they have heard so far, pay to be settled in paper notes."

"Then when you next set foot among them say that the Great Khan has saved this announcement for a most propitious time and that time is now. All men who fight well will be rewarded just as I have said. Officers will receive more as fitting their rank." That should light a fire under the hearts if not the buttocks of a defeated army that had lost its honor and its land with its emperor. Nodding, Fan bowed his way out as well.

That left only Admiral Hong. The man had opened a window on the stern and sniffed at the night sea air. Hsin joined him. "It was a storm that drove off the last landing," he said.

"And now is the season when more storms may come," answered the Admiral from Koryu.

"And should a storm come," Hsin said, remembering in his mind's eye what now he spoke in prophecy, "men will flee for the nearest ship. An army that is already in flight is already lost and I need no scribbling on a scroll to tell me that." With the admiral alone, he could toss some hard words the general's way.

The admiral shared a short laugh, then grew very serious. "Are you prepared to land your army, empty the holds of my ships, and be quit of their sails?"

The Mongol general answered slowly. "I would be, once fully ashore. No fighter stands strong who has one foot in a boat and one on land."

The man of the blue sea turned from the window. "There will be no storm tonight, but one can never say, even those who study the urine of a great Sung general, how long it will be before angry seas beset us. Certainly no sailor can. So let us land you on firm land, and let the great ships sail off to Chinese ports to carry the great words of what the great general of the Great Khan offers soldiers who stand in service to him."

"That would free my soldiers from the sight of large sails."

"Small fighting sails must remain close at hand. If you gallop the plains of Honshu, the warriors of Zipangu will seek to sail back to their homes, to stand there against you. My ships can keep them in port or fight them if they sail. Those exploding jugs you Mongols throw are fully strange to see. But on a wooden ship, they are hard and then some. My sailors would share a great laugh as Zipangu pirates burn alongside our ship."

"And what pay will your men want to spur their laughter?"

"There will be many ships to take, much plunder. And I would like to rule one of these Japanese islands. If not Honshu, then Kyushu."

"Hum," Hsin said, slowly stroking his beard. "Ships, peasants, and the mud they grub in, these are minor things that a general may give. The rule of an island. That is for the Great Khan to decide."

"But he will listen to the advice of his victorious general, will he not?"

"I think we understand each other."

Low did the Koryu admiral bow as he made his retreat from Hsin's presence.

Two turnings of the glass later, after Hsin had smashed much priceless porcelain and shredded many valuable silks, after he had been washed and scented to remove the stench of the Sung and Koryu dung he swallowed, Hsin strolled around the deck of his flagship to smile and nod to his guests.

The gold-teethed pirate of Zipangu had sent ashore for a man, a Buddhist priest by dress, who bowed low and thanked the general in horrible Chinese for the honor of carrying word to the true emperor in Kyoto that the Mongols and Sung had come as allies to set the proper emperor on the throne and restore Buddhism to its traditional purity. Hsin considered the garbled message and decided it was as close to the truth as he wished it to be and sent the monk on his way with a small sack of silver.

Now Hsin withdrew to the stern of his flagship to meet with Admiral Hong, his captains, and the Zipangu pirates to select a place to land. Hsin listened as the pirates argued in surprisingly good Chinese for one of three landing sites.

"Ujina is a good port," the gold mouthed man pointed out. "The Castle of Hiroshima is close at hand. You should have little trouble bringing its walls down if your engineers are as good as we have heard at smashing Sung walls," he said, grinning wide at Fan. The general reached for his sword, but Hsin silenced the men with a flick of his small left finger.

"There is Osaka Bay," another man offered. "Land your army there and it is only a short march to

Kyoto." A glance at Admiral Hong's superb map showed an open area of blue at the far end of what it called the Inland Sea.

"A long sail among many rocks," Hsin observed.

"If that sail is long, there is a shorter one. Why go farther than Hirado Jima," a better dressed pirate said with a lower than usual bow. "Once you seize the mouth of the Gulf of Imari, you could come up behind the Samurai, the servants of the Shogun, surprise them, and smash them where they stand. Then all of Zipangu will lie open to you for the taking."

Hsin watched the sailor with soft hands as his fingers walked around Hong's map, highlighting the places that Hsin knew too well from his disastrous campaign.

"I like a path that does not put these ships too close to rocks eager to rip their bellies open," Hsin said, quoting himself as he committed his army to defeat and ruin. "Go now to your ships. I will raise the flag tomorrow and you will all follow in my wake," he finished.

Beside him, Admiral Hong's nostrils flared, his eyebrows flinched, but he regained control, bowed low, and said. "We will do as the Great General of the Great Khan orders." That also had been his reaction the last time Hsin issued those orders.

The Zipangu pirates made to argue among themselves. Either they had not heard Hsin's order or they did not know that to hear was to obey. Either way, guardsmen with pikes moved forward to see that they took their stinking presences elsewhere now that Hsin had issued an order. Hong began to back out, bowing, but Hsin nodded at him and waved a small finger to make him stay as all others left them.

"You wish something from me, my general?"

"That other pirate. Do you know his name?"

"The one who suggested we sail for Hirado?"

"Yes, that one."

"No, I do not know his name. Would you have me call him back, my Lord General?"

"No, the sooner that one is gone from my sight, the better my digestion will be. No. Have two of your captains, ones with small and swift ships, follow that one if he leaves our anchorage tonight. Do not intercept him, but I would know where he goes."

Almost Hong grinned. "It will be done."

"And tomorrow, your flagship will lead the way for the entire fleet. Set your course for Ujina Bay. Have ships with our engineers and siege train not far from the front. I do not want to take a lot of impudence from those who huddle in Hiroshima castle. Let them surrender or die quickly."

"That will be done, my general," the man said, the wide grin of a tiger soon to be fed on his face. "With great joy."

General Hsin of the Ever Victorious Mongol Army patted the neck of Black Lightning. The war stallion snorted with impatience to be off. Hsin shared that impatience, but one more time he led the horse in a wide circle.

To the east rose the walls of Hiroshima castle, gray stone against gray sky. Before it, crows picked at the carrion on wooden gibbets. Those fools had made a sally the third day of the siege, charging Hsin's engineers. The Zipangu had fought well, man for man, but not well as a formation. Mongol horses rode them down. He'd had their bodies mounted for all in the castle to see. Some had not been corpses yet when they went up to feed the crows. The castle opened its gate next morning. Hsin had those men in chains, having not yet decided if they surrendered quickly enough.

Fan's flag flew over the castle now. He and a small contingent would hold this place while Hsin led the rest of the army north. It seemed to the Mongol that Sung soldiers fought better with a roof over their heads. Now some were under such a roof. Others could look to them and look forward to a roof of their own. A roof over their heads and land under their feet made for a happy Chinese pikeman.

In the harbor, the last of the large ships was getting under sail, its cargo unloaded and being hauled by peasants into the castle. Maybe there were more soldiers to be had among the defeated Sung; Hsin did not know. What he did know was that come storm or shine, his army would not look to its back for salvation. No, they would look to their horse and to their sharp swords. It was folly for a soldier to look anywhere else.

There was no sign of Hong's flag. He'd changed from the large ship he'd sailed in to a small one before the castle fell. He'd also put aside robes of gold and silk for a fighting man's armor. He'd offered Hsin a box: pine, unpainted. It held the head of one Zapango. "No pirate that one, but a spy. He sailed from Iki almost before you asked me to have him followed. My watch ships saw him to Hakata Bay, then followed him back. I assure you, he sent no message to Kyushu before we took him in sight of our fleet. And now I sail for Kyushu to take my own message for them. Many thanks for the gunpowder jugs. It will be a laugh watching those landsmen when we toss a couple of those at them as they try to grapple and board."

Hsin liked the feel of that one when he sailed away. There was one who well deserved his share of this glory and an island to rule. That was a suggestion to lay before the Great Khubilai Khan.

Now he let his horse free, let it gallop for the north. Beneath its hooves was good black earth, showing solid sprouts of wheat. The warhorses would eat well, grow strong, and charge hard. And if the storm blew, well, what was a little rain to a warrior raised to a harsh life. Black Lightning galloped. Hsin enjoyed the taste of a breeze of his own making, and all was well as he led his army off to conquer, pillage and burn.

General Hsin-tu debased himself before the Great Khan. Around him, slaves held silks, jewels, gold, the riches of Japan. Before him, Kubilai Khan slurped from a golden wine goblet and bade Hsin rise to his knees. With one more profuse bow to the floor, the general settled comfortably into reverence to his great lord.

The man had changed much in the two years since Hsin sailed for what he now thought of as Japan, for the people of that land did not name themselves Za-pangos as the court of the Great Khan thought, but

Japanese. Here, before the Khan, Hsin would call them whatever the Khan wished.

"You have done very well, my general," Khubilai said, as a slave wiped his mouth of some wine that had missed his gullet.

"Thank you, my great Khan," the general said, wondering if the man could get his wide behind on a horse these days. Yes, the years had not been kind to the Khan. The man who commanded armies in all the lands under heaven apparently could not command himself to stop drinking or feasting. There were also rumors that Hsin had heard as far away as Japan that the Great Khan trusted his finances to men who served him no better than his own cooks and wine servants. If the man could not discipline himself, maybe an old soldier should do him the service.

Having seen what passed for an emperor among the Japanese, Hsin could well understand why an old soldier might considered it a service to his lord and his people to discipline one who would not discipline himself, to rule him who would not rule himself.

Hsin let nothing that passed through his mind show on his face. He nodded and bowed and thanked the great Khan as he bestowed honors and the rule of Kyushu on Hsin. Shikaku went to Admiral Hong, at Hsin's suggestion. This general of the Mongols now saw the value of a good man of the sea at his back. Fan could warm his backside, if he could find any warmth, on the cold island of the north. Still, Fan did get his island to rule.

Long, boring hours later, Hsin was allowed to stand and bow his way from the presence of the Great Khan.

A soldier presented himself and offered to lead Hsin to his rooms where he might prepare for tonight's banquet. The man looked familiar.

Alone in rooms fit for a prince, the guard did not make to leave. The general tossed his escort a small golden goblet, then half filled it from a bejeweled wine jug. Without asking the soldier, Hsin toped the cup off with water, then filled another golden goblet in like fashion for himself.

"To victory," Hsin said in salute, then took a small sip.

"Victory is so much better than defeat, isn't it?" the guard said, giving him a knowing look as he also sipped his wine. The man was short with round eyes, not unusual in an army that drew its men from everywhere under heaven. What was surprising to Hsin was the pale, bald head that showed under the helmet.

"I am grateful," Hsin said, not really sure what he meant by that, but feeling that somehow those were the right words here.

"Not nearly as grateful as some others. General Short or Admirals Gormley and Phillips, to mention only a few." The man easily got his mouth around such strange words.

"No?" Hsin said, knowing he was more puzzled by the man's statements than enlightened. Yet he was unwilling to let go of this one connection to an hour only he seemed to still remember.

"Entire history of the Pacific rim is drifting on the wind," the man said. "No one's quite sure where it will wander off to," the man continued, downing the last of his wine. "You are a very unusual man, General Hsin. You took advantage of your second chance to shake the very roof of heaven. I salute you," he said, lifting his glass, then setting it on a small lacquered table. With no further words, he left.

General Hsin turned to a leather campstool that stood incongruously in the middle of the room. It was the kind a Mongol of old might have in his simple felt yurt on the steppe. Among the ornate wall hangings and silks, it was completely out of place. Still, it seemed at home with the empty brazier of blackened iron that stood beside it.

Hsin poured himself another glass of wine, mixed it evenly with water, and went to sit on the stool. Had he shaken the very roof of heaven? The bitter memory of defeat was harder and harder to remember. It was always easier to recall victories, but something stranger deepened the shadows around those dark recollections.

Shaking his head, Hsin tossed off those useless thoughts. He was a soldier. He served the khan. And something was wrong with the khan. What might a true Mongol soldier do for him?

Slowly Hsin sipped at his drink and thought as the sun set lower in the sky.

Jesus H. Christ

Laura Resnick

It ain't exaggerating to say that me and the Boss got a checkered history together.

Some guys (like that polenta-eater, Adam) thought the Big Guy would never get over being pissed off about the time He caught me sending Lucifer a cut of the souls I skimmed off the Road to Salvation. Now, just to be clear, I wasn't culling no souls that we'd actually want intermingling with the general population in Heaven. I was just doing my job according to an individual interpretation of my duties that, unfortunately, the Boss didn't wind up sharing when it come to light. The way I seen it, I was just relieving Saint Peter of the burden of having to request back-up when he was forced to deny some sorry chump's entry past the Pearly Gates after double-checking their particulars the way a good archangel should. Heaven's a very high-class place. You don't want just *anybody* getting in. We gotta have standards, same as any other swank operation.

See, people spend a few eons in the Purg, and sometimes they come out smarter about how the afterlife works. You understand what I'm saying? Sometimes, they get on the Road to Salvation just *pretending* like they're all cleansed of their wickedness and ready to start doing better. Because they've figured out that, once you leave the Purg, there's only two places to go. And the other place don't have no room service.

Well, me, I'm kind of an expert in human frailty. My boss on the earthly plane, Carmine "The Undertaker" Corvino, counted on me to know who'd be a stand-up guy no matter what, and who'd sing like a canary the first time some assistant district attorney squeezed his balls a little. Mr. Corvino also counted on me to know when the second kind of guy would be relaxed and easy to whack out. So, what I'm saying is, I got a lotta background in knowing the human heart. Plus, while I was still alive, I watched a lot of *Jerry Springer* that time I was in the joint on a bum rap. So, I'm telling you, I can spot an insincere soul faster than a Fed can threaten to ruin your kid's Christmas.

And whenever I recognized a soul on his way to Salvation who wasn't straight up penitent . . . Okay, maybe sometimes I gave Mister Lucifer the heads up. Let him in on an easy mark. Split the swag in exchange for greasing the wheels. Because sometimes, you know, I knew someone who'd maybe taken a wrong turn on his way out of the Purg and needed special dispensation to get outta Hell. For example.

It was just business.

When the Maker of All Things figured out what I was doing, He never questioned my judgment about the souls I skimmed. I want to say that up front. The Boss always thought I had a good eye; it's why He sprung me from the Purg and made me a soldier in His outfit. But He blew His stack when He found out about my little arrangement with the Prince of Darkness. Talk about two guys who got some *history* between them.

So that was the real problem with that business. I couldn't have chosen nobody worse to work that deal with. The Lord of Hosts didn't really care that I had a little side action going. And when Adam told people that the Lord God was mad that I wasn't giving Him any vig off the top before moving the swag, well, that was just spite—and, frankly, exactly what you'd expect from that little piss-ant, Adam "The Woman Made Me Do It" of Eden. No, what made Mister Yahweh mad enough to condemn me to Eternal Damnation was that I was doing business with His old archnemesis, the devil himself.

To be honest, that was just petty of Him. I say that with no disrespect, just telling it like it is. Yahweh took it personal, and there was just no reasoning with Him after that. So I got cast out of Heaven.

Like I said, we got some holy water under the bridge, me and the Boss.

So, in retrospecting certain choices I made in Heaven, I gotta acknowledge that maybe dealing under the table to Satan wasn't the smartest thing I ever done. But, like my old man used to say, a stand-up guy keeps getting back on his feet until the day six of his buddies carry him away in a box. And when I was down and out of Heaven, Mister Lucifer didn't forget who his friends were. He offered me a job, and in no time at all (and through some judicious whacking of a few demons) I became his *consigliere*, his right-hand soul, one of the most important entities in Hell.

Unfortunately, I wound up having a slightly checkered career with the devil, too. No need to go into details, but it involved televangelists, so it was a pretty dirty business. (And, yep, it involved that jerk-off, Adam, too. Don't even get me started.) Anyhow, the deal went sour, and I got asked nicely (considering the source) to leave Hell pronto.

So there I was, with a rap sheet in Eternity, kicked outta the only two places to go. Well, I sure as shit didn't want to get sucked into Limbo (what a mess *that* whole scheme was), and I happen to know that the Master of the Universe is very big on giving people second chances. So I went up to the Pearly Gates to petition for an audience with the Lord God.

"Vito!" Saint Peter blurted, ushering some penitent souls into Heaven when he saw me approaching. "Where in Eternity have you been? I haven't seen you in yonks!"

"You ain't heard?"

"Heard what? Last thing I recall, you were . . . *Oh!*" The saint's eyes got real big and round. "That's right. You . . . " He gulped. "Down *there*?"

"Uh-huh."

"With, er . . . the entity whose name we try not to mention in this or any other dimension, lest it enrage the Lord God beyond reason?"

"Yep. That's who I was with."

"I see. So how's he keeping?" Saint Peter asked. "I haven't seen him since, obviously, you know . . . the Fall."

"He's fit. Works out. Still single. A little moody."

Saint Peter rolled his eyes. "*Tell* me about it."

"Huh?"

Saint Peter whispered, "The Heavenly King."

I frowned. "You're saying the Big Guy's in a snit?"

"Remember the Blessed Virgin in her ninth month when Joseph put her on that donkey and announced they were heading for Bethlehem?"

In the earthly plane, that was almost two thousand years before I was born. In the Heavenly plane, though, time gets a little jumbled up, so I'd had to babysit Yahweh's first (and only) kid in that smelly manger while Mary was recovering from childbirth and Joseph was fighting with the innkeeper about the bill.

I asked, "You're saying Yahweh's in *that* mean a mood?"

"Even worse."

"What's got Him riled?"

"Three guesses."

"Well, *I* don't know, I been in Hell for the past . . ." I caught Saint Peter's eye, and the truth hit me. "Oh, for heaven's sake."

"Uh-huh. You got it."

"*Still*?"

The saint sighed. "I know, I know."

"I swear, some things never change," I said. "Not on the earthly plane, and not on this one, neither."

"You said it, Vito."

"Well, I picked just a *great* time to come back and plead for mercy and redemption."

"Is that why you're here?" When I nodded, Saint Peter grimaced. "Bad timing, indeed."

"I thought this kind of thing would be behind Him by now."

"I'm beginning to think it'll *never* be history."

"Maybe I should come back another time?"

"This is Eternity, Vito. There *is* no other time."

"I didn't mean technically. I just meant—"

"You would *think*," said Saint Peter, "that the Maker of All Things, the Master of Creation, the Omnipotent and Omnipresent Ruler of the Universe would be able to control his own son."

"Ah, give the Big Guy a break, Pete," I said. "You ever had children? I raised two, and I'm telling you, there ain't *no one* that can control a teenager."

"You *have* been away a while," said the saint. "That lad's not a teenager anymore, Vito. He's a grown man."

"Already?" It hadn't felt like I was in Hell that long, but I guess time flew down there.

"He's over thirty now."

"That skinny kid is over thirty? Last time I saw him, his voice was still cracking!"

"They grow up so fast," Saint Peter said sadly.

"Has he moved outta his mother's house yet?" I asked.

"His stuff's still there, but he's on the road almost all the time these days."

"And he's still fighting with the Big Guy all the time, too, huh?"

Saint Peter nodded. "As you noted, even in Heaven, some things never change."

"That kid . . . I'm telling you." I shook my head as memories came back to me. "Remember when Yahweh found out he was skipping temple to watch chariot races?"

The saint nodded. "Remember when he started wearing his hair like a Roman?"

"Remember the *toga*?"

Saint Peter guffawed. "Oh, no! The *toga*! You *had* to remind me!"

There are some things in eternal life that you just don't want to remember.

The saint asked, "Were you still here when Yahweh found out he wasn't keeping kosher anymore?"

"No, I missed that one." And I was glad. Yahweh could be pretty rigid about tradition.

"That means you weren't here when he started dating the harlot, either."

"He's dating a harlot?"

"Uh-huh. And the *fight* he and Yahweh had about it . . . Which the boy won, by the way. I swear, he should have been a lawyer."

"Well, his mother would have liked that." The Blessed Virgin had never been shy about making that clear.

"You should have heard the arguments he made to silence the Lord God's objections to Mary Magdalene. Brilliant! Even Yahweh wound up having to agree that loving and comforting the most outcast among mankind was in perfect keeping with His plans for the boy's career."

"He got Yahweh to *agree* to him dating a harlot?" I said in surprise. The Big Guy was also pretty old-fashioned when it came to women.

"The Blessed Virgin even had the girl over to dinner," Saint Peter said.

"Sounds serious."

"I know what you're thinking, but the lad's destiny comes before marriage, Vito. Or, well, hmph! So we had hoped."

"There's a new problem," I guessed.

"Is there *ever*. I swear, Vito, if that boy would bring half the effort to saving mankind that he does to fighting with his Father, we could wrap up Judgment Day by this time next year. But the way things are going . . ."

"So what are they fighting about this time?"

"Get this. Jesus doesn't want to die for mankind's sins."

"*What?*"

"I got this straight from the savior's mouth."

"You're kidding me!"

"Nope. This is on the level, Vito."

"But . . . but . . . that's his *destiny*," I said. "It's what he was born and raised to do!"

"I know, I know."

"It's Yahweh's grand plan," I said. "For the salvation of mankind!"

"I hear you."

"It's what's supposed to get the world out of the dung heap that that loser Adam left it in when he screwed up in Eden!"

"You're right, you're right," said Saint Peter.

"And the kid's saying he won't do it?"

"That's what he's saying."

"Unbelievable."

"Intolerable," said Saint Peter.

"Yahweh's tried to talk him round?"

"Yahweh shouted so long and loud, my ears are *still* ringing."

"And Jesus wouldn't budge?"

"Stubborn." Saint Peter shook his head. "Just like his Father, really."

"So he's not gonna die for mankind's sins," I said, stunned.

"Nope."

There was a long silence while this news sank in. Poor God. What a blow this must be to Him.

"Well," I said at last, shaking my head. "Kids. Whaddya gonna do?"

"Well, if You're Yahweh, what You're going to do is make eternal life miserable for every angel, saint, and cherub in existence." Saint Peter looked around, then leaned over and whispered. "Honestly, Vito, if things gets any worse around here, even *I* may go apply for a job in, you know, the other place."

"I *heard* that!" a voice thundered from on high.

Saint Peter grimaced at me, then shouted aloft, "Please forgive me, Lord God!"

"Yeah, yeah, whatever," Yahweh responded, His eternal voice echoing through Heaven.

The saint added, "We have an unexpected visitor, Lord!"

"So I apprehend," said the Almighty, sounding a little peevish. "How are you, Vito?"

"I'm keeping fit, thank You, Lord. And Yourself?"

"What are you doing at the Pearly Gates?" Yahweh demanded. "Didn't I damn you for all Eternity?"

"Yes, Lord, You did. But I was hoping maybe You'd reconsider."

"Why would I do that?"

"That second chance thing," I said. "Mercy and forgiveness?"

"Not now, Vito," said the Lord God. "I've got real problems on My hands."

And then I knew what it was going to take to get me back into Heaven and soldiering at the right hand of the Father. "I hear Your son's being a little rebellious again," I said. "I raised two kids of my own, you know. Got some experience in this area. Maybe I could help You out with this problem, Lord."

That offer got me a sitdown with Yahweh. And I gotta say, with just one look, I could see how much the strain was wearing on Him.

"If you don't mind me saying so, Lord, you don't so good."

"Go raise children," said God morosely.

"I hear Your son don't want to shed his blood for all mankind."

"I don't understand him," said God. "I've *never* understood him!"

"No, Lord."

"We talked about this. We went over the grand plan many times. He knows what's at stake! He knows how much I've invested in this!" God tore at his silvery mane. "Does he think a virgin birth is an easy thing to bring off? Does he think that a world-changing religion can be cultivated from just *any* obscure Middle Eastern cult?"

"Did he say *why* he—"

"You want to know what he said to me?" God cried. "He said, 'I want my own life. So go make my brother the sacrificial Lamb of God.' Uh-huh. That's what that ingrate said! His *brother*."

"He ain't got a brother," I said, confused.

"That's my point!" God thundered.

"Oh."

"He's mocking Me! Me, the Master of the Universe. Mocked by His own son! His own ungrateful, irresponsible, rebellious child."

"Yes, Lord."

Yahweh scowled. "This is all his mother's fault."

"When You and Your son talked about this, Lord, was there any particular—"

"She spoiled him," God said. "I tried to tell her, but would she listen to Me? Noooo, I'm only his Father! Only the Lord God Almighty! What would *I* know about raising the boy?"

This went on for a long time. It was a while before the Big Guy calmed down enough to tell me the root of the problem.

"He . . . wants to be a klezmer musician?" I said.

"Uh-huh."

"Klezmer," I said again. "That music from the old country that was playing at Nathan Kugelman's kid's bar mitzvah when they arrested him?"

God said, "The Kugelman boy was arrested at his bar mitzvah?"

"No, Nathan was. The kid never spoke to him again."

"That will be my fate, too." Yahweh's eyes got a little misty. Okay, sure, they fight like cats and dogs, but the Big Guy loves His kid.

"No, no, Lord, we're gonna straighten him out. I promise."

"I've tried, Vito. He won't listen to Me."

"Let me give it a try, Lord."

"Do you really think it'll do any good?"

"Well, as You know, Lord, I got a long history, on more than one plane, of convincing guys to do stuff they maybe wasn't that eager to do before I shown them the light." I nodded. "Yeah, I think maybe I got a chance of bringing the kid around to a better understanding of his responsibilities."

If you ever get the chance, in any plane, dimension, or existence, to visit Judea under Roman rule, my advice is: DON'T.

What a miserable time and place. And the food! Let's just say that I could've ended the Corvino-Matera war real fast if I'd ever served the Matera family a banquet of the food they got in Jerusalem circa 30 AD.

As soon as I was back there for the first time in yonks, I remembered what a scrappy kid Jesus had become due to growing up in an environment of such unfortunate violence and social unrest.

"You keep looking at me like that, buddy, and I'll blow your brains out," I said to a zealot who was staring at me. "You understand?"

Well, maybe he didn't, since my Aramaic's not so good. But I showed him my piece, and even though he'd never seen a gun before, I guess he got the idea. He backed off real fast and went about his business. I started searching Jerusalem for the kid.

"Excuse me," I said to a beggar. "I'm looking for the Son of God."

"Who?"

I handed him a coin. "The Lamb of God. The King of Kings. The savior of all mankind."

He frowned. "I'd like to help, but I don't think I—"

"Goes by the name of Christ, Jesus H. Christ."

"Oh! Right! He's hiding out in that house over there."

"Thanks."

"So . . . that's for real, then? He's not just saying it?"

"Saying what?"

"That he's Yahweh's son."

"That's *Mister* Yahweh to you. And, yeah, it's for real." I turned to go.

"Wait! What's the 'H' stand for?"

"Hyman."

"Oh. You probably want to keep posterity from knowing about that."

I shrugged. "It was his mother's father's name."

"Still, take my advice about this. Really."

I found Jesus hiding in the house the beggar had pointed out to me. Some of his disciples were with him. A lotta stories been told about those guys, but they was basically an okay crew. Mostly stand-up guys. Except for Judas "The Rat" Iscariot, of course. But, hey, for every dozen guys you got on the payroll, one will be ready to betray you. That's human nature, right?

And, after all, human nature was why Yahweh thought Jesus needed to set such a tough example for us.

Jesus' jaw dropped when he recognized me. "*Vito*?"

"Hey, kid!" I gave him a slap on the back. "How ya been?" He'd filled out real good, a nice looking guy. But he needed a haircut real bad, and I wasn't crazy about the beard.

"Vito," he said, "I thought you were in Hell with Lucifer?"

There was a clap of thunder and the house shook a little.

"You *gotta* say the name out loud?" I said to the kid. "You couldn't be a little discreet?"

Jesus looked Heavenward with an expression that was real familiar to me, since I seen it often on the faces of my own offspring. "It's been eons!" he shouted up at his Father. "Get over it already!"

"Introduce me to your friends," I said, hoping to distract him.

"John, Paul, Thomas," Jesus said, "this is Vito 'The Knuckles' Giacalone. Used to work for my Father." He gave me a hard look. "And apparently he's been rehired."

I shrugged. "Yahweh forgave me. It's what He does." I said to the guys, "Would you excuse us, please? We got some family business to discuss."

They looked a little annoyed. Paul said, "We're supposed to be rehearsing."

"Rehearsing?" I said.

"Our klezmer band. We call it Jesus and the Apostles."

"So you were serious about the klezmer thing?" I said to Jesus. "You didn't just say that to drive your Father nuts?"

"*Yes*, I'm serious!"

Paul said, "We've got a wedding in Cana to get ready for. We're the headliners."

I said, "And that's a real big responsibility compared to, oh, *saving mankind*."

"Don't start with me, Vito," Jesus warned. "I know why He sent you, and I don't want to—"

"But I guess you forgot why He sent *you*," I snapped.

"Vito, this is none of your—"

"John, Paul, Ringo," I said. "Get the fuck outta here. I gotta have a sitdown with your lead singer."

"But, er, it's hard to rehearse without Jesus, he—"

"You see this?" I showed him my rod. "It can blow a hole through all three of you that no one in this eon knows how to fix, and just in case my aim's bad, I brought extra clips."

John said, "We'll just, uh, be outside. If you need anything, Jesus. No rush, of course. Take your time." John wasn't no dummy.

When we were alone, Jesus said, "A *gun*? You brought a gun here? *Vito*."

I shrugged. "It's a dangerous place."

"Well, it certainly is *now*. Give me that."

I brushed away his hand. "What, you gonna *shoot* your way out of destiny?"

"Do you know what He has planned for me?" Jesus said in outrage. "Did He tell you?"

"He don't have to tell me, kid. I was raised a good Catholic."

"Oh, is that why you grew up to be a killer and extortionist?"

"Okay, let's stay focused on you," I said.

Jesus sat down and put his head in his hands. "I'm sick of Him running my life, Vito. Sick of it!"

"So you decided to become a musician, knowing that would drive *any* parent nuts."

"I'm good at music!" he said defensively.

"So instead of being mankind's savior and the object of a worldwide religion steeped in faith, hope, and charity, you want to pass the hat at weddings, bar mitzvahs, and funerals for the rest of your life?"

"We've got some good gigs lined up," he insisted.

"At?"

"Um . . ." He sighed. "Weddings and bar mitzvahs."

"I guess it's hard to book funerals in advance," I said.

"Well, yes, unless you're a soldier in the Corvino family, *for example*, it's hard to predict exactly when people are going to die." He shook his head and gave me another of those looks. "Why did you go back to work for Him, Vito? I thought you liked it in Hell."

"Who said that?"

"Cherubim talk."

I shrugged. "Hell's okay, kid. But not for all Eternity."

"So now what? You get back into Heaven if you make me behave?"

"Something like that."

"I'm too old for this, Vito. When is He going to let me live my life?"

"Ain't never gonna happen, kid. You're dreaming if you think it will."

"All I want—"

"All you want is to be someone *else*."

"Yes! Someone *ordinary*! Someone who can get married, have children, gamble, and play in a klezmer band! Someone who can attend the funeral of his own father and, while mourning, be secretly relieved that he never again has to hear about what a disappointment he is to the old man!"

"Jesus," I said in disgust.

"Yes?"

"Er, I meant . . . good grief."

"What's that supposed to mean?"

"It means, *grow up*! A normal life ain't among your options. It never was, and it's time you got used to that! You're the son of the don. That decides your life for the *rest* of your life. No way around it. Like it or not, that's how it is."

"I've put up with this for thirty years! But now I've finally had it, I tell you! Do you know the grand finale?"

"You're the son of God, you were sent to this plane to suffer for our sins," I said.

"I don't want to be crucified, Vito! Have you ever *seen* anyone die on the cross?" He looked a little sick.

"Our sins are pretty bad," I admitted. "Dying for them ain't gonna be no picnic."

"Why do I *have* to die for your sins? Why can't *you* die for your sins?"

"I already died for mine."

"Oh. Right. You were executed in a restaurant on Mott Street, weren't you?"

"Jesus," I said, trying to make him understand, "this is bigger than my sins. This is about all our sins put together, plus ones that ain't even been committed yet. That means you don't get to die in bed surrounded by fat grandchildren."

"Why not?" he pleaded. "Why aren't there *any* perks in being His son? Such as, oh, long life, happiness, and a peaceful death?"

"Well, I—"

"I won't die on the cross, Vito. I *won't*. He can shout about what an irresponsible ingrate I am until His hair falls out, I won't do it."

"Oh, boy," I said. *Stubborn* was right. Just like his Father. "Okay, let's look at this your way for a minute. Let's say you apologize to Pontius Pilate, the Pharisees, the Sadducees, and everyone else you've been pissing off. You quit teaching The Word. You talk your way out of crucifixion—which, if Saint Peter is right about you, you can do."

"That nattering gossipmonger," he muttered.

"And pretty soon, your followers move on to the next guy, whoever he is. Probably some zealot who wants to commit mass suicide at Masada."

"Huh?"

"I'm just guessing," I said. "You go on the road

with your band. You even make a modest success of it. You marry the harlot."

"Her *name* is Mary Magdalene."

"And you have a decent life. Relatively speaking. I mean, considering that we're in a time and place where you can't get a decent meal, there's no such thing as a movie, and this whole city is going to be sacked in about forty years."

"Your point?"

"This ordinary life you want . . . that would be it, right?"

"*Without* mass suicide at Masada and the sacking of Jerusalem following in my wake, yes, that would be it."

"And then what?"

"Then . . . *what*? I live and die as an ordinary man. That's all."

"Right. Your Father's heart is broken—"

"Oh, for the love of—"

"So He never sires another child or tries again to save mankind by sending us His son."

"It was a terrible idea to begin with."

"We're never redeemed. Christianity ever exists. The Roman Empire never converts. The Catholic Church ain't never founded—"

"You say that like it's a *bad* thing."

"And the world just keeps going down the drain from here on out."

"Oh, come it's . . . it's not that bad." But he looked a little guilty.

"Have you walked around the streets lately? Taken a good look at how much hopelessness and misery there is?"

He shuffled his feet. "That's not my—"

"Picture things being exactly this way for the next ten thousand years. No relief in sight. No hope at all."

He was silent, looking down at his bare feet.

"But, hey," I said. "What do you care? *You* got to lead an ordinary life, after all. *You* got to die old and in bed. So that's all just fine, I guess."

He gave me a dirty look. "You could've been my mother."

"I ain't a virgin."

"I meant—"

"I'm just pointing out a few facts that have escaped you in your moment of crisis," I said nicely.

"Bastard."

After a moment, I said, "Klezmer music?"

He grinned. "Really drove Him *nuts*, didn't it?"

"So . . . you know what you gotta do, right?"

"Yes." He sighed. "I've got to go die horribly on the damn cross."

"Good boy."

"But, Vito, this is the last thing I'm doing for Him. I mean it. Enough is enough."

"I know it's a raw deal, kid, but you'll get back at him someday."

"How?" Jesus shrugged. "He's God Almighty, Master of the Universe. I'm just the savior of mankind."

"You'll see," I promised. "Just be patient."

Needless to say, Yahweh was thrilled that I'd knocked Jesus into line. So I got back into Heaven with full status, and I been kind of a favorite with the Big Guy ever since. Him and Jesus still fight like all get-out, of course, but the Son is seated at the right hand of the Father, where he belongs.

And about fifteen hundred years or so after all this went down, which is just the blink of an eye in Eternity, Protestantism was born. It drove Yahweh *nuts*.

Jesus, of course, was tickled to death about that.

AUTHOR NOTES

Liz Holliday is a Londoner whose fiction has found wide acceptance in a number of genres. She's done a number of novelizations, and her short story "And She Laughed" was shortlisted as a Golden Dagger Nominee.

Dean Wesley Smith is the bestselling author of over seventy novels and many short stories. He has also served as an editor for several different book houses, and currently edits one anthology a year called *Star Trek: Strange New Worlds*. He wrote the novel for the Hallmark miniseries *The Tenth Kingdom*, the novel for the first *X-Men* movie, and many *Star Trek* novels. He lives on the Oregon coast with his wife, Kristine.

Kristine Grayson is the author of several award-winning humorous fantasy romance novels. Publisher's Weekly calls the series "delightful." The most recent book is *Absolutely Captivated*. The next, *Totally Spellbound*, will be published in August 2005.

When not working as a rocket scientist, **Daniel M. Hoyt** writes fiction, poetry, and music. His short stories have sold to markets as diverse as *Analog Science Fiction & Fact* and *Dreams of Decadence*. He currently lives in Colorado Springs, Colorado, with his wife, author Sarah A. Hoyt, two rambunctious boys and a pride of cats. Catch up with him at http://www.danielmhoyt.com.

Jay Lake is the winner of the 2004 John W. Campbell Award for Best New Writer, as well as a nominee for the 2004 Hugo and World Fantasy Awards. His stories appear in half a dozen languages in markets around the world, as do his collections *Greetings From Lake Wu*, *Dogs in the Moonlight* and *American Sorrows*. His novel *Rocket Science* came out in mid-2005. He lives in Portland, Oregon. Jay can be reached through his web site at http://www.jlake.com/

Ray Vukevich is the author of *The Man of Maybe Half a Dozen Faces*, and *Meet Me in the Moon Room*, a collection of short stories. His short fiction has appeared in *The Magazine of Fantasy and Science Fiction*, *Asimov's*, *Rosebud*, *Aboriginal Science Fiction*, *Pulphouse*, *Talebones,* and a number of anthologies, including *Twists of the Tale*, *The Year's Best Fantasy and Horror 12,* and both volumes of *Imagination Fully Dilated*.

Jody Lynn Nye lives northwest of Chicago with two cats and her husband, author and packager Bill Fawcett. She has published thirty books, including six contemporary fantasies, four SF novels, four novels in collaboration with Anne McCaffrey, including *The*

Ship Who Won; edited a humorous anthology about mothers, *Don't Forget Your Spacesuit, Dear!;* and written over seventy short stories. Her latest books are *The Lady and The Tiger,* third in her Taylor's Ark series, and *Myth-Taken Identity* cowritten with Robert Asprin.

Loren Coleman is the author of over twenty novels, including *Blood of Wolves,* which lead the relaunch of fiction novels for the world of Conan, and *Sword of Sedition* for the MechWarrior: Dark Age line. He also writes a great deal of short fiction for http://www.battlecorps.com/ and is working on a new original novel. When he isn't writing, Loren Coleman coaches local sports and collects DVDs. He also holds a black belt in traditional Taekwon Do, which he considers mandatory for any father with a daughter. His personal website can be found at http://www.rasqal.com/.

Brenda Cooper has published fiction and poetry in *Analog, Oceans of the Mind, Strange Horizons,* and *The Salal Review,* and been included in the anthologies *Sun in Glory* and *Maiden, Matron, Crone.* Brenda's collaborative fiction with Larry Niven has appeared in *Analog* and *Asimov's.* She and Larry have a novel, *Building Harlequin's Moon,* coming out in 2005. Brenda lives in Bellevue, Washington, with her partner Toni, Toni's daughter Katie, a border collie, two gerbils, and a hamster.

Depending on whom you talk to, **Christina F. York** is either a romance writer who does science fiction, or a science fiction writer who does romance. Either way, she finds it difficult to color within the lines. Her first work was self-published at ten. Finding she wasn't a publisher, she retired to complete grammar school. Since then she has sold nonfiction, short stories, and novels, and worked as a technical writer. Her latest novel *Dream House* is a December 2004 release, and Enigma Ship, in collaboration with her husband J. Steven York, is included in *Star Trek S.C.E.: Wildfire* (November 2004). The Yorks live on the Oregon Coast, where Chris has a view of the ocean from her office window. She and her husband split their time between solo and collaborative work, and serving their two feline masters.

Annie Reed lives in Northern Nevada with her husband, daughter, and several high-maintenance cats. In addition to science fiction, she writes mystery and mainstream fiction. Her short fiction has appeared in *Ellery Queen Mystery Magazine* and *Strange New Worlds Vols. 6, 7*, and *8*, and in 2005 she received a Literary Artists Fellowship award from the Nevada Arts Council. A former musician and radio DJ, she watches far too many movies for her own good and is a font of useless movie trivia.

Susan Sizemore lives in the Midwest and spends most of her time writing. She works in many genres, from contemporary romance to epic fantasy and horror. She's the winner of the Romance Writers of America's Golden Heart award, and is a nominee for the 2000 Rita Award in historical romance. Her books include a dark fantasy series, *The Laws of the Blood*, other science fiction, and several electronically published books and short stories. Susan's email address is Ssizemore@aol.com, and her webpage address is: *http://members.aol.com/Ssizemore/storm/home.htm*

Sarah A. Hoyt is the author of *Ill Met By Moonlight*, *All Night Awake*, and *Any Man So Daring*, an acclaimed trilogy that undertakes a fantasy recreation of Shakespeare's life. She's currently working on a time-travel/adventure novel with Eric Flint. She has also sold over three dozen short stories, some of which have appeared in magazines like *Absolute Magnitude*, *Analog* and *Asimov*'s. Sarah lives in Colorado with her husband, two sons, and four cats.

Kristine Kathryn Rusch is an award-winning fiction writer. Her novella, *The Gallery of His Dreams*, won the Locus Award for best short fiction. Her body of fiction work won her the John W. Campbell Award, given in 1991 in Europe. She has been nominated for several dozen fiction awards, including the MWA's Edgar award for both short fiction and novel, and her short work has been reprinted in six Year's Best collections. Before that, she and her husband Dean Wesley Smith started and ran Pulphouse Publishing, a science fiction and mystery press in Eugene. She lives and works on the Oregon coast.

Mike Moscoe writes from the Pacific Northwest. He's been nominated for the SFWA's prestigious Nebula award three times since 2000. Among his recent novels are the series he writes under the name as Mike Shepherd: *Kris Longknife—Deserter* (December 2004) and *Kris Longknife—Relieved of Command* (November 2005). He's retired from 30 years with the federal government spent building databases on spotted owls and other forest critters.

Laura Resnick won the 1993 John W. Campbell award for best new science fiction/fantasy writer. Since then she has never looked back, having written the bestselling novels *In Legend Born* and *In Fire Forged*, with more on the way. She has also written an account of her journey across Africa entitled *A Blonde in Africa*. She has written several short travel pieces, as well as numerous articles about the publishing business. She also writes a monthly opinion column for Nink, the newsletter of Novelists, Inc. You can find her on the web at www.sff.net./people/laresnick.

CJ Cherryh
Classic Series in New
Omnibus Editions

THE DREAMING TREE
Contains the complete duology *The Dreamstone* and
The Tree of Swords and Jewels.   0-88677-782-8

THE FADED SUN TRILOGY
Contains the complete novels *Kesrith*, *Shon'jir*, and
Kutath.   0-88677-836-0

THE MORGAINE SAGA
Contains the complete novels *Gate of Ivrel*, *Well of
Shiuan*, and *Fires of Azeroth.*   0-88677-877-8

THE CHANUR SAGA
Contains the complete novels *The Pride of Chanur*,
Chanur's Venture and *The Kif Strike Back.*
                                         0-88677-930-8

ALTERNATE REALITIES
Contains the complete novels *Port Eterntiy*, *Voyager in
Night*, and *Wave Without a Shore*   0-88677-946-4

AT THE EDGE OF SPACE
Contains the complete novels *Brothers of Earth* and
Hunter of Worlds.   0-7564-0160-7

To Order Call: 1-800-788-6262

MERCEDES LACKEY

The Novels of Valdemar

To Order Call: 1-800-788-6262

DAW 25

Mercedes Lackey
& Larry Dixon

The Novels of Valdemar

"Lackey and Dixon always offer a well-told tale"
—*Booklist*

DARIAN'S TALE

OWLFLIGHT
0-88677-804-2

OWLSIGHT
0-88677-803-4

OWLKNIGHT
0-88677-916-2

THE MAGE WARS

THE BLACK GRYPHON
0-88677-804-2

THE WHITE GRYPHON
0-88677-682-1

THE SILVER GRYPHON
0-88677-685-6

To Order Call: 1-800-788-6262

DAW 26

Tad Williams

THE **WAR** OF THE **FLOWERS**

"A masterpiece of fairytale worldbuilding."
—*Locus*

"Williams's imagination is boundless."
—*Publishers Weekly*
(Starred Review)

"A great introduction to an accomplished
and ambitious fantasist."
—*San Francisco Chronicle*

"An addictive world ... masterfully plays
with the tropes and traditions of
generations of fantasy writers."
—*Salon*

"A very elaborate and fully realized setting
for adventure, intrigue, and more
than an occasional chill."
—*Science Fiction Chronicle*

0-7564-0181-X

To Order Call: 1-800-788-6262

DAW 45

OTHERLAND

TAD WILLIAMS

*"The Otherland books are a
major accomplishment."*
–Publishers Weekly

"It will captivate you."
–Cinescape

*In many ways it is humankind's most stunning
achievement. This most exclusive of places is also
one of the world's best-kept secrets, but somehow,
bit by bit, it is claiming Earth's most valuable
resource: its children.*

CITY OF GOLDEN SHADOW (Vol. One)
0-88677-763-1

RIVER OF BLUE FIRE (Vol. Two)
0-88677-844-1

MOUNTAIN OF BLACK GLASS (Vol. Three)
0-88677-906-5

SEA OF SILVER LIGHT (Vol. Four)
0-75640-030-9

To Order Call: 1-800-788-6262